W9-CNP-594

"Captures the commitment and dedication of Agency analysts beautifully and makes the reader wonder— could this really happen?"
—Barbara McNamara, former Deputy Director of the National Security Agency

"A very rare, eye-opening peek into the ultrasecret world of the National Security Agency. Harrigan has distilled her twenty-seven years with the NSA into a powerful novel of suspense that could only have been written by an insider. Some of the fun of this novel is trying to guess what words the NSA blacklined before publication."
—Nelson DeMille, *New York Times* bestselling author of *The Gate House*

"*9800 Savage Road* gives you a never-before-seen look at the inner workings of the nation's premier— and most secretive—intelligence-gathering agency. Harrigan's fascinating novel puts you in the middle of the cloistered world of electronic spying few people ever experience. A must-read."
—Bill Gertz, national security reporter for *The Washington Times* and author of *The Failure Factory*

"I was gripped from start to finish by this amazing story. Harrigan has achieved a perfect balance between a truly exciting piece of fiction and the authentic background of the mighty U.S. SIGINT System."
—Dick Williams, Officer of the Order of the British Empire and former Senior Intelligence Officer at the U.K.'s Government Communications Headquarters

9800 SAVAGE ROAD

A NOVEL OF THE NATIONAL SECURITY AGENCY

M. E. Harrigan

A TOM DOHERTY ASSOCIATES BOOK
NEW YORK

This is a work of fiction. All of the characters, organizations, and events portrayed in this novel are either products of the author's imagination or are used fictitiously.

9800 SAVAGE ROAD: A NOVEL OF THE NATIONAL SECURITY AGENCY

Copyright © 2009 by M. E. Harrigan

All rights reserved.

A Forge Book
Published by Tom Doherty Associates, LLC
175 Fifth Avenue
New York, NY 10010

www.tor-forge.com

Forge® is a registered trademark of Tom Doherty Associates, LLC.

ISBN 978-0-7653-5752-6

First Edition: September 2009
First Mass Market Edition: July 2010

Printed in the United States of America

0 9 8 7 6 5 4 3 2 1

In memory of my father, James Mears Sheen,
1914–1971.
The greatest man of the "greatest generation."

ACKNOWLEDGMENTS

My first and greatest thanks go to my husband, Bill, who read and commented on every version of this book—and there were many. He calmly encouraged me to continue during the turbulent periods of rejection letters (or no letters) and joyously celebrated with me in the times of good news. He is, indeed, my sunshine.

Special thanks to my agent, Joe Vallely of Flaming Star Literary Enterprises, who patiently guided me through the process of writing, rewriting, and, finally, finding a publisher. He is the best! And thanks also to my editor, Bob Gleason of Forge/Tor Books, for his exceptional advice and feedback, wealth of knowledge, and good humor. Thanks to Eric Raab, editor at Forge/Tor, for his support, talent, and expertise. And kudos to Ashley Cardiff, a truly excellent editorial assistant.

Others who supported me by reading the manuscript, providing inspiration, or suggesting changes include my daughters, Jamie Welch and Melissa Kelly; Gayle Jeffries; Kay Koontz and her sister Evelyn Musavi; Chary Izquierdo; Rosanne Greco; Chris and Jim Beck; Gary and Betsy Clark; Shari Schneider; Linda Dinan; Slim and Maryann Webster; Mary Lynn Qurnell; my "spy sister" Kay Sullivan; Unit Ten and Friends Book Club members; Patricia Mulcahy; Kim Lionetti; Sue Case; and Sue Fisher.

Many special thanks to Bill Gertz, *Washington*

Times analyst and reporter, who helped me find my agent; to John McGinty, who pulled up floor tiles in an NSA office area to see if a person could fit in the sub-floor grid area (yes!); to Rich Baillieul, for all the names; to the real Carter Giles for graciously allowing me to use his name; to Gary Holmes, DVM, of the Columbia (MD) Animal Hospital, for information about canine injuries due to a fall; to Sandria Johnson, for information about lockers at Union Station; to Cathy Hill and Bob Hardy, for legal advice; to Jim Doyle and Woody Dawes and Pat DeCillis and all the members of the REPG, for teaching me the wonders of technical ELINT; and to Mary Lott and Connie Molter, without whom this manuscript (and I) might not have survived the NSA prepublication process.

AUTHOR'S NOTE

9800 Savage Road is a work of fiction set at a defining moment in our country's history. The glimpses I provide into the nation's least known intelligence agency are realistic insights into what kinds of activities took place at NSA, the various personalities and character traits of the people who worked there, and what the complex looked and felt like during the timeframe of this novel. This realism was confirmed by an early pre-publication reviewer who told me, "You can't publish this! Reading it is just like walking in to work."

The characters in this novel are all fictional, with the exception of several scenarios that include actual persons (such as Usama bin Laden) and a few passing references to other actual persons (such as Dick Lord, founder of the National Security Operations Center).

Although the book's NSA Director (DIRNSA), Lt. General John Murray, is also a fictional character, he was modeled after a real-life DIRNSA, General Michael Hayden. General Hayden was a breath of very fresh air during his term as DIRNSA (1999–2005) as he led an agency in turmoil and disarray through a period of enormous change both before and following 9/11. I admired General Hayden enormously for his integrity, openness, and his active role in returning the National Security Agency to a modern defender of our country's security. I am proud that he chose to include some of my recommendations for NSA's "transformation" in a briefing he presented to Congress.

I readily acknowledge that some of the dialogue between the characters in chapter 27 has been paraphrased from General Hayden's *Statement for the Record Before the Joint Inquiry of the Senate Select Committee on Intelligence and the House Permanent Select Committee on Intelligence, 17 October 2002*, which is posted on NSA's website, nsa.gov. As it is a public record and not copyright protected, and as General Hayden said it all better than I can, I borrowed part of his speech and gave it to the fictional NSA Director, Lt. General Murray.

My career at the National Security Agency was both rewarding and challenging, with incredible intelligence-gathering victories and frustrating setbacks and a lot of hard work in between. I can't imagine having done anything else. I salute those who remain at NSA; they are smart (often brilliant), patriotic, hardworking, and very human people who would, with few exceptions, volunteer to work 24/7 until they dropped if a crisis demanded it.

You will discover a few redacted areas in this book. They represent words or phrases that have been deleted by the National Security Agency because of security concerns.

One last note: the last three paragraphs of *9800 Savage Road*'s epilogue describe a reportedly true occurrence. We should all be so brave in such a crisis.

9800 SAVAGE ROAD

PROLOGUE

Operations Building 1, National Security Agency
Wednesday, November 29, 2000
Afternoon

"Come here and look at this!"

The NSA escort glanced up from her book and saw one of the workmen she was chaperoning peering through a hole in the wall on the other side of the hallway. A second workman walked over to see what was going on and whistled quietly in surprise. Both men started pulling away strips of plywood and throwing them on the floor. Soon a space big enough for a person to squeeze through appeared, and the men shined a flashlight into the opening.

"You know, I think it's a kitchen," one of them said, amazement in his voice. "What would a kitchen be doing here?" He slid through the opening, tripped over a step down he hadn't seen, and disappeared into blackness.

The escort put her book down on the floor and stood up from the metal folding chair she had been sitting in for the last two hours. She would have to investigate. The workmen were "red-badgers," uncleared contractors working on Agency renovations, and she was responsible for their actions.

Everyone who works at NSA wears a badge, usually

on a chain around his or her neck, an immediate symbol of the individual's status. Fully cleared government employees wear blue badges. NSA senior executives have badges with an American flag in the background, immediately distinguishing them from the rest of the pack. Green badges are worn by cleared contractors, blue-striped badges by newly hired govies waiting for their final clearances, yellow badges by Defense Intelligence Agency personnel integrated into the Agency, purple badges by rehired annuitants working for the heady sum of a dollar a year, and on and on. It's an arrangement that neatly delineates a caste system as intricate and hierarchical as any in the world.

The very bottom of the heap is the red-badger, an uncleared person who has to be accompanied every minute by an NSA employee—usually a junior employee who isn't in a position to decline the chore. It's a boring job, and this escort, a recent graduate of Columbia University with a degree in advanced mathematics, was glad for the distraction.

"Move out of the way, please," she ordered, taking the flashlight and looking into the ragged doorway. The man inside had picked himself up and stood looking around at the small room.

"It's a kitchen, all right. Looks like it hasn't been used for a very long time. Did you know this was here?" he asked the escort.

"No," she said. "But I've heard things like this have happened before. Last year, some men were working over in the old headquarters building and found a walled-up office complete with a desk, a chair, and a typewriter. Apparently it had been closed up for quite a while." She giggled. "I suppose they were lucky there wasn't a pile of bones in there, too."

"What a system," the workman said. "If you don't

need it anymore, just rebuild around it." He shrugged and asked the escort, "Is that what we should do here? Just close it up again?"

The escort brushed her hair back from her face and thought a moment. "I'm not sure what you should do. I'm going to have to ask my boss." Fancy degree or not, she wasn't ready to make decisions about things like this.

She walked the men through the breezeway out to Gatehouse 2, not far from where they were working, and ordered them to stay with the two guards stationed there while she left to talk to her supervisor. She went back into the building and walked down another hallway to the nearest office with a secure phone, mumbling under her breath the whole time. "The entire damn world has cell phones, but can we use them here at the 'ultra high-tech National Security Agency?' No, we can't. Only hardwired desk models for us." She sat at a desk and frowned at the squat, gray telephone and its curled corded handset. "At least the thing is push-button," she muttered as she punched in some numbers.

When the gray, secure phone on my desk rang, I picked it up and answered distractedly. I was deep in thought, trying to make sense of a sheaf of intercepted conversations, all related to our newest antiterrorist program. It appeared at first glance that an al Qaeda member named Khalid Sheikh Mohammed (known within NSA as KSM), currently going under the alias Abdul Majid, had left a safe house in Germany and was traveling to France for at least the second time this year. He was *such* a bad guy—despite his extensive education in the U.S.—that seldom in my career had it been so important to track someone down.

Of course, even if we actually found him, it would take a mighty effort to convince anyone in the government of France to arrest the guy. The damn French were reportedly still selling spare parts, through front companies, for Mirage fighters and Gazelle attack helicopters to the Iraqis, and God knows what else to who else. The French were, in fact, reluctant to piss off any potential customers—a *franc* in the *banque* seemed to be their main goal. I wondered wistfully if CIA still had ultrasecret hit squads to deal with situations like snatching KSM from wherever he was. *Ah, well, one problem at a time.*

I was making lists and checking maps and routes, so involved in my work I felt like I was just behind the elusive KSM, running hard to catch up. The phone call barely interrupted my concentration. It took a moment to realize the voice on the other end was that of my latest employee, a new hire who needed someone to supervise her until she entered the Cryptologic Mathematics Intern Program scheduled to start at the beginning of the new year.

"Ms. O'Malley? It's Lucy—you know, the intern who's escorting the workers in OPS 1?"

After a few moments, I willed myself back into the present and answered. "Please call me Alex," I reminded her automatically. I wasn't ready to be called Ms. O'Malley or even Alexandra yet. Maybe when I turned forty—or fifty. "What do you need, Lucy?"

She explained about the discovery of the old kitchen and asked me what she should do.

"Lucy," I said, anxious to get back to the intercepts, "I'll walk down there with someone from Logistics as soon as I can and take a look. In the meantime, tell the men to bypass it and work farther down the hall."

"Should we board the doorway back up?" the escort asked me.

"Don't bother," I said. "Put up some 'Do Not Trespass' tape at the end of the hall. No one will wander back there before we know what to do next."

That decision was a mistake, a genuinely unintentional mistake, but one of the biggest in the almost fifty-year history of NSA. In a little more than forty-eight hours, the newly uncovered kitchen area would be a gruesome, blood-splattered murder scene that would rock the Agency and foreshadow a series of events that would change the world.

1

A furious wind raced across the wintry Maryland countryside, spinning drifts of dry early winter snow into swirling squalls. The wind whipped down from the hills and through the acres of parking lot surrounding the National Security Agency, battering cars, people, and the dilapidated old trailer balanced on concrete blocks outside the chain-link fence around the complex. The trailer's faded gray siding shuddered in the gusts, and a sign that read "Visitors' Center" hanging over the entrance banged against the door frame.

Inside, two Federal Protective Service officers checked identifications and handed out official white visitors' patches to nearly a hundred guests who would be attending the promotion ceremony in the Operations Building 1 auditorium. The two guards were busy, and they were cold. Both wore puffy down-filled uniform jackets, collars zipped up to their chins. The faded green indoor-outdoor carpeting was worn bare in many places, and the outside cold filtered in through the shabby floorboards. On either end of the trailer, bracketing the guards' workspace, window glass rattled incessantly as gusts of cold air hissed through the cracks around the frames. A total of four ancient chairs lined one short wall, each with its own particular idiosyncrasy: a missing arm, a short leg, a cracked seat, a bent back.

The trailer was NSA's official Visitors' Center, hauled in on a flatbed several years earlier when Security decided it was too risky to process visitors inside the OPS 1 building as we had been doing for many years. Now, visitors to any of the four buildings in the main complex—Headquarters, OPS 1, OPS 2A, and OPS 2B—were funneled through the ramshackle shelter. Construction of a permanent center had been delayed by what had become a yearly budget crunch. The run-down temporary structure was a poor introduction to one of the world's most powerful intelligence organizations. It may have been well into the first year of the new millennium, but you would never guess it from that place.

Dr. Jamal Rashiq, perhaps the day's most distinguished visitor to the Agency, was not a bit impressed by this first view of NSA, the place he had wanted so badly to see for himself. He had pictured a shiny, modern entrance staffed by poker-faced guards with automatic weapons. Banks of computers and mirrors and video cameras everywhere. He saw only two older model Sun workstations and no surveillance equipment. The guards did have handguns tucked into holsters on their belts, but they were friendly and welcomed each guest despite the cold and the conditions.

This made Jamal Rashiq uneasy. It was not at all what he expected. Being with his adoptive parents for the first time in several years made him uneasy, too. They had flown in from San Diego to attend their daughter's promotion ceremony, and they had been

ecstatic at the sight of Jamal, the boy they had saved
from the refugee camp in Pakistan and welcomed into
their family years before, waiting for them in the NSA
parking lot. His mother fawned over him, kissed his
cheeks; his father looked at him proudly. His son the
famous virologist—and the elder Rashiq never thought
of Jamal as anything but his true son—was right there
for him to touch. Jamal could almost hear them thinking, *Perhaps this family will be reunited now.* Probably
his "sister," Mariam, was thinking the same thing.
She had been so shocked, and then so pleased, that
he had responded yes to the invitation to attend her
ceremony.

He had been stunned by her invitation, especially
after Mariam told him the actual ceremony would be
followed by a tour of the building. It was, he knew, a
sign that his special mission was divinely blessed. Access to the complex was a spectacular gift, astonishing and unbelievable. He would be able to go past the
fences, past the guards, past the dogs, and into the
NSA buildings. He would be able to inspect and ap-
praise for himself one of the world's greatest enemies
of Islamic supremacy. He would use his time inside to
try to find a way to destroy the buildings and everyone
working in them. He shivered a little in anticipation of
the next hours.

Official Agency escorts chaperoned the visitors in
groups of ten as they left the trailer and walked briskly
across the parking lot into the gatehouse at Operations Building 2B. Just outside the gatehouse, a large
American flag snapped in the wind, its metal clip hooks
clanging against the pole. In just a few minutes, the
visitors walked through double-glass doors and into
one of the country's most secluded and best guarded
government structures.

Rashiq watched closely as the guards at the gate-house lifted a rope to allow the visitors to bypass the normal procedures that all entering NSA employees followed. Each employee slid his badge into a machine, punched in a pin number, and then passed through a turnstile. Rashiq carefully observed his sister as she went through this operation, noting the numbers she entered on the keypad. He also noted that the guards paid little attention to this ritual; the machine—called CONFIRM, according to the sign overhead—did all the work of employee verification.

He memorized another sign, posted off to the side of the check-in area:

ATTENTION RMAC AND ALL CRISIS ACTION CENTERS:
During the Month of December, only Gatehouse 2 will remain open for the 0300–0400 early shift changes. All other gatehouses will be closed from 2330–0400.

After the group of visitors walked slowly past the guards, they were ushered down the halls and up the escalators to the Friedman Auditorium, cocooned deep within OPS 1. The William J. and Elizabeth S. Friedman Auditorium, once named only for William, world-renowned for his skills with codes and ciphers and for being the NSA's first chief cryptologist, but re-named in the last few politically correct years to include his also cryptologically accomplished wife, had a seating capacity of about three hundred people. The Friedman was plushly decorated in a bright mauve and charcoal gray, with a thick carpet and velvet stage curtain, and was the site of all important gatherings or formalities, especially those involving family members. But whomever the outside guests might be, the

welcome was always gracious—and temporary. Believe me,

At NSA, you're either One of Us
or you're not.

At two o'clock, the huge curtain slowly parted, revealing a large American flag twinned with an equally
large Agency flag, each on either side of a table stacked
with gold-embossed promotion certificates. The table
was draped with a rich blue covering, a large seal of
the National Security Agency on the side facing the
audience. A cobalt-blue vase filled with gaily colored
flowers stood in front of the podium at the left of the
stage. The whole scene was brightly lit and remarkably impressive.

Lt. General John Murray, the new Director of NSA,
or DIRNSA—everyone who works at NSA and most of
the Intelligence Community calls the Director DIRNSA
because this abbreviated form of his title appears on
each message sent to or from the Agency—walked
across the stage and greeted the visitors. "I am proud
to have you here at NSA today," he said. "Our mission
could not operate successfully without you—family
and friends—to support these wonderful folks who will
be receiving the promotions they so richly deserve."

Dr. Rashiq stirred in his seat. Next to him, his parents were rapt; bewitched by the scenario before them
and clearly euphoric their daughter was part of such a
place.

The general continued. "We'll be handing out the
certificates shortly, but first you're going to see a little
about the important work these people have done here."

The lights dimmed and a short video on the activities of the Agency started. Making and showing a film on NSA and its mission, unclassified or not, was a big change in policy—the new Director's attempt to show a more human and open side of the Agency.

A woman's voice began: *"The National Security Agency: A Vital Asset for our Country in the Information Age."* She spoke solemnly as a huge picture of the NSA seal, with an American eagle glaring proudly and fiercely at the world, filled the screen.

"On October 24th, 1952, President Truman signed the memorandum which established the National Security Agency to consolidate the collection and reporting of foreign electronic intelligence for the United States. We call that electronic intelligence SIGINT, or signals intelligence, because it comes from sources such as phone calls or telemetry monitoring devices or data from radars."

The insignia faded and a video fly-by of NSA's Fort Meade campus replaced it. The narrator continued. *"Since that time, the National Security Agency has provided America the decisive information advantage through the exploitation of SIGINT."* Scenes of serious people doing serious work attested to the words.

"How does NSA exploit SIGINT, or signals intelligence?" The scene shifted to a laboratory filled with intent-looking analysts staring at dots flashing across oscilloscopes.

"Both the United States and its adversaries create an electronic blizzard of signals." A spinning blue earth, encircled with chains of silver dots, appeared and disappeared.

"Signals emanate from everywhere: phones, fax, television, computers, and missiles." Each was accompanied by an appropriate example: TV commentators,

rows of computers, a cruise missile bursting from its ship-borne launch platform.

"Through code breaking and other sophisticated techniques, the National Security Agency uncovers the information in foreign signals and provides its critical intelligence to customers throughout the government." Hundreds of ones and zeros floated across the screen, evolving slowly into reports stamped "Secretary of Defense Eyes Only" and "White House Highest Priority."

Dr. Rashiq grew restless. There would be no real information in this video, he was certain of that. Nothing about the millions of phone calls and e-mails he was sure the Agency intercepted and stored. Nothing about the hundreds of satellites orbiting around the world furtively sucking up private conversations. Nothing about the way NSA targeted everyone everywhere, just in case they might need the data later. And nothing, for sure, about how NSA shared all its dirty little secrets with the Jews so they could kill Muslims all over the globe.

The film was winding down. The seal reappeared, its white border revolving around the eagle. *"A strong National Security Agency means a strong America in the information age."* The tape ended, and bold letters on the screen pronounced, *"Information Superiority for America and Its Allies."*

The lights went up, and DIRNSA took his place back at the podium and spoke to the assembled visitors. "Let me just give you a short, real-life example of how important SIGINT is to the protection and defense of our country. I'm sure none of you in this audience is old enough to remember World War Two," the general stopped to wait for the light, but appreciable, laughter, "but without the role that signals intelligence played in the battle of Midway—which, as you know, turned the tide in the Pacific theater—we might all be speaking German or Japanese today.

"How did that happen? In the late spring of 1942, the Allied war effort in the Pacific was in a precarious state. Admiral Yamamoto had scored victory after victory against our naval forces led by Admiral Chester Nimitz. We were in the desperate position of facing a blow that would be fatal to the Allied war effort in the Pacific if we didn't know when and where the next strike would occur.

"A Navy radio intelligence group was tasked with providing communications intelligence on the Japanese navy. The Japanese command code they were working on was superenciphered, using an additive table, and was incredibly complex. The best our guys were able to do was make educated guesses based on the code, but it turned out to be enough. Through a combination of determination and skill, with a bit of trickery thrown in, the navy team was able to figure out that Yamamoto's next attack would be against the island of Midway. And they knew when: the third of June. Admiral Nimitz moved his carriers to a point northeast of Midway and lay in wait. When the day was over, Nimitz's forces had sunk all four of the Japanese aircraft carriers and put Japan on the defensive for the rest of the war.

"Now, I know," General Murray continued, "that this happened quite a while ago, but believe me such things continue today. How cryptology won the battle of Midway has been declassified, so I can talk about it now, but plenty of other SIGINT victories have occurred since then that I can't tell you about. At least, not yet."

DIRNSA looked out at his audience, all listening intently. "The National Security Agency is here to serve the American people, to make sure our country continues to enjoy the freedoms our constitution guarantees us."

He put up his hand. "But enough talk about NSA and its mission. Let's get back to the business at hand. Before we hand out the certificates to these exceptional people in the front rows, let me tell you a few things about them as a group."

He looked down at the promotees and smiled. "Never before in our history has it been so difficult to get promoted. Only forty-eight people are receiving promotion certificates today, less than three percent of those who are eligible. Twenty-one are women and four are racial minorities." He paused and looked out over the audience again. "The National Security Agency has a better educated and more diverse workforce at all levels than ever before in our history. We are proud of that."

After a few more words about special skills and accomplishments, the promotees filed out of their seats a row at a time to walk across the stage as their names were announced. A well-dressed, handsome man wearing dark glasses and led by a black Seeing Eye dog joined the general on the stage to help hand out the promotion certificates. He was Barry Ballard, NSA's deputy director for security and the workforce's favorite senior executive. Tall and slender, in his midforties with silver hair and a strikingly handsome face, he looked more like he should be on a movie set than working at the Agency. Of course, his impeccably styled Armani suit, as out of place at NSA as Donald Trump at a yard sale, didn't hurt his image at all.

He was also blind and had been since birth. It was a handicap he smiled through and got on with. Because of his popularity, Barry Ballard often took part in official Agency ceremonies, especially those involving visitors.

Jamal Rashiq saw his sister Mariam's delighted look as she received her certificate from the handsome deputy director for security and had her picture taken shaking hands with the Director of NSA. Jamal could feel his parents lean forward in approval at their daughter's success.

After cake and coffee in the main cafeteria, the visitors who wanted to tour the building were divided into groups of fifteen. Jamal's parents stayed behind to visit with Mariam, and he joined the first group out. It was made up of several families, including two young boys, a little girl, and two teens. The tours, like the movie, were new, an attempt to provide more access and openness—but only to those who were direct relations of the NSAers: spouses, children, parents, siblings. Security opposed it initially, as they do everything that provides any insight into the Agency's mission or layout, but they finally decided that these relatives would pose little threat. After all, they would have been included in the employee's recurring five-year security updates.

The group's guide was a boyish-looking air force captain. "Please call me Greg," he said. "We won't be using last names today. The first place we're going is the spookiest area of NSA—the basement." He grinned at the kids and added, "Once, many years ago, the basement was the place with the deepest, darkest secrets in this place. Every entrance was guarded night and day. You had to have very special clearances to go down there. Now," he shrugged, "now it's pretty much just a basement, but you'll see why it's still spooky. Follow me," he said, moving toward the cafeteria door. "We're on our way to the Classified Waste Disposal Center. Please stay together."

The group, each wearing a round, white visitor's badge, followed the captain down a long hallway, much of which was undergoing massive remodeling.

"NSA is famous for this hallway," the captain said as they walked. "It's 980 feet long—that's like three football fields, folks. It's the longest unobstructed corridor in the country, maybe the world."

"I wish I had my rollerblades with me," one of the boys said.

Captain Greg laughed. "Lots of employees here have said the same thing."

At the end of the hall, he directed them into a stairway leading to the basement. The stairwell was clean and white with blue trim, and it was brightly lit by big, round spaceship-shaped lights on the walls. It smelled of new paint and rubber stair treads.

The basement was neither clean nor brightly lit. It was shabby and dull. Dr. Rashiq looked around in the dim light at unpainted cinder block walls and naked steel T-shaped braces shoring up the building as they walked through a maze of boxes, forklifts, and hallways of differing sizes. *Is this where the first mighty Cray Supercomputers once broke codes at the rate of 420 million operations per second? Hard to believe.* He looked again at the myriad of steel braces. *The whole place must be ready to fall in on itself.*

He wasn't the only one to notice. "Why are those steel beams all over the place?" one of the men asked.

Captain Greg wrinkled his forehead. "This building is almost fifty years old and supports a lot more weight now than it was designed to carry. Last year, unfortunately, part of the OPS 1 cafeteria floor started to sag.

Within days, a bit of it actually caved in. No one was hurt, but, believe me, there was a very quick response. These guys," he touched one of the braces, "popped up like weeds down here. As soon as we get the money, Logistics will install some kind of permanent fix. For now, they're just part of the basement ambiance."

Off in the distance, a man wearing a hard hat drove a small, bright yellow golf cartlike vehicle, outfitted with a flashing light and emitting an annoying beeping noise. Most of the people in this shadowy, unrepentedly blue-collar underworld were men wearing the green badges of government contractors. They were intent on stringing cable, moving great stacks of equipment, and minding their own business.

This will be the last place at NSA targeted for restoration and new technology, Rashiq thought. *The basement is not worth my time. Not for what I'm going to do.*

The group turned down a corridor that was narrow and dim. Piled high on one side were pallets with boxes in pink shrink-wrap labeled "Acoustic Ceiling Tiles." A forklift was parked between the stacks. They turned another corner and ahead of them was a glassed-in area with a sign stating it was the "Classified Material Conversion Center". An authoritative sign on a pedestal in front of the door read "Do Not Advance Beyond This Point."

"Okay, folks, here we are," announced the captain. "As you can see, nobody aspiring to an exalted position at NSA is going to spend much time down here in the cellar. This is definitely no place to get 'face time' with the Agency rulers."

He gathered them in front of the center. "Every day, the people who work at the Agency throw their classified waste into something we call 'burn bags.' When they have a cartful, they take the bags to little rooms—cleverly called Burn Bag Rooms—on each floor of the various buildings and toss the bags down a chute in the wall. The bags collect in one of these Conversion Centers, and several times a day huge shredders like the ones behind this door slice the bags and their contents into slivers, ready to be mixed with a thick gray substance in huge vats to become pulp for recycling. NSA processes some forty thousand pounds of classified documents this way every single day. Would you like to see how that happens?"

The group nodded. A man dressed in a white lab coat and wearing a headset opened the door to the glassed-in area and led the way toward a thick, steel door. Suddenly, the noise in the room increased to a level of roaring blasts. Each person took a turn looking through a window in the door to watch the enormous razor-sharp shredders slice their way through mounds of paper.

Back outside in the relative quiet, the captain told his awed followers that in the Agency's early days the Waste Disposal Centers actually burned the trash instead of shredding it. "People who have worked here a while have told me that sometimes wisps of smoke would escape from the burn bag chutes and fill the halls with fumes. Not pretty. Now, the worst problems they have are the nonclassified stuff people put in the bags, even though they're told not to do that."

"Like what?" a small girl asked.

"Oh, like combs and calculators and items of clothing. Hats, bras, shoes—there's no telling what might show up and cause the whole system to grind to a halt. But eventually all this stuff gets processed and sold to paper companies that turn it into things like pizza boxes. Think about that next time you call Dominos."

Most of the visitors found it all very interesting. Dr. Rashiq did not; he needed to have very different information. He stepped to the front of the group and spoke. "This is quite impressive, Captain. Quite an operation. It must be just as big a job to keep this complex of buildings heated and cooled and supplied with a constant source of electricity, isn't it?"

"You are so right," Captain Greg replied. "We have generators, of course, to back up the Headquarters building and the three Operations buildings in case of an outage, and it's surprising how many times they have to be used. Especially in thunderstorm season. Our heating and cooling plant is enormous—in fact it's down here in this part of the basement someplace. Did you see the big boxy structures on top of the buildings when you came in?"

Rashiq had not only seen them, he had counted and noted the position of each one.

"No," he replied. "I didn't."

"Well, they're the air handlers. We moved them up there several years ago for security reasons."

Rashiq wanted to know—badly—if the air handlers for the four buildings were interconnected. It seemed obvious to him that the corner stairwells in this building would provide access to at least one set of them, but perhaps not to all of them throughout the complex. He asked carefully, "Is it harder to heat and cool the tall buildings than the lower ones?"

"Nope," the captain said. "They're all wired through the same system."

Bingo.

"Thank you, Captain," Dr. Rashiq said, gloating behind expressionless eyes.

Behind them, the shredders continued their din. Greg smiled at the group. "Come on, kids, let's go back upstairs where it's not so scary. We'll take the escalator this time."

Stop number two was a shock to Dr. Rashiq: DEFSMAC, the Defense Special Missile and Astronautics Center. Nobody, he had thought, ever got into this place without Top Secret/Sensitive Compartmented Information clearances and very compelling reasons. In fact, he knew that it was only because of his preoccupation with NSA and his hours of research that he had ever heard of the cryptic organization called DEFSMAC before this moment.

The guide reached into a metal box set just below a red seal, punched in a series of numbers, and pushed open the door, and the group walked unchallenged into one of the most secret and restricted organizations in the U.S. Intelligence Community. A short, very friendly man with a head full of curly black hair welcomed them and led them into the watch area, heart of the center. "My name is Andy," he said. "I'm the mission director here today. I'll talk a while and then you can ask me questions. First, let me step up on the dais so I can be the tallest person in the room." He chuckled as he hopped onto the elevated platform filled with several computer workstations and specialized displays—all dark. Signs over three of them read: INTELINK, ANCHORY, and WRANGLER.

"We don't get uncleared visitors here," he said. "In fact, you might be the first—except for that Polish general who came through after the Cold War ended." He wiped his brow. "That was a challenge! Two years earlier we would have just shot the guy.

"Anyway, you'll notice the screens on the wall are turned off and all the analysts in here are whispering into microphones. We can only go so far with openness, you know." He laughed again. Andy was enjoying himself.

"DEFSMAC," he said, "is what I always call the premier organization at the National Security Agency. Our mission is to coordinate collection against foreign missile and space launches, and we do it very well. But, we have an advantage. DEFSMAC is a joint organization, not just NSA, but DIA as well, and we go back to 1964. The Defense Intelligence Agency folks add a lot. They allow us to go well beyond just signals intelligence, or SIGINT—collecting phone calls or radar data or telemetry signals. We can also delve into the often weird world of HUMINT and multispectral, fast-framing, staring-sensor technology and terra bands and pixels and lots of other fun things. Most of us love our jobs and wouldn't work anywhere else for anything."

He didn't mention the two suicides and several severe nervous breakdowns that DEFSMAC personnel had suffered over the past thirty-five years. Nor that the stress of working in a near real-time environment, fun or not, takes a toll.

Andy spoke for a short time, really saying very little but making it sound like a lot. "Now it's your turn," he said. "But remember, I can't give away any secrets."

A man in the front row spoke out. "Do you control all the U.S. satellites up there spying on Americans? You know, the ones the newspapers call odd names like JUMPSEAT and TRUMPET?"

"Ah, I do love the easy questions," Andy said, grinning. "First, none of our satellites spy on U.S. citizens, and, second, I don't control anything, I just strongly recommend."

"Can you watch other countries launch spacecraft

and missiles? How do you know when they're gonna do it?" one of the teenagers asked.

"That's the toughest part of our job," the mission director said to the boy. "Knowing when, and exactly where. We have to find indicators, or what we call 'tip-offs.' We work very hard at that. And we get a lot of help from people at various sites all over the world, as well as some artificial intelligence input from systems like MASTERSHIP over there." He pointed to a work-station covered with a black cloth. "But can we actually watch the launches? Only on the TV news next day, like you."

"Do you have any astronauts working here?" the boy asked.

"Our last DEFSMAC director was an astronaut-select, but never went into the program. But she was truly a rocket scientist!" A look of amusement crossed his face at the thought of some past incident.

Suddenly, a red light high on the wall pulsed and an alarm went off.

"What's that?" a woman asked.

"That's the end of your tour, I'm afraid. Looks like there's a launch in progress."

The mission director, suddenly a professional intelligence officer rather than an amusing host, pulled on a set of earphones and barked orders to his crew. The guide led the group out of the area as people began jumping between workstations and pulling the black cloths off the wall displays. Outside in the hall, Captain Greg said, "You guys are really lucky to be in there during a launch sequence. You must be living right."

He led them back down the hall and up the steps to the second floor. "Next stop: NSOC. I can't believe they're letting you into NSOC, but you're definitely not the first. Reagan's been in, so has Cheney, at least one news anchor, and even James Bamford. I figure the Dixie Chicks will probably be next. But what do I know? I just follow orders." He grinned. "Follow me."

NSOC, the National Security Operations Center, was NSA's primary watch center and the soul of the Agency during its off hours. NSOC was the place that took care of the business of signals intelligence while the world outside slept. Every Agency office had a desk officer on duty in NSOC at all times: Middle East, Russia, China, ELINT, World Wide Weather, Counterterrorism, Counterintelligence, and many others. Here, emergencies were handled routinely, crises were coordinated with other watch centers, reports were issued, and people were constantly on alert.

Because of the frequent periods of high tension in NSOC, sneaking off into a remote corner to smoke was tolerated as a stress breaker, although, like all other Agency areas, it was officially a smoke-free environment.

After passing through two doors with combination locks and being warned to speak in whispers, the group entered one of the most exclusive places in the intelligence world. They stood in the rear of a huge room, dimly lit, surrounded by walls of electronic maps. Normally, each map would flicker with color-coded lights portraying different types of activity. But, while the visitors were there, the maps would stay dark. The guide told them that NSOC was by far the largest of NSA's watch centers, with a workforce of dozens of civilian and military employees on each eight-hour shift keeping track of any threatening activity anywhere in the world.

Cubicles filled the center of the room. Workers sat at desks, talking into headphones to communicate with each other as they had in DEFSMAC. It was remarkably quiet. The guide explained that when no visitors were present—nearly one hundred percent of the time—the headphones were put aside and everyone chattered constantly. "The place can sound like a madhouse," the guide said. "Especially when the bad guys cause trouble out there someplace." He pointed to one of the maps highlighting the Middle East.

Jamal Rashiq's eyes narrowed. *Bad guys? You have no idea just how bad,* he thought. *And one of them is standing right next to you.*

A tall, silver-haired man in a suit and tie walked out from a glassed-in office and approached the visitors. "This is the senior operations officer, also called the SOO," said the guide. "He is in charge of NSOC whenever he's on duty, and he is in charge of the entire Agency when he's on duty and everyone else has gone home. He's going to talk to you in the conference room."

When they were all seated, the man introduced himself as Tom. "I'm the SOO today," he said, "and I welcome you all to my world." He swept his hand around the conference room.

"You cannot imagine the secrets that have been discussed in here," he said, slowly shaking his head.

"Like what?" one of the teenagers asked.

"They wouldn't be secrets if I told you," the SOO said. "But I bet you can guess what some of them are. Shoot, half of them are probably PlayStation games by now." He looked over the group. "Okay, what questions do you have for me?"

"Do you ever get death threats from people who hate what the NSA does?" a man asked.

The SOO named Tom thought a moment. "Not really death threats," he said, "but we get some very strange phone calls from disturbed or angry people calling the Agency to complain about being watched or followed or having their phones tapped. Or that we've put computer chips in their brains so we can read their minds. Usually they call at night, so the SOO on watch gets to handle them; otherwise the folks in Public and Media Affairs get the honor."

"Oh," the teenager bounced with glee. "What's the worst call you ever got?"

Tom looked grim. "The worst thing I ever had to deal with wasn't a phone call, it was a series of home videos from some seriously disturbed person that mysteriously arrived in NSOC in the middle of the night instead of going to Public Affairs during the day as it should have. Videotapes of the man reading a newspaper, cooking hamburgers, reciting poetry, and, no doubt as a crowning touch, sitting on the toilet for a couple of hours. I sent that one off to Security pretty darn fast."

"Any more questions for the SOO?" asked the group's guide quickly. "Maybe something more mission-oriented?"

"How about e-mails? I know you spy on people's e-mails because it said so in the movie we just watched. Are you guys reading all my e-mails?" one of the teenagers demanded.

"Not all of them," the SOO answered. "Just the ones you send to terrorists or drug dealers or alien smugglers or Russian spies after you've renounced your American citizenship and you're living in a foreign country."

The teenager rolled his eyes. "Geez, you could've just said 'no we're not,'" he mumbled.

"I could have," the SOO grinned, "but nobody ever believes me when I say that."

A woman raised her hand. "Do you get information

from the grocery stores' computers about what we buy? Do you know all the things I've gotten at, like, Safeway, in the last year?"

The SOO laughed. "Okay, I'll try the simple way this time. The answer is 'No, NSA does not do that.' Interesting question, though. I've never heard that one before."

"Well, I'm sure you're going to say NSA doesn't listen to all of our phones calls, either," another woman said. "But, do you *want* to listen to all of them? That's what the newspapers say."

"The newspapers say that to sell newspapers," answered the SOO. "The truth is that NSA wants the same thing that all of you want—a safe and secure country where we're all free to pursue our lives."

Jamal Rashiq asked softly, "But NSA *could* listen in to all our calls if they wanted to, couldn't they? You have the *capability* to do that, right?"

"Well, sir," the SOO asked just as softly, "what do you do for a living?"

"I am a medical doctor. I specialize in researching and preventing hemorrhagic viruses," Rashiq replied proudly.

"In that case, Doctor," the SOO said, "I'm sure you deal with some very deadly diseases in your work. You have chosen to use your skills to save lives, but you probably have the *capability* to use your knowledge to do a lot of evil if you wanted to."

"A very good point," Rashiq said, nodding at the man. "Nicely put."

As the group filed out of the conference room and walked back to the cafeteria to meet up with their sponsors, Jamal Rashiq scowled. *What I'm going to do isn't evil. It's justice, and these people will soon face its full force.*

Rashiq met his sister and parents back in the cafeteria. They were sitting at a table drinking coffee and talking to a red-haired lady holding a framed promotion certificate. Rashiq had noticed her when she walked across the Friedman stage earlier. *She's the most attractive woman here,* he had thought, looking approvingly at her long legs and cascading crimson curls.

He approached the table with a charming smile.

"Alexandra O'Malley, this is my brother, Dr. Jamal Rashiq," Mariam said to the redhead with a pleased look on her face. "Alex was promoted today, too," she told Jamal as the two shook hands. "In fact, Alex is a very important person at NSA. She's in charge of Agency reporting these days. It's a big job."

She won't be doing that much longer, he thought.

The redhead smiled broadly as they finished shaking hands. "Mariam does a wonderful job here, Dr. Rashiq. You should be very proud of her." She looked over at the black-eyed linguist. "As proud as she is of you."

"Oh, I certainly am," he said, nodding his head. "And I'm so pleased to meet you, Alexandra. A friend of my sister's is a friend of mine."

2

Directorate of Operations Conference Room,
National Security Agency
Friday, December 1, 2000
Morning

NSA is in deep trouble, **I thought, for perhaps the**
third time today, and a quick glance at the clock told
me it was only seven-thirty-three a.m. Twelve of us
were seated around the Directorate of Operations' polished wooden conference table waiting for our daily
staff meeting to begin. Nobody spoke, but I could almost hear eyes flicking back and forth as we waited
for Sally Epperson, DO chief of staff, to arrive. I wondered if everyone else in the room was as aware of
the precipitous downward slide of the National Security Agency as I was. *Even if they are,* I thought, *denial would be their first response; stonewalling their
second.*

I may have come to work for NSA fourteen years
ago with a degree in political science rather than eco-
nomics, but I could easily tell what the effect of the
past decade of budget cuts had been on the Agency.

Anyone could see it by just looking around: Outside, several light posts in the parking lots had cracked
and not been replaced. Huge boulders painted white
had been put in a ring around the complex, apparently

cheaper than permanent fencing. The effect was un-professional and a bit kooky. Not as unprofessional, however, as the decaying old trailer that was currently the Agency's Visitors' Center.

Inside the main buildings, uncompleted remodeling and repair projects had left large areas gutted and austere. Hallway lights had burned out or flickered uncertainly. The atmosphere was chilly and forlorn, especially after daylight hours and in the older parts of the complex. Many of the ladies' rooms had hand dryers that hadn't worked in months and faucets that were out of order. Not wanting to become known as "Alexandra O'Malley, plumbing inspector," I hadn't asked any of the men about the state of their bathrooms.

Less than a year ago, the entire NSA computer infra-structure had collapsed, putting every office in the Agency effectively out of business for an unbelievable four days. Actual *collection* of intercepted phone con-versations and other signals intelligence information didn't stop, but this harvest of data piled up in electronic bushel baskets with no way for analysts at Fort Meade to process or report it. A group of renegade Russians could have been plotting to nuke New York City, and NSA wouldn't have had a clue.

Computer crashes were still common, leaving en-tire floors of buildings without connectivity for hours. Morale was so low that people huddled together in small groups in the halls, the cafeteria, and even the credit union to grumble and fret about the lack of di-rection and to grieve for our lost days of glory.

And they *were* glorious: nearly fifty years of pro-viding an incomparably valuable source of intelli-gence to those at the head of the U.S. government and military organizations. Now, however, recognition of

our achievements and praise from the highest levels
had slipped away into increasing criticism and funding problems.

A man across from me coughed, interrupting the
tense silence in the conference room. I checked the
others' faces for signs of life, found little, and went back
to my musings.

The National Security Agency was, by anyone's assessment, an elite American government organization.
Introverted cousin to the Central Intelligence Agency,
it remained an unknown entity to much of the country.
And no wonder: dashing, daring, swashbuckling CIA
agents got all the press as they pursued their undercover quests. NSA analysts (with a few extraordinary
but carefully hidden exceptions) were much more sequestered and hidden from publicity. *"Keep a low pro-
file. Never comment on anything,"* security personnel
and posters reminded NSA's workforce daily. And the
workforce listened. For years we joked that NSA stood
for "No Such Agency" or "Never Say Anything."

But don't doubt for a minute that CIA and NSA
were intimately entwined as they went about their
business of intelligence gathering. The primary mission of the National Security Agency was intercepting
foreign phone calls, faxes, e-mails, telemetry, and radar
transmissions. Collection of this data could result in
a treasure trove of signals intelligence, or SIGINT,
which provided actual transcripts of the enemy talking about their plans, sometimes real-time, in their
own words. Nothing could compete with it for reli-
ability and accuracy; few other sources could provide
such knowledge and insight.

NSA SIGINT supported many CIA programs, just
as CIA human intelligence (HUMINT) provided the

basis for new or different approaches to signals collection. This interdependence was the way the Intelligence Community was designed to work, not just between CIA and NSA, but for all its members.

The National Security Agency was America's cryptologic organization, and the country could not survive without it. But the end of the Cold War and the cutbacks of the 1990s had cast NSA adrift on a sea of severe budget cuts, constant reorganizations, a dwindling workforce, and deepening malaise. SIGINT didn't seem quite so important to anyone anymore. In many ways, our success was our downfall.

It was not just NSA that lost its focus when the Soviets drew down the curtain on their decades-old socialist experiment. Turmoil and uncertainty raced through the corridors of every agency concerned with intelligence collection and analysis. Of course, we still had plenty of collection targets:

rogue states
weapons of mass destruction
nuclear proliferation
terrorists
illegal drugs
cyber crimes

But we knew that the dogged determination with which we had pursued our former archenemy had waned. Along, of course, with our funding.

God help us when the next global crisis explodes, I thought. *It will take a lot of work to bring the community back together again. I don't know how we'll do it.*

And a crisis was bound to happen. I knew it, but

nobody wanted to believe it. The complacency level, even in the Intelligence Community, was way, way too high. At every level.

Sometimes I thought the only thing people in this country cared about in this first year of this new millennium was the continuing prosperity generated by an ever-rising stock market.

I looked at the clock again: seven-thirty-seven. In the old days, two weeks ago, the daily Operations Directorate staff meeting started at the crack of seven-thirty, no matter what. Of course, those meetings also used to be tiresome, tedious, and sometimes interminable, but no longer. Our new Director, Lt. General John Murray, had seen to that. Charged with transforming NSA from an agency that had lost its way into a sleek provider of intelligence information, he now sent daily demands to the Directorate of Operations— the DO—staff to address.

This personal attention from DIRNSA had terrified most of the executives required to answer his questions and carry out his orders. Previous DIRNSAs had always been a bit, oh, ethereal. They dwelt "up there," enjoying their final tour before retirement, meeting with presidents and secretaries of defense, and testifying before congressional committees. They didn't, for God's sake, actually *read* NSA reports and comment on them. Or trouble themselves with what the *workforce* thought.

This DIRNSA was different. A graduate of the Air Force Academy with a master's degree in military history from Duquesne University, General Murray did not strut around the NSA hallways with an entourage of aides like many of his predecessors. Rumor had it that he walked to the barbershop alone, stopping to shake hands with and talk to NSA employees he met in the hall. The general was a sturdy, balding man with a pleasant smile. He looked like a good guy to go fishing with. No one underestimated his power, however. We knew he didn't get to the rank of three-star without plenty of determination and grit. Most people were still trying to figure him out.

In one of his first e-mails to the workforce, he stated:

> We must change how we behave, think and feel at NSA. This is more than just "culture"; it is "ethos," the complete thought process of our workforce. We must make this change so that we can reenergize our mission. If we circle the wagons one more time, we will begin to resemble the Donner Party—with, perhaps, the same consequences.

In a truly amazing departure from historical precedence, General Murray had invited, encouraged even, everyone who worked at NSA to send him e-mails with their concerns and advice. And they had responded: he got hundreds of them daily and answered each one personally.

I checked the time again: seven-forty, bordering on a new record. Sally Epperson, Directorate of Operations chief of staff, entered the room and took a seat at the head of the polished wooden conference table. In front of her was a stack of paper, mostly intelligence reports NSA had issued the previous day, all notated in red ink and signed with DIRNSA's initials. Still silent, she began to skim the papers to decide who should get each action. Most of the people at the table looked like they were holding their breath, probably wondering if it would ever be safe to breathe again.

I watched this process as serenely as I always did, undisturbed by the tension in the room. I was pleased that the Director was involved in our future and that he was asking questions and talking to us all. It wasn't a threat to me; frankly, I found it challenging, exhilarating. And, in this case, necessary. Nearly everyone else was scared stiff.

There was a reason why. Most of these people were currently living outside their comfort zone, afraid they might be asked to do something different from what they had always done. Afraid they would be encouraged to embrace NSA's new concept of individual empowerment. Perhaps above all else, NSA employees did not like to be held personally responsible for making decisions.

This should be no surprise to anyone who has worked here.

Before we were hired by NSA, we were given a battery of tests: psychological, IQ, mental acuity, aptitude. If we made it through that process—including the "lifestyle" polygraph, which is another story altogether (Have you used drugs? Had sex with animals? Think God speaks to you through the metal in your teeth?, etc.)—and were hired, we were given more tests. Perhaps the most interesting, and the most revealing about the nature of NSA employees, was the Myers-Briggs personality assessment.

We took this test because long ago someone in Personnel decided that it would help us understand and value one another for our differences. After the results were in, we were each given a small sign with the four-letter designator indicating our personality type. We were told to put the sign on our desk so that those who come to see us could instantly identify how best to communicate with us. Or at least to know who the heck they were dealing with.

This exercise was not much of a challenge at NSA. Desk after desk displayed the designator "ISTJ," letters which stood for an Introverted/Sensing/Thinking/Judging personality type.

ISTJs, translated from the official jargon, tended to be

introverted
serious
orderly
responsible
impersonal
inflexible
aloof

They loved details and clung insistently to the long-established ways of doing things. They wore white shirts (well, sometimes light blue) and gray suits and never ate a peach. They were, above all else,

careful.

This particular personality type comprised a near-majority of the people at the National Security Agency and a supermajority at all levels of management.

Even the blatantly odd employees—like the aging hippie with the gray-streaked ponytail that fell to his waist; the mathematician who mumbled to himself in the hall but refused to speak to his colleagues, providing his amazingly brilliant discoveries in longhand on sheets of yellow legal paper; the man who breathlessly counted each step he took in the stairwells and always walked in the exact middle of the stairs—at heart, they were as conservative as anyone else who worked at the Agency.

Last year, the Agency published its *National Cryptologic Strategy for the Twenty-First Century.* An unclassified version was posted on the Internet. One sentence read: *"Our forward thinking, innovativeness, and willingness to take risks keep us at the forefront of our business."* I don't know who wrote that, but it was largely untrue. In fact, it was largely a joke. Risk taking, no matter how measured, was not something many NSA employees wanted to think about, much less do. For the most part, staying "at the forefront of our business" had been achieved through determination and hard work, not through brilliant flares of creativity or imagination. Traditional ideas, rules, patterns, and old ways of doing things have always ruled at the Agency.

Whether DIRNSA knew it or not, this was the ethos he wanted to change at NSA. He was going to have a tough time.

Myers-Briggs was a test I failed badly, at least from an NSA perspective, but I guess I wasn't surprised. My mother, Molly, a retired NSA senior executive, had always told me I was much more of a freethinker and nonconformist than most of the other people at NSA. I turned out to be an "ENTP," an Extroverted/ Intuitive/Thinking/Perceiving personality type who was bored by routine and was not always careful to follow all the rules.

The test administrator defined ENTPs as having been put on this earth to drive ISTJs crazy. I was undisturbed. I already knew I wasn't like the rest of the people I worked with.

I was an extrovert. I liked new ideas, adversity,

tough problems to solve. I wasn't afraid to make decisions. I hated red tape and often ignored it. I liked to
improvise. I could handle details just fine when I had
to, but I didn't let them slow me down. I always wanted
the big picture, and I wanted it fast. It was either a
miracle, or a disaster, depending on your viewpoint,
that I was hired by NSA and continued to work here.
But I loved it. Maybe it's the never-ending challenge
of making new things happen against all odds.

There were a few more like me here, but not many.
Most had left or had hidden their damning tempera-
ment indicators and pretended to be more like everyone else. To fit in. And get ahead.

This was the current I swam against every day. It's
a good thing I was a strong swimmer.

I looked around as the chief of staff continued reviewing the papers, dividing them into piles. This room
had been recently renovated and was often a meeting
place for visitors who were important but not quite
director-level. The gray-blue carpet still looked new,
and a matching set of drapes covered two large projec-
tion screens at the end of the table. Six rows of tasteful
wooden chairs with burgundy upholstery filled one side
of the room. There were no windows, but the lights
were almost endlessly adjustable. It was a pleasant
place usually, unless, like now, you were waiting for the
crap to hit the fan.

Sally pushed a stack of papers my way. "Alexandra
O'Malley, again you win the prize for getting the most
actions," she said.

I looked at the first report on the pile: General Murray had written across the top, *"I can't understand this.
Where is the background? What's the context? And
what does the title mean?"*

No wonder he was confused. The subject line

contained thirty-seven words and two semicolons.
This title was so jumbled I couldn't determine if the
article was about bioterrorism or drug smuggling.

The other eight were afflicted by a variety of problems, some similar, some not. The most disturbing to
me, and to the general as well, was a description of a
conversation between a well-known terrorist and another man in Saudi Arabia who was planning a trip to
the U.S. *"Why was this issued five days late?"* the red
ink demanded. *"Did someone at least call the FBI and
tell them about these plans?"* I hoped so, but almost
certainly that hadn't happened. NSA was forbidden by
law to provide phone tip-offs unless the information
had already been officially reported in written format
to the Intelligence Community. This kind of dilemma
is an excellent example of how Congress tied our hands
after the Church Committee investigations in the 1970s.
I sighed. This one was a real problem.

I handed it to the chief of the Office of Counterterrorism, seated just to my right. "I'll need to see you
at my one o'clock meeting today, Henry," I said. "Please
have an answer to this question. And these other two."

Henry, a longtime senior executive, barely looked
up from the papers. "I'm busy at one. I'll send my
deputy."

"No, I need you there," I said, without elaboration. I
have found it's better to say as little as possible to the
powerful. Henry Trotter was, apparently, unimpressed
with my new title, assistant director for agency reporting.

Or that I had now been a GS-15, just one grade
below senior executive, for all of twenty-four hours.
But he must have heard that the Director himself had
picked me to reenergize NSA report writing; he
shrugged his agreement.

I, on the other hand, was equally unimpressed with his reputation for sexual prowess or with the rumor that he had been caught by a guard after hours last year boffing his administrative assistant in the comfort of his oversized office. Not that he was the only one doing it; sex between NSA coworkers was commonplace, even at the highest levels. Having sex *inside* one of the buildings—even if it was just with your own husband or wife—was considered a major achievement. It was the NSA version of the "mile-high club."

Sally picked up another paper, this one torn from a notepad embossed at the top:

DIRECTOR, NATIONAL SECURITY AGENCY
9800 SAVAGE ROAD
FT. GEORGE G. MEADE, MD 20755–6000

"Good Lord," she said, looking over the writing on the paper, "DIRNSA wants to know why the library doesn't carry the newest edition of the *International Electronic Countermeasures Handbook*. Where does he come up with these things?" She handed it to her deputy. "Cliff, please take this down to the head librarian right away."

Cliff nodded slowly and stood. He didn't want to miss the rest of the meeting and its potential for emotional frenzy. After all, half the people in the room were senior executives, a group known for its haughty exclusivity. Many of these folks had gone beyond *careful* to full-blown *defensive* as the new Director began his transformation campaign, and there was no telling what they might do.

For some, the lines between NSA and real life had blurred to the point that their job had *become* their life. A few years ago, in the middle of the post-U.S.S.R. downsizing of the Agency, the previous Director had asked a senior executive to retire. He didn't take it well. He ended up sobbing and screaming and threatening people, and the Federal Protective Service guards had to go up to DIRNSA's office and carry him out of the building.

Nobody wanted to miss that kind of show. No wonder Cliff was reluctant to leave.

Sally moved on. The next item was a thick, bound document titled "U.S. National Intelligence Estimate on the Ballistic Missile Threat." It was so highly classified I wondered exactly who could read it.

NIEs were prepared by the CIA, often in response to a request from a high-level policy maker, and must be coordinated with all the other Intelligence Community agencies. NIEs often showed up for coordination late on a Friday afternoon, ensuring a weekend of work for the NSA point of contact and hardly endearing their producer to the response team. They could be very interesting, however, because they differed from most other intelligence products, which merely assessed current issues: NIEs actually *forecasted* future developments and covered a wide range of concerns— from military to technological to economic to political trends.

On the front of this NIE, DIRNSA had scribbled, *"See pg 14."* On page 14, the note continued. *"Are we ready for this? Let's not miss it like we did the India nuclear test two years ago."* Unspoken were the words: *"Not on My Watch."* A short highlighted paragraph was circled in red:

███████████████████████ missile, which is capable of reaching parts of the United States with a nuclear weapon-sized (several hundred kg) payload, appears ready for flight-testing.

Sally read this out loud and passed the document to the director of DEFSMAC. I had heard some of the visitors at the promotion ceremony yesterday had been taken on a tour of DEFSMAC, but I could hardly believe it. The center was hidden deep inside Ops 1 and was inaccessible to most other employees because of its extreme sensitivity in the missile and space world.

Director Vince Morelli smiled as he took the NIE. He was on top of this one. Director of DEFSMAC is a plum assignment and, for Vince, his preretirement tour. He had had a distinguished career at the National Security Agency, and he damn well meant to keep it that way. He had already held meeting after meeting with his mission directors, branch chiefs, collection specialists, and analysts on the subject of ████████████ missile launches and their indicators. Vince could write the answer to this DIRNSA question in his sleep.

Sally picked up the last paper from the pile. The group at the table leaned forward as she said, "This one is really unusual. It's an e-mail to the Director from two analysts. It's been forwarded to us from his executive assistant. She says DIRNSA is at another emergency meeting at CIA, but she's sure he will want to know the answer to this when he returns. I'm afraid I don't understand what it's about, so you will have to decide whose action it is."

It was very short, and she read it to us. "General Murray: We are concerned that the new Project Meridian communications have gone silent. We don't know who else to ask about it. Can you help?"

I couldn't believe I had heard her correctly. A chunk of ice the size of New Jersey formed in my stomach. If what the e-mail said were true, we were facing a disaster of massive proportions. If it were true, NSA's greatest achievement in years, perhaps decades, had been compromised. Tiny hairs on my arms rose chillingly as I thought about the consequences.

Only two people in the room were cleared for the Meridian project—me and the man sitting across the table from me, Navy Captain Kip McColloh. Captain McColloh was the chief of the Operations Collection Management Center, or OCMC. He made a choking noise and reached out his hand toward the e-mail Sally was holding. "I'll take that, please," he said. His face was ashen.

3

Forty minutes later our group had gathered in the Project Meridian office. The tiny space, carved quickly from a storage room in the basement for the ultra-secret Meridian project, was designed to hold three analysts, four at the most. Instead, nine stunned people had crammed into the small area. An angry silence hung in the air as we all stared at the transcript of a phone call intercepted just two days before. Only a few words long, its impact on the people in the room was stunning.

"Stop using these phones now. They are not safe. We have ... [unknown number of words garbled] ... *Meet at two o'clock Sunday at the Uncle's house for new plans,"* the words, translated from Arabic, read. After that terse call, there had been no others between the al Qaeda headquarters in Afghanistan and the terrorist cell in Germany that NSA was targeting.

"Is there any way this could be just some kind of test?" In the middle of the anguished group, Mike Faure, security officer for the project, looked over at the two NSA Project Meridian linguists hopefully.

"Don't think so." The voice came from a massive

black man in air force fatigues who stood near a desk filled with headphones, magnetic tapes, dictionaries, a computer, and an array of miscellaneous paraphernalia.

"But could it mean they stopped using the GlobalSat phones? That they just switched to some other satellite company?"

"Don't know for sure," the Pashtu and Arabic linguist said. His nametag read "Jackson." "But we've been doing this long enough to guess what they're up to. We're pretty sure they know they've been betrayed."

Navy Captain McColloh, Operations Collection Management Center chief, slammed his hand down on the desk. "Goddamn it," he snarled at Mike, displaying his famous brusque and blustering persona, "stop trying to put a happy face on this thing."

I grimaced. Mike Faure was my ex-husband and we were still friends. I knew he was cringing at this furious criticism.

The captain continued. "There's no other possible interpretation. They've found out we can unscramble their calls and they aren't going to be using those phones or any other damn phones again during this operation. The only reason they even went to the GlobalSats was because they were convinced they were completely secure. Now they know better and we're screwed. And that little bastard in Germany was about a gnat's eyelash away from blabbin' the details of their plan. You could tell just reading the transcripts of the most recent calls that he's a braggart. A couple of more intercepts, and he would have given us something good."

The captain's face twisted with anger. "But not now. Now, thanks to someone who knows what Project Meridian is all about—and that has to be one of us, Goddamn it—a lot of people are probably going to die and we can't do a freakin' thing to help stop it."

The rest of us nodded our agreement. The end of these intercepts would be a lethal blow to one of NSA's greatest successes; a success so huge it was a miracle, really. Project Meridian was a cover name for the recent recovery of the communication network used by the terrorist leader Usama bin Laden, traditionally referred to as UBL by the Agency workforce.

"We can't look at it that way." An elegantly dressed man sitting on the room's other chair spoke for the first time. He was Barry Ballard, the deputy director for security who had handed out promotion certificates at the ceremony the day before. He had been involved in the Meridian project from its inception.

Lying at his feet was Barry's constant companion, an unusually small black guide dog with a bright red kerchief tied around its neck. The dog opened an eye from time to time to check that all was in order and then fell back asleep, head against Barry's foot. We were all used to seeing them together in the halls as the dog guided its master unerringly through the maze of passageways that made up the four main NSA buildings. Their bond was clearly a very special one.

"Why the hell not?" the OCMC chief demanded. "It's a disaster. What other way can we look at it?"

"Well," Barry replied, "we said the very same thing in 1998 when those press leaks alerted UBL that we were listening to his ████████████ phones. He stopped using them immediately, remember? We knew he had to communicate with his al Qaeda cells somehow, but nobody here could figure out how he was doing it. And all the speculation—e-mails, a new satellite system, couriers, microwave, smoke signals. Remember that?"

We all nodded slowly. Yes, we remembered. Just like now, we all knew then that thousands of lives could depend on regaining the terrorists' communications.

"It took two years," Barry continued. "But we never gave up and we did find the answer." He smiled. "Well, actually, we found a 'mole' inside bin Laden's camp, and he gave us the answer. And then we developed Project Meridian. It's been one of NSA's most effective programs in the history of the Agency. We didn't give up then, and we can't give up now."

Barry's smile faded. "And by the way, while we're all sitting here feeling sorry for ourselves about losing the comms, you might take a minute and say a prayer for that inside guy because if the poor SOB is not already dead, he will be soon."

"Yes, you're right. We should do that for sure," Captain McColloh said quietly. "Finding that guy was a hell of a coup. He was very good to us. He doesn't deserve what's going to happen to him."

A quiet pause. Then, "Yes, may we all be so courageous when we need to be," said Barry.

Project Meridian was born in the fall of 2000 after a bin Laden aide named Ajmal, in agony over the accidental death of his son at a UBL-funded terrorist training camp, turned against the al Qaeda leader and his cohorts. He confided his anguished feelings to his brother-in-law Bashir, and Bashir, an occasional CIA-financed proxy operative, asked him to help work against the terrorists. Ajmal jumped at the chance for revenge.

Ajmal was not in the inner circles of the al Qaeda band. They did not share their plans with him. But he was a trusted servant, a friend of bin Laden's for several years. He had free rein of the compound, cooking, cleaning, getting supplies, and, most important, performing the daily morning test of the new satellite phone system linkup with its outposts. He knew exactly how the terrorists were talking to each other, and he told CIA, through Bashir, how they were doing it.

He passed on to Bashir that bin Laden, flush with funds (more than you could say for NSA) simply switched from the ████████████ phones he had been using before the 1998 press leaks to something much more advanced: GlobalSat, a new generation satellite phone system. And the digital version of GlobalSat, with its specially designed crypto-key plug-in, allowed his network to become secure and robust. UBL's conversations, no longer readable by NSA, had continued undetected by us via satcomm links.

Satellite phones were used by tens of thousands throughout the world who spent their lives beyond the reach of ordinary telecommunications. They were the cell phones of the civilization-challenged. Unless you're actually in the polar regions, GlobalSat's constellation of eight geosynchronous satellites would give you instant communication capability anywhere in the world. They're used by navies and police forces and fishermen and inhabitants of remote villages . . . and terrorists. Pop in a smart card called a Subscriber Identification Module, and your phone became secure from most listeners; add the crypto plug-in, and it was impregnable. For most users, GlobalSat was a lifesaver. For UBL and his network, it was a weapon.

Ajmal's information that UBL was using GlobalSat was a stunning breakthrough for us; one we would never forget.

"But remember," Barry said, "that even after Ajmal told us which phone system UBL was using, the usual times of day he used it, and even what frequencies it was on, we still couldn't read his conversations. We could intercept them all right, but we couldn't decipher them."

"Oh, yes, I remember that part," the man beside him answered. "Our damn supercomputer couldn't break the encryption system, and I had to go to Congress and beg them for money to buy a new one. One of the senators on the committee actually asked who Usama bin Laden was and why we cared what some terrorist in a cave in Afghanistan was doing. Too regional, too primitive, he would never affect us on American soil, he said."

The man speaking was Paul Eckerd, PhD and deputy director for operations—DDO. He sat on one of the two desk chairs and looked thoughtfully at the people in the tiny room. He was the third most powerful person at NSA after the Director and the deputy director, in charge of the directorate where all the SIGINT collection strategies were designed and the Agency's analysis and reporting took place. The DDO position could be a stepping stone to deputy director of NSA, and the incumbent always had DIRNSA's ear.

Paul had been with the Agency for nearly forty years, and he still loved everything about the place. He had risen quickly through the ranks, checking all the necessary boxes (shift work, staff officer, field service) to make sure nothing stood in his way. He had been a brilliant analyst and theorist during the first half of his career. Unfortunately, like so many other brilliant analysts, he was moved into management, where he no longer shined. The workforce saw him as a brainy but remote senior exec and interacted with him as little as possible. It seemed obvious to us that his wife must dress him; otherwise he would surely wear plaids and stripes of clashing colors and forget to comb his hair as he had in his early days with the Agency. No one was sure how he had gotten to the very weighty post of DDO, and we hoped, with his incredible lack of people skills, that he wouldn't ever be the deputy director.

"The committee wouldn't give us a cent," Paul said. "Not for that, not for much of anything except retirement incentives. All Congress wanted was for NSA to reduce its workforce, not to spend money for new computer capability, no matter how critical it was. And it's definitely critical."

He was so right: NSA's latest Cray supercomputer, so powerful and fast it was nicknamed Hercules when it was acquired in the mid-1990s, could not break the rotating cipher-generating algorithm in bin Laden's new satellite phone. Modern encryption techniques long ago had abandoned the realm of one-time pads and code books; today it's all done with computer chips. But keeping up with the latest systems that power the chips is expensive, and, despite pleas from NSA management, money for a supercomputer upgrade was not on the congressional horizon. Even a long horizon.

"But we found a way around that, too, didn't we?" Barry asked us. "We developed another method to read the comms."

And we had done just that. As it turned out, NSA cryptographers didn't have to depend on Hercules to break the sophisticated cipher or for money to buy new computing hardware. Our cryptologic engineers devised an alternative, bold scheme with an incredible payoff, and Ajmal, devoted Muslim and grieving father, carried it out under bin Laden's nose. One early morning while he was testing the new communication system, Ajmal replaced the crypto card in UBL's

GlobalSat phone with a fake one, which, instead of choosing a random algorithm, chose the same one each time. NSA listeners were back in business: we could break this code as easily as if there were no encryption at all.

It was a maneuver so clever, so immediately successful that everyone involved considered it the cryptologic achievement of a lifetime.

Now, after only a few weeks, the comms had apparently been compromised again.

"And now we're back in the dark. What are we going to do? I can't even imagine what we can do, Barry, despite your optimism." The OCMC chief continued his hand-wringing.

"We must find a way," Barry said, twisting his coffee cup on his knee. "We have to. Everybody in here knows that."

Silence filled the small space. The magnitude of this loss was beyond words. Everyone in the room knew we had been on the verge of discovering the details of a plot that was savage, huge.

Project Meridian might not have been prodigious in its output, but what it did provide was pure gold: names and aliases of al Qaeda terrorists, ████████ transactions, detailed personal information, and, because it was a satellite system, links between terrorists in Afghanistan and al Qaeda cells all over the world. Sometimes UBL himself spoke to his followers, obscurely discussing various nefarious plots. The transcribers recognized his voice easily now.

Most recently, the intercepts revealed strong hints that a major operation was in the final stages of planning. UBL and his cohorts referred to the operation as *al-Buraq*, named, apparently, for the winged steed that carried the Prophet Mohammed through the skies

on his so-called spiritual Night of Power some fourteen centuries ago.

Much of the chatter on the network, whether it was
from the Taliban, who used mainly Pashtu, or al
Qaeda, who spoke primarily Arabic, dealt with matters
other than *al-Buraq*, so we had very few intercepts
dealing directly with the plans. A few phrases or
strangely worded sentences indicated a preoccupation
with explosions, thousands of deaths, a worldwide reaction of massive proportions including, perhaps, military retribution. This theme definitely got our attention;
we had not heard conjecture quite like that before. It
seemed to us that whatever murderous schemes the al
Qaeda teams had dreamed up had evolved into an operation of grandiose scale.

We reported these intercepts in our special channels, but we had no real facts and no time line and no
idea what the discussions really meant—except that
the level of excitement among the terrorist satcomm
users was rising by the day. Collection on this link had
been as dedicated as any outside of outright conflict,
but we were still missing details. We knew *al-Buraq*
was serious, and we worried that this time the terrorists would be able to follow through.

We debated among ourselves if naming the operation after a flying horse had any real meaning. Did
they plan to use missiles? Aircraft? Bombs? What was
the target? Something symbolic as was often the case?
Where? Europe? The United States? Surely a major
strike against the U.S. was impossible. We talked and
worried, talked and worried.

We began to have meetings among the Project Meridian members from other agencies to discuss what
UBL might be planning. We invited experts from other
agencies to address specific questions as they arose. We

discussed the various possibilities: dirty bombs, chemical or biological warfare, hijacking, suicide bombers.

But our biggest fear was that bin Laden had managed to get hold of materials to build a small nuclear weapon, especially since the speaker on one intercept referred to the *al-Buraq* plan as "another Hiroshima." We knew from a very sensitive and reliable informant that, in the mid-1990s, agents of al Qaeda had tried repeatedly, but without success, to purchase highly enriched uranium in South Africa, Europe, and Russia. What if a source for HEU, the essential ingredient of nuclear weapons, had actually been found? Obtaining this material would be the hardest part of making a small nuke, so long as the Pakistanis, or a renegade scientist from another nuclear program, were willing to help them. It might be crude, bulky, and low-yield, but the terrorists could deliver it to our shores by container ship and then drive it by truck or van to strike a blow so devastating the world would never recover from its consequences. A nuclear scientist we brought in to the Agency from DOE put it in stark terms.

"If the men who detonated the car bomb under the World Trade Center in 1993 had had a small nuculear weapon—one that would fit in a van-sized vehicle—instead of the urea nitrate-fuel oil device they used, it would have been a whole different story. As it was, only six people died and the North Tower didn't collapse as planned. With a small nuke, ten kiloton yield or smaller, not only would the WTC buildings have tumbled but the whole southern tip of Manhattan would have disappeared. Thousands and thousands would have died or wished they had. But the terrorists have to be able to get the plutonium to make such a nuke."

We wouldn't be so worried if we didn't know plutonium and HEU were available in several facilities, in a number of countries, with security ranging from excellent to flat-out scary. Would someone in one of those facilities sell this material to terrorists, even knowing what might happen? You bet.

Perhaps it could be even simpler: Pakistan's Inter-Services Intelligence Directorate had been complicit in everything over the years, from heroin smuggling to assassinations to aiding North Korea in its nuclear program to funding UBL's training camp at Zahawa, in a border area between Pakistan and Afghanistan—until it was destroyed by U.S. cruise missiles in August 1998. Supplying al Qaeda with an already built small nuke seemed within both ISI's capabilities and interests.

We scoured the intercepts for any hint of such a thing, any carefully worded phrases that could indicate al Qaeda had somehow received such a weapon or any of its parts. We had found nothing yet except for the references to thousands of deaths, which was enough to keep us very alert. We had hoped bin Laden would call someone besides his regular group; someone outside Afghanistan whom he would need to brief on this operation. Perhaps then we could get details. God forbid this new contact would be in the States—then we would have to stop recording the conversation until the FBI investigated the citizenship of the person being called. If he turned out to be a U.S. citizen or green card holder, then we would have to go to a special court for a warrant. It's damn hard to get all that done in time to discover anything useful. Most likely the first call would be the last call, and all we would have of that would be very little.

NSA intercepted hundreds of calls between various terrorist cells making threatening statements, planning acts of destruction, and talking about killing Jews,

Americans, and just about anyone who was not one of them. They were a normal, everyday kind of collection. UBL's comms were different, and we thanked our good fortune every time we intercepted them. The world hadn't taken much notice of him yet, but we knew he was the big guy. He had struck before and he would do it again. The drumbeat of intrigue and scheming associated with the *al-Buraq* operation had intensified to the point where everyone in the know from DIRNSA to the White House was demanding more information. We desperately wanted to provide it.

We begged other members of the Intel Community— those receiving our special channel reports—to add any information they had. As usual, sharing data was problematic; everyone wanted to keep control of what they collected and dole it out only in extreme circumstances. As always, we didn't know what they wouldn't tell us. *We need a place for all related information to come together and be assessed,* I thought again, as I had so many times.

We had worked so hard on this, and now, apparently, it was over.

Paul Eckerd stood up and squared his shoulders. "We need some time . . . we have to think this through . . . find out the details . . ." He sat back down in the chair.

"Damn it, Paul, the details aren't going to matter a bit. The comms are lost, gone as of now, and we're in shit up to our elbows." The speaker was Lester Krebbs, a short, plump angry man with thinning hair. He was the oldest person in the room, almost sixty-five, ten years past retirement age, a careerist who couldn't imagine a life after the Agency. His position as chief of Covert Assurance Operations gave him access to the Project Meridian clearance—his group of engineers had designed the special crypto card that Ajmal had placed in UBL's GlobalSat phone. Lester was sexist, bigoted, pugnacious, and often boorish, but smart enough to know who he could insult with impunity.

I had often wondered if his early life as an enlisted man in the army had somehow forged him into the bigot I had come to know and dislike. Or if his lack of a college degree in a place where most of us have not just a bachelor's degree but also a master's had made him so defensive he overreacted with bitter hostility. In any case, he had left an icy trail of misogynistic destruction behind him—he had consistently gone out of his way to block promotions and advancements for females through rumors, sneers, and backstabbing lies.

I had no doubt at all that he had attributed my recent promotion to me sleeping with someone (everyone?) in my promotion chain. I recently overheard him talking to one of his cronies in the hall about the "slut" who got all her promotions on her back. They both snickered as I walked by. I knew he could have been talking about me or any other woman who had advanced past GS-5 in the government pay scale.

After the "shit" comment, Lester turned to his side and mumbled, "Sorry, Alex. Forgot you were here." He didn't bother to apologize to the other woman in the room; she was just a lowly linguist and dark-skinned besides.

I was standing near the door, watching everyone's reactions to the news about the lost comms. "Lester," I said. "I've heard the word 'shit' before."

"The real question is, who gave us away? Ames, Walker, and those two commie fags who defected back in the sixties were bad, but this is worse than any of them," Lester continued with his usual lack of even basic sensitivity. "We've got to find the nutcase who betrayed us."

"The only good news is we should be able to figure out who that is," Mike Faure said. "There just aren't that many people who could have done it."

Project Meridian was so secret it was in the VRK— Very Restricted Knowledge—program, and only about twenty people at NSA had been "read in": DIRNSA, of course; the deputy director of operations; the deputy director for security; the OCMC chief and his staff; a program security officer; an Operations Security guy and his engineers; and two Pashtu/Arabic linguists, a crypto-engineer, one COMINT signals analyst, and me, the newly appointed assistant director for agency reporting.

I was involved in Project Meridian because it was my job as Agency reporting guru to make sure the information from the project was disseminated to the right people in the right way.

All NSA employees held clearances at the Top Secret SCI (Sensitive Compartmented Information) level, which gave them access to much of what was collected and reported at the Agency, including intercepts that came from NRO-designed and -operated satellites. However, there were plenty of special VRK programs with access doled out only to those with the "Need to Know," a hugely important concept at NSA. At its most basic level, the Need to Know directive meant you were not allowed to share any intelligence information with anyone else unless you were positive that person must have it to do his job. Even if he had the same clearances you did, even if he was working on the same targets you were, even (perhaps, especially) if he was your counterpart at CIA or some other agency.

Need to Know was everything. A Need to Share

concept had not yet entered our culture in a meaningful way.

Some projects were so sensitive, and so exquisitely
esoteric, that candidates for the access had to pass a
private, rigorous polygraph and a series of security
interviews before they were "read in." Believe me,
this stuff was beyond anything Tom Clancy could
think up.

Reporting information from these programs to
authorized customers in the Intelligence Community
always presented special challenges. Each time the
Meridian analysts decided to issue a report, they sent
it to me by Agency e-mail, encrypted under the NSA-
created Icarus protocol. I read it and made sure it
made sense, stated everything in context, referenced
any previous related activity, and included any perti-
nent "collateral"—any bit of amplifying information
other than SIGINT. Most important, I decided the
proper recipients and how to notify them. Twice I have
hand-carried publications to the White House office
of the president's national security advisor, an unusual
method of delivering reports used only for extremely
sensitive material.

"Right!" The voice came from Jackson, the air
force sergeant in the fatigues. "Mr. Faure is right! We
should be able to find out who did this. All we have to
do is polygraph everyone with the Meridian clearance
and we'll know who the leak is."

"Won't work, Jacks." The second Pashtu linguist sat
cross-legged on top of her desk to make space for the
others. She tossed back her long, black hair and looked
at the air force sergeant fondly. "At least it won't work
quickly. There are more of us than you think."

The linguist, Mariam Rashiq, had started her career
in the air force studying Middle Eastern languages at

the Defense Language Institute when she was nine-
teen years old. Born to Afghan natives who had emi-
grated to the U.S., she had grown up speaking Pashtu
and Dari as well as English and French at home, and
she quickly picked up Arabic. She was so proficient at
these languages that the air force stationed her at their
school in Monterey, California, to teach others. She
soon tired of teaching and the constraints of military
life and sent out her résumé to civilian agencies. NSA
snapped her up so fast nobody else had a chance, and
she had worked here for several years. She was much
more aware than Sergeant Jackson, who was relatively
new to the Agency, how the bureaucracy worked. I had
been very pleased to see her receive a promotion at the
ceremony yesterday.

"I'm afraid Mariam is correct." Barry Ballard put
his coffee cup on the desk and slowly shook his head.
"Remember," he said, "there are at least another twenty
people at CIA with the clearance and then there are
a few collectors and lots of people who get our reports
who have to have this VRK. It's not impossible, of
course, and I'm sure DIRNSA will ask us to try it, but
working through fifty to seventy-five polys is going to
take time."

"It'd help if they start with the most likely candidates," Lester sneered, glaring at Mariam.

My eyes widened in shock. Jacks pushed his way to
Lester and grabbed his arm, hard.

"For God's sake, people," Paul Eckerd jumped to
his feet and yelled. "Lester, stop that. We have enough
problems today without your nonsense."

Lester pulled away from the sergeant's grip and
rubbed his arm. "Where is General Murray anyway?
We have to tell him about this."

"DIRNSA's down at CIA again, talking to the DCI

and the director of ops. He's going to meet with all of us tomorrow," Paul said. His brow furrowed. "I have a feeling DIRNSA may already know the comms are lost. We have to help him come up with a new plan. Figure out how to recover from this."

We all turned and looked at Barry. He couldn't see us, but he knew we expected him to speak to us, to continue his encouragement. "We all know this is very bad," he said. "And Paul is right—we must find a way to recover the comms. The good news is that the people in this room are among the best in this Agency. If you folks can't find another way to listen in on those guys, nobody can."

One by one, the crush of people filed out of the office until only Jacks, Mariam, and I were left.

"Alex, sorry we had to e-mail DIRNSA. We tried to call you several times late yesterday afternoon when we realized what was happening," they both said all in a jumble.

A twinge of guilt stung me: I had been so consumed with my own promotion yesterday I had been unavailable to these people who needed me. Mariam had gone back to work after the ceremony; I hadn't. I shook my head. It was done; move on.

"Also," Mariam said slowly, "Mr. Eckerd was right. Jacks and I think you should know that DIRNSA has probably been aware for several days that this was going to happen."

"What! How?" I looked at the two of them and the answer popped into my head. "Oh, of course, CIA's proxy agent in Afghanistan. I bet he got word back that Ajmal had disappeared, right? But how do you know that? Nobody at CIA would pass on agent information until it was approved—and releasing this can't possibly be approved. It'll be in Blue Border files for years."

Jacks looked uncomfortable. "A friend," he said. "This morning. No details. But we thought you should know."

"Thank you," I said. My mind was already racing, wondering just what CIA was planning to do next. But I was pretty sure I knew. No wonder I hadn't heard from Gabe in two days. This was the disaster he had warned me about; the catalyst that would force CIA to insert an agent into Afghanistan to set up a new way to listen to what the terrorists were saying. Operation Minaret. I had been read in on it months ago, before Ajmal helped us find a better way. Now, I was betting, it was being put back in place despite the terrible danger, and Gabe was the agent who was going in.

Jacks and Mariam apparently had been told of my relationship with the CIA agent and wanted to tip me off if I didn't already know what was happening. I shook my head. *No secrets in the intel world.*

But I also knew CIA would take action immediately, no matter how it impacted me—or anyone else—personally. The loss of the Meridian comms was much too devastating.

The three of us stayed in the room for a while, still mourning the terrible loss. We looked at each other bleakly. We knew something big was going on, perhaps on the level of the Cole or worse; we had prayed more intercepts would give us the details.

Now, unless Gabe was successful in replacing the Meridian comms with whatever other communications system al Qaeda might be using, there would be only silence.

4

Southeastern Afghanistan
Saturday, December 2, 2000
After Midnight

"Get ready ... hook up ... stand by ... go!" commanded the jumpmaster. He added, quietly, "God be with you." His voice echoed in the huge cargo bay; this extended-range C-130 transport held only one paratrooper rather than the usual sixty. The crew was at its leanest. The mission, which began at the U.S. naval facility at Diego Garcia and would end when the aircraft landed at Shaikh Isa Air Base, Bahrain, was too dangerous to risk any unnecessary lives.

The man in the back of the aircraft followed the orders as they were given, closed his eyes, and fell dreamlike through the open cargo door into the immense darkness of the night. "*Inshallah,*" he murmured. God be willing. A rush of wind smacked him, then he free-fell, heart racing, until the black silk of his parachute slipped out behind him and tugged him up by the safety of its canopy.

The man's name was Zafir, Arabic for "victorious." He had selected it himself, hoping it would be a good omen. Zafir would be his only name; where he was going, many people used only one. He relaxed in his harness, enjoying the rocking, soothing descent.

Zafir was not the man's real name, but it would be for the next few days, and so he thought of himself as Zafir. He was, in fact, Gabriel Ayala, an agent of the Central Intelligence Agency, a volunteer for this mission, and uniquely suited for it. Gabe spoke both Pashtu and Dari and many of their dialects as well as Arabic and several other languages. From the time he was a small boy, he had had the remarkable ability to learn languages the way others learn breathing. He was dark-complexioned with intense black eyes, inherited from his Jewish ancestors. He had grown a mustache and full beard. Under his ebony jumpsuit he wore a long shirt over baggy pantaloons and a striped wool coat and carried a turbanlike *pakol* hat to replace his jump helmet.

Gabriel Ayala's mission, code-named "Operation Minaret," was to parachute into a remote area northeast of Kandahar, Afghanistan, land undetected, and meet his Afghan contact, a man named Babrack. With Babrack's help, Gabe planned to tap into the Taliban-operated microwave telephone system NSA thought bin Laden must be using now that he knew his satellite phones had been compromised.

When the Taliban took over the country in the mid-1990s, they inherited a communications disaster. Telephones were few, radios fewer, and TVs and newspapers almost nonexistent. The new fundamentalist regime didn't care at all about increasing the availability of mass media—it might, after all, contain Western "propaganda"—but they desperately needed to be able to communicate with one another. They had to have a telephone system that worked.

Just before they left Afghanistan, the Russians had started to modernize its unreliable and antiquated landline telephone system by building a network of land-based microwave towers. They placed the towers twenty-five to thirty miles apart, sometimes closer, in order to maintain line of sight for beam transmission. But the Russians never finished the project, and the Taliban was faced with an alarming situation to fix.

The easy solution, using cell phones, was not a possibility because of Afghanistan's mountainous terrain. An outrageous number of cell phone towers, at an equally outrageous price, some at the top of twenty-thousand-foot mountains, would be necessary for a workable system. A second option, laying cable for a land-based phone system, was also much too expensive.

Finally the Taliban decided to complete the Russian-built microwave communications system using mainly inexpensive off-the-shelf equipment with the help of technicians from Pakistan. Much of the simple point-to-point network between Kandahar and Kabul was already in place, and the Taliban slowly expanded it to reach more remote areas of the country—areas considered important because of their strategic location, political base, or terrorist camp population.

In the meantime, with contacts outside the country and cash in hand, bin Laden's al Qaeda network had bypassed all the difficulties of a cell phone network or the time and expense of building land-based microwave towers by simply buying and using satellite phones. Satellite phones didn't need any kind of towers, just line of sight to one of the many geosynchronous satellites that passed the comms from place to place. And, best of all, they provided both in-country and international calling capabilities.

But now al Qaeda knew those satellite comms had been compromised by Ajmal, and NSA was betting that UBL's terrorist groups would be forced as an alternative to use the Taliban's newly constructed microwave system to plan operations and send *jihadists* on their deadly missions. Bin Laden had a compound near Kandahar, and the Agency knew he must be talking to his Afghan al Qaeda camps somehow. The microwave system wouldn't provide international communications capability like the satcomms, but it would give bin Laden a usable phone system in the country. And, for now, it was all he and his network of fanatics had to use.

For NSA, the easiest way to intercept microwave transmissions was to collect the spillover, or sidelobes, of the beams as they were rebroadcast from tower to tower. Afghanistan's mountainous terrain dispersed the sidelobes and made this impossible. That, along with the physical inability to access switches and lines, was a showstopper for the Agency's ability to eavesdrop. Gabe was parachuting in to put in place another method of monitoring the terrorist comms.

Microwave systems do not use standard landlines but instead employ tall towers to relay signals between two or, with switching stations, more than two locations. The only way for NSA to listen in on a call sent over this system without collecting sidelobes would be to physically place intercept equipment on one of the towers that was being used to relay the al Qaeda phone calls.

Gabe's primary mission was to climb a strategically located microwave tower with a switching station, one which imagery had determined to be the critical transmission point for the targets of interest: the microwave communications link between Kandahar and Kabul, and the new extensions from Kandahar to the camps at Khost and Herat. He would tap into that link and set up an antenna to capture the transmissions as they were passed through the tower. The antenna would swivel every hour to rebroadcast the stored, encrypted data to a satellite for relay back to the U.S.

Operation Minaret was not an entirely new scheme. It had been originally proposed and planned shortly after UBL's phones were compromised the first time, back in the fall of 1998, when NSA first concluded he was using the microwave comms so recently installed by the Taliban. Despite the plan's urgency, it had taken a year and a half—until May 2000—for CIA to get approval and financing for Operation Minaret. Never before had an American agent been put on the ground in post-Taliban Afghanistan; it was considered much too risky, and "proxies" had always been used instead. But this mission demanded a specialist who could deploy the unique intercept gear, and even their most trusted proxy had neither the equipment nor the skills to install it. The decision makers were terrified that the mission could fail and that their agent might be found out. But finally the benefits of regaining UBL's comms outweighed the perils, and Gabe, the agent they selected for the treacherous assignment, began his intense training during the summer of 2000.

After all the weeks of planning and training, the operation had been scheduled for early November. Gabe had been so ready he twitched with anticipation. And then, at the last minute, Ajmal, bin Laden's aide, told NSA the terrorists were using GlobalSat instead of the microwave system. Because GlobalSat was a cutting-edge satellite system that promised them the security they needed for international as well as in-country calls, the Taliban-operated microwave system had become merely a backup. With this news, Operation Minaret was put on hold and Project Meridian, which targeted the satcomms, was born in high hopes that the terrorists' plans could be discovered without risking an agent.

With no small measure of disappointment, Gabe had ended his training as Zafir the Afghan and reappeared in Langley as CIA agent Gabriel Ayala, sitting behind a desk instead of jumping into a danger zone.

Now that the project to intercept the GlobalSat comms had failed after only a few weeks, Operation Minaret had once more become essential.

Two days ago, early, Gabe had been called at home and told to come to work immediately. When he arrived at CIA, he learned he was meeting with the director of Central Intelligence and the head of CIA's Directorate of Operations, the clandestine, "spooky" side of the agency. Gabe was ushered to a plush chair in the DCI's office beside windows overlooking the wintry Virginia landscape. An aide brought coffee to the three men and quickly left the room.

Louis Hahn, the DCI, was a stocky, square-faced man who spoke his mind carefully but firmly to the press, the secretary of defense, and even the president, if necessary. He inspected his young agent, nodded his head, and said, "You went through some rigorous training not long ago. For Operation Minaret?"

"Yes, Sir," Gabe answered. "I remember it well."

As if I could forget even a minute of it. Those weeks would be with him forever: The grueling, extreme exercises with Special Forces soldiers at the JFK Special Warfare Center at Fort Bragg, North Carolina, and the perilous high-altitude parachute ops with the "Nightstalkers" at Fort Campbell, Kentucky. Drills, harsh obstacle courses, runs so long he collapsed at the end, sleep deprivation, navigation, night vision and fieldcraft skill development, weapons training, mission rehearsals. He hadn't known anything could be so severe, so exhausting, so terrifying.

Afterward, they sent him to the National Cryptologic School for intensive instruction in microwave communications principles and practice. Blindfolded, he learned to dismantle and assemble the specialized gear designed for his mission. Then back to Fort Bragg for more drills and rehearsals, climbing high structures with bulky packs full of tools and antenna parts that he put together and deployed over and over and over.

Yes, he remembered it all in great detail. But he answered only, "Yes, Sir." He waited for the next, expected words.

"We need you for that mission again," the DCI said. "Project Meridian has failed. We know one of our Afghan agents has been betrayed and because of that the al Qaeda comms have been lost again. We *must* recover them. We *must* know what they are doing. Now. Those bastards are planning something big, and we have to find out what it is. We need to put you on the ground to tap into the microwave system the way we planned to do last month."

"Yes, Sir," Gabe repeated. His body tingled with excitement.

"We will support you in every possible way." The ops directorate chief spoke for the first time. "But it's really up to you." Left unsaid was the gruesome reality that if Gabe were captured, the U.S. government would deny that he was an American much less an employee of the CIA.

The DCI stirred in his seat. "I can't tell you how important this is," he said. "This country needs your help. We must get the comms back."

"I'm ready," Gabe said.

The next hours were a whirlwind of preparations. Now he was on his way. He was grateful someone had decided at the last minute that this would not have to be a HALO jump—high altitude, low opening. Jump at thirty thousand feet, where the aircraft is just a dull murmur above the clouds, and scream down to fifteen thousand before you pull open your chute. Gabe had done it in training, and both times he had had the distinct feeling he was about to die. He would never admit it, of course, but the experience had always left him shaken for hours. The jump he had just made—out the bay door at fourteen thousand feet—was much easier on his nerves; in comparison with HALO jumps it was almost fun despite all the other dangers.

Gabe, now Zafir once again, checked the altimeter strapped to his hand; he would soon be on the ground. There were no lights anywhere to break the awesome darkness, but that was the plan—to land undetected in a remote area northeast of Kandahar.

Zafir carried with him enough dried food for ten days, but he hoped he would be back home much sooner. He also had special comms equipment, folded and packed carefully in his carryall, a primitive woolen bag he would sling across his shoulders.

He checked the altimeter again, and prepared himself for touching down. In moments he was on the ground, rolling and pulling in his harness and canopy. Far to the north and west stood the majestic and rugged Hindu Kush mountains, the *Koh-i-Baba,* or "Grandfather," range deep in snow and impenetrable until warmer weather arrived. In the area where Zafir landed, the ground was barren and brown. Here the snow melted almost as soon as it fell. No trees, no vegetation of any kind. He buried his parachute rig and jumpsuit in a pile of rocks, straightened his rucksack and clothes, and became just another Afghan traveler.

Zafir looked at his GPS receiver and began to walk to the west, searching for the hut he would use as a base. His contact, a man named Babrack, should be there waiting with the horses they would need for their ride tomorrow to the switching station. It was cold, but not terribly so. There were no landmines in this area, Zafir had been told, but he wondered how they knew for sure. He knew the Russians had left thousands of the deadly things behind them. He had been warned to watch for packs of wolves.

After an hour of walking across the rutted, desolate country, checking his bearings often, Zafir found the hut. Two horses stood in an improvised corral, their breath frosty in the darkness. *Good, Babrack is here already,* he thought. Zafir moved silently to the dwelling, a deserted mud-brick structure surrounded by crumbling walls. He stepped through the open doorway. Suddenly a bright light flashed. A fierce and dirty man with a bandolier across his chest and a dagger in his belt pointed a rifle at Zafir's chest. Zafir turned his head at a noise behind him, and a second menacing figure raised his rifle, laughed, and spat, in Pashtu, "You are a dead man."

5

Operations Building 1, National Security Agency
Friday, December 1, 2000
Evening

Eight o'clock at night. I was still at work. The thou-sands of people who filled the halls and offices during the day were gone, leaving the business of SIGINT to NSOC and a few other watch centers scattered throughout the complex. An eerie stillness had settled over the buildings.

I liked the sense of tranquility the silence brought. The day had been demanding, with disagreements and aggravations lurking at every crossroads, to say nothing about the alarming Project Meridian situation.

And then, of course, there was Gabe.

I had tried twice during the day to call him at his office at CIA and was amused, as usual, when the woman answering the gray, secure, interagency phone simply said "Hello." No name, number, or hint of location. Just "Hello," as though she were home in her kitchen. Very weird. At NSA, as is typical throughout business and government, the traditional greeting was a name or office identifier.

I wasn't so amused by the response. On the first call, I was told Gabe wasn't in, on the second, that he had left "on assignment."

At eight-fifteen, I picked up the black, unsecure phone on my desk and dialed his home number. It rang on and on; finally a recording droned out the usual "nobody is available." I hung up.

"Damn it, Gabe," I mumbled, "I know where you are. I wish you had called me before you left."

I shook my head, forced myself back into the present, and looked around. I had just finished fixing up my new office, a perk of my promotion to grade fifteen. The sign outside the door said, "Alexandra O'Malley, Assistant Director for NSA Reporting."

I had embellished the stark, white, windowless cube with a blue accent rug, a green-shaded banker's lamp, a corner table, and two chairs liberated from a deserted conference room, along with several colorful prints and pictures. From the World War Two Army recruitment poster that my grandfather had had in his newspaper office fifty-five years ago, a weary, wounded soldier, his head wrapped in a bloodstained bandage, stared out at the world asking, "Doing all you can, brother?"

"Yes, we sure are," I mumbled again.

Especially Gabe. He was on his way, I knew, to an incredibly dangerous mission to try to recover the lost terrorist comms. CIA wasn't wasting any time going back to basics. I wouldn't have known what was happening except for my special bond with the CIA agent.

I had met Gabriel Ayala a month ago at the first Project Meridian meeting, held at CIA's Counterterrorism Center at their headquarters in Langley, Virginia. The center was the obvious place to hold the meetings since it was convenient for the DCI to attend. Despite the extraordinary presence of such a high-ranking government official and the serious topic, I soon noticed the man with a dark beard sitting in a corner, quietly watching the others argue and debate. I leaned forward a little to see him better. His teeth were white against his tanned complexion, the left front tooth overlapped the right slightly . . . and, I thought, sensually. His dark hair curled down nearly over his ears, and his eyes were very black and very bright. He didn't look terribly tall, less than six feet, and his shoulders and arms were muscular and strong under his lightweight coat. He was probably in his late twenties.

All things considered, looking at him was even better than eating a Ben and Jerry's Peace Pop. I had to force myself to concentrate on the discussions.

He saw me, too. As we left the conference that first day, he slipped a note in my hand. *"Meet me for coffee tomorrow morning? Silver Spring, Tastee Diner, ten o'clock?"* The note was signed *"Gabriel Ayala."* The next day was Saturday. I nodded faintly in his direction; we were, after all, intelligence agents and not about to advertise our attraction to anyone around us. It just wasn't done.

Coffee stretched into lunch, and then a leisurely walk to my car. We were hooked. I smiled, remembering how fast we were drawn to each other, how quickly we had started a relationship that was as bewitching as it was passionate. It wasn't like me. Not at all. Not since my troubled and short marriage to fellow NSAer Mike Faure had failed three years ago. I had been much too dedicated to my work to sustain such a commitment. I knew it, accepted it, and had put all thoughts of romance behind me. Until now.

Our attraction blossomed despite our differences: Gabe was twenty-nine, I was thirty-five, perhaps not as significant in our competitive world as my grade fifteen to his thirteen. He made up for it in languages: he spoke six and was learning a seventh. His family background was Jewish, mine was Irish Catholic; and, of course, there was the whole CIA-NSA rivalry. We didn't care. We spent as much time together as we could in the past few weeks, growing closer with each encounter.

I had stayed at his town house in Virginia the past weekend and we spent most of Saturday afternoon in our own special world, touching and kissing and whispering and laughing and finding the exquisite joy that comes with new love. Gabe was a delight, touching my hair and arms in long, languorous strokes and, eyes half shut, telling me that I was beautiful; the loveliest, softest, most wonderful woman he had ever known.

We finally got up at seven-thirty that evening, starvation driving us from the snug haven of his warm bed. Bathed and dressed and on our way to dinner, we both jumped when we opened the front door and a blast of frigid air and white flakes blew through the foyer. I looked at Gabe. He shrugged his shoulders and I grinned. I hadn't noticed it was snowing either.

Our relationship had quickly become one of astonishing trust and intensity—and shivery excitement.

Well, I won't see him for quite a while now. He had warned me that if the Meridian comms were ever compromised he might be sent on a mission to replace them. I already knew someone had been trained for that mission; I had just never known who it was. As professionals, we accepted the risk. As lovers, we hated it. Soon—if not already—he would be halfway around the world, in a strange and dangerous place in a time zone nine and a half hours ahead of D.C.

I reached behind my neck and pulled the blue NSA picture badge and chain from my back where I had tossed it to keep it out of the way while I moved furniture, pounded nails, hung pictures. I had pulled my glossy red hair back into a ponytail, but I was barefoot, dressed in silky shorts and a T-shirt emblazoned with the CIA logo on the front, clothes I had changed into two hours before when I went to the NSA SHAPE fitness center to work out. It was my favorite shirt to sweat in, as I had met few CIA employees who weren't arrogant enough to declare their superiority over all other government employees, American or otherwise. The Intelligence Community's nickname, Christians in Action, was a good one for the sanctimonious agents, I had often thought.

Except Gabe, of course. Maybe I should exchange this for an FBI T-shirt. I smiled again.

I wiggled my bare toes and tossed several stray red curls out of my eyes. I wanted to call my hair a sophisticated "auburn," but it was truly as Irish red as an Aer Lingus poster child's. Some days, when I spent the time, it was long and silky and not so unruly. Tonight I had pulled it into a ponytail, and humidity had kinked the ends into damp curls.

"Gabe, you'd better come back from this alive," I muttered.

"Hey, Alex, are you talking to yourself? Is that what getting promoted to GS-15 does to people?" A young woman stood in the doorway, popping the top of a Coke can and looking amused.

"Kai. It's great to see you." I pulled myself back from my restless thoughts again and forced a smile. "What are you doing here?"

"I'm working swings in NSOC. I took an eighteen-month gig as the ELINT Watch Officer, remember?"

"Of course. How's that going?"

"All right. It's not what I'm used to, but it's interesting. And a nice break for a while."

Kai Kalani was a beautiful woman, the kind who

caused NSA men to trip all over themselves when they saw her in the halls. Her mother was part Hawaiian, and she had given her daughter exotic eyes, radiant tawny skin, and lustrous black hair that Kai wore long and straight. Men fell at her feet, begged her for dates, even tucked bouquets of flowers in her car door handles out in the parking lot, but since I had known her she had only had eyes for Zachary Becker, a cryptologic mathematician with shaggy hair and dark-rimmed glasses who looked exactly like the classic distracted scientist.

Kai was an expert in ELINT, electronic intelligence, one of the three pillars of SIGINT, along with COMINT (communications intelligence) and FISINT (foreign instrumentation, usually telemetry). She was part of a select, technical, and underappreciated group that worked long hours in darkened labs watching green lines dance across oscilloscope screens. By studying the attributes of a radar signal, she could— given enough intercepts and time—assess the capabilities of an entire weapon system and the interaction of all its component parts.

Kai had done just that two months earlier, astounding the Intelligence Community when she discovered that a key foreign missile system, the ███████████████ that specifically targeted United States strategic strike capabilities, had stopped calibrating its radars. No more daily test modes, no more tracking ███████ or other objects, just an occasional unmodulated emission. Kai knew, and she said in her report, that it's impossible for complex missile systems to work as designed if their radars aren't calibrated properly.

I had helped Kai write her startling communiqué. I was on a six-month tour in the W9D ELINT organization when she made her discovery, and I convinced her how important it was to get a report out quickly that would tell those who needed to know what it all meant. It wasn't easy. Technical ELINT analysts love to write about things like new linear frequency modulation on the pulse or new modes of pulse repetition interval ramping on a target tracking radar or amplitude variations and PRI dwell and beam position changes.

But they hate to say what the changes *mean*: they could Get in Trouble for that.

The news of Kai's discovery aggravated the hell out of the Weapons Analysis Center, the Scientific and Technical Intelligence Center officially responsible for making final assessments on the system. In fact, they were furious with us. The analysts there had missed all the changes in the level of activity, then denied they had happened, and finally tried to downplay their importance. The WAC analysts were thoroughly upstaged. Suddenly, their jobs and reputations were at stake. Especially when Kai told them we were going to *interpret* our SIGINT data and tell people what it meant.

I knew the rest of the world would have a very hard time understanding this issue. After all, most people were accustomed to newspaper and magazine articles that discuss the *who*, *what*, *when*, and *where* but focus intently on the *why* of a story. In fact, without a *why*, most stories were not worth telling. But in the Intelligence Community, only a few agencies thought they were qualified, or legally blessed, to tell the *why* of intelligence analysis.

As a consequence, many of the analysts within the Community hated it when NSA analysts included *any* non-SIGINT information or meaningful analysis in their reports. There were a variety of reasons. Some of them simply believed "all-source" analysis was solely within *their* purview and therefore NSA should report SIGINT only. The all-source analysts would figure out what the SIGINT *meant* within the context of other information. Also, an NSA report was often the initial report on a subject, and if that report was too detailed or complete, there could be little or nothing left for the all-source analysts to add in follow-up reporting to justify their existence. Last, but certainly not least, there was always the possibility that an all-source analyst's boss might ask, "Why didn't you figure that out before the guy at NSA did?"

And so, over the years, Community analysts have been quick to complain to NSA authorities anytime they feel a SIGINT report has impinged on their turf. NSA analysts, quick to realize a losing battle when their own weak-kneed management would not support them, gradually accepted the "go along to get along" philosophy and included analytic comments only when they were not likely to offend.

But this time, Kai and I wrote up her analysis in a clearly stated, nontechnical publication that both military and policymakers could understand. We showed them the graphs and we showed them the imagery and we told them exactly what it all meant. And they listened.

When the report was published, it included a sentence in the comments section that stated the stark bottom line: "The ███████████████ missile system is almost certainly no longer fully operational." A furor of excitement bordering on hysteria blazed throughout the community. If we were right, organizations could lose funding; analysts could lose jobs.

The S&TI Center screamed bloody murder and demanded a conference on the subject. It was held at

CIA and the room was packed. Analysts from all over the Intelligence Community and their contract colleagues, Brits from both Government Communications Headquarters (GCHQ, NSA's counterpart) and the Ministry of Defence, a representative from USSTRAT-COM, and several from government budget offices filled the seats and overflowed across the back wall.

The S&TI Center sent two people: Malcolm Breuner, chief of the Missile Division, and Dixie Baker, the analyst who had the primary responsibility for the missile target at the vortex of the recent controversy and who had failed to notice the changes that were occurring until Kai reported them.

The CIA moderator, George Tisby, was a white-haired missile analyst with a PhD in physics and a calm air of authority. He had been around for years; a respectful, thoughtful, and knowledgeable man who put up with guff from no one. He had been specially selected by the chief of the Intelligence Directorate to keep a firm grip on the potentially contentious proceedings. Dr. Tisby summarized the controversy, then invited NSA to make the first presentation.

Kai walked to the front of the room and put a viewgraph on the machine. A brightly colored graph of radar activity filled the large screen. She pointed to it with a laser pointer. "Here you can see that, on every day of the week except Sunday, these radars have been tested on average about two hours a day. This has been going on for years." She talked about the background of the system, what the testing meant, and why it was critical to have the radars perform their acquisition, scan, and track modes.

She flipped up a second viewgraph, dated January 2000. The radar activity had completely ceased except for a few minutes every Wednesday morning.

"This is what has happened since the beginning of this year," Kai said to the audience, suddenly stunned into silence at the magnitude of the change depicted by the graph.

"You can see from the activity levels that something drastic has changed here," Kai said. "We must investigate why this is happening to this weapon system. I must tell you that my interpretation . . ."

"No! You must not!" Malcolm Breuner leaped to his feet and bellowed. "We do not want any more of your 'interpretations.' The National Security Agency is *not* responsible for making intelligence assessments. Only technical centers like ours can do that. This is all a collection problem, which you clearly do not understand. It's not radar activity that's changed, it's collection activity. You have made a huge mistake and you are embarrassing the United States government in the process."

The audience, braced for a squabble but not a brawl, gasped in unison. This was bad, and headed for worse.

George Tisby stood up from his seat in the first row and walked to the front of the room next to Kai, whose cheeks had reddened and whose hands had become white-knuckled fists. The moderator touched her shoulder reassuringly, narrowed his eyes, and spoke to Breuner.

He did not raise his voice, and the audience strained to hear his words.

"Malcolm, I have known you for nearly thirty years. You are perhaps the last person I would expect to act the way you are acting. This is a forum for people to exchange views, calmly and respectfully, no matter how controversial or heated the subject. I know everyone has strong opinions on this issue, but we will not use this conference to make personal attacks. No matter how upset or stressed we might be. If you do anything like that again, I will ask you to leave."

He didn't have to ask: Malcolm Breuner and a smirking Dixie Baker stood and walked out of the conference room.

Kai turned and asked, "Should I continue?" George Tisby opened his arms in a question to the audience, which, slowly, still stunned, stood and began to applaud.

The day after the conference, the S&TI Center sent a harshly critical message to DIRNSA as well as the DCI:

1522Z 2 OCT 2000
FM SPECIAL SECURITY OFFICER/WeaponsAnalysis Center
TO NSA/DIRNSA/DCI/NSC/NSOC/OCMC/SIRVES/DDO/ DDP
TOP SECRET ZARF TALENT KEYHOLE CHANNELS
SUBJECT: Evaluation of product serial number: K/OO/946-2000
(TOP SECRET ZARF) Intelligence significance: this report has negative value. It is based largely on speculation and very little on SIGINT data and analysis. It makes unwarranted assumptions about our collectors and uninformed assumptions about the operation of these critical missile systems. Furthermore the report contains hearsay and quotes finished intelligence out of context.
(CONFIDENTIAL) This report should be cancelled immediately. In the future Ms. Kalani and Ms. O'Malley should report SIGINT facts only.

But these SIGINT facts were undeniable, and when the two of us were summoned to DIRNSA's office, we had no problem convincing him it was not a collection issue. Two days later, we were in a staff car with DIRNSA headed downtown to brief the director of Central Intelligence and State Department Seniors, who told us repeatedly that this was exactly the kind of information they expected and needed from NSA. General Murray was elated.

That was the end of October. Three weeks later, the Agency Promotion Board added my name to its list of newly minted GS-15s. It was barely two years since I had been promoted to GS-14, the absolute minimum eligibility time. I had become the youngest GS-15 in the history of the Agency.

Reporting the decline of the weapon system and its consequences was the catalyst for my quick promotion. It was also why DIRNSA appointed me as head of reporting for the Agency, which led to my role in Project Meridian.

Kai was famous from Washington to London. She was pampered and praised by the same managers who had cringed and wrung their hands when the report was first issued. They promised her a promotion the next quarter. We both wondered if it would happen; promoting ELINT analysts is hardly high on the priority list for NSA executives.

She decided to take a sabbatical from the W9D ELINT organization and go to NSOC, where she switched from assessing the capabilities of large missile systems to tracking small ones as they moved from place to place. She had been doing that for several weeks now.

Kai sipped her Coke. "Lester Krebbs is the SOO tonight. Want to come over and say hello?"

"Maybe not," I said. "That would be twice I've had to see him today."

Not only did Lester dislike all women who aren't

secretaries, he had a special dislike for me. It's an ex-trapolation of his hatred of my mother, Molly, a re-tired NSA exec. The two of them had worked together for several years in the 1980s and early 1990s, and when Molly advanced to the exalted rank of senior executive and he found himself actually working for her, he began a bitter feud that now extended to her daughter.

Of course, I disliked him as well and took a great deal of pleasure in the fact that my recent promotion distressed him terribly.

"Why doesn't he retire, anyway? He's sure old enough," Kai said.

"NSA is his life. He can't imagine doing anything else." I shrugged. "There are lots of people around here like that. But, at least we don't have to put up with him very often anymore."

At some point in the past two years, someone in management had been savvy enough to recognize Lester's many imperfections and had moved him out of the SIGINT side of the business and into Opera-tions Security, the other side of the NSA mission. OPSEC, instead of exploiting targeted communica-tions, made sure nobody could exploit U.S. secure comms. OPSEC engineers designed and implemented security solutions for everything from computers to audio and video communications. They even had their own microelectronics—computer chips—production facility.

But few people who have tasted the sweet world of signals intelligence want to work in OPSEC. Lester was no exception, although he bragged unceasingly about his new position, chief of Covert Assurance Op-erations, a position that, to my dismay, made him part of the Meridian team.

This week, however, he was filling in for a senior operations officer who was recovering from gall bladder surgery. As such, Lester was in charge of the National Security Operations Center and, really, the whole National Security Agency during the time his shift was on duty after normal workday hours.

NSOC SOOs like Lester answer only to God when a crisis strikes in the middle of the night.

Kai shook her head and changed the subject. "What a great promotion ceremony you had yesterday! And weren't you glad Barry Ballard helped hand out the certificates? Isn't he wonderful?"

"Yes, he is," I answered. "It's great the way he loves those two little kids of his. He's always showing their pictures to anyone he talks to." I laughed. "Besides, tell me someone else in this 'Land of Bad Clothes' who dresses with such style?"

Over the years, NSA had become famous for the variety of attire worn by the extraordinary, but often quaintly unconventional, analysts who worked here. Anything goes if you weren't attending a meeting downtown: ripped sweatshirts, shabby blue jeans, baseball caps, mismatched shoes, stained ties, even a few pairs of shorts in hot weather.

When analysts got moved into managerial positions, which happened much too often, they often "upgraded" to shiny suits from outlet stores and some of the most amazing shoes seen outside of Family Dollar. The few well-dressed employees stood out like show dogs among pound pups.

Nobody did this to purposefully look bedraggled. NSA analysts were much too busy worrying about things like elliptic curve factoring algorithms, the revival of digital steganography, and the challenge of influencing the huge number of competing collection priorities pouring in from various agencies. (Solutions include, in order of "legality," beg the OCMC, bribe the OCMC, threaten the OCMC, skip the OCMC and call the field site directly and ask your friends there for help. The last method, although against all the rules, is often the most productive.) In the face of these challenges, sartorial correctness was far down on analysts' priority lists.

"It's true," Kai said. "Barry is great. He's not like the rest of the damn seniors. They are just so, you know, egotistical." She sipped her Coke again. "It's awful that Barry's blind. They say he never complains about it though. Was he born blind, Alex, do you know?"

"That's what I've heard."

"What a guy." Kai crumpled her Coke can and turned to leave. "Back to Lester and the bunch. Hey, maybe you can afford to get some dress-up clothes now that you've been promoted." She looked at me and laughed as she slipped out the door. "And some shoes," she flung back over her shoulder.

6

Operations Building 1, National Security Agency
Friday, December 1, 2000
Evening

I reached for the remote control and clicked on my
new TV, mounted high on the wall opposite my desk.
I shook my head, still amazed by such an extravagant
symbol of my elevated NSA lifestyle. A private office
and a television set? So very rare. I basked in the wonder of my newfound abundance as I watched the screen
spring to life.

That didn't last.

The blue and white seal of the National Security
Agency, a large eagle staring fiercely from its center,
filled the background of the studio of *CNN Headline
News*. I turned up the volume.

The anchor was excited, eyes darting from his notes
to the camera and back as if he couldn't quite believe
what he was about to say. ". . . According to the report
from National Park Police headquarters in Greenbelt,
Maryland, Stanley Freemont, a senior executive at the
supersecret National Security Agency, was arrested
late this afternoon at a rest stop on the Baltimore-
Washington Parkway. Mr. Freemont has been charged
with 'offering to pay for, and engage in, an act of lewdness' with an undercover male police officer."

I grimaced as a mug shot of Stan Freemont replaced the proud eagle and the seal. I knew him slightly; he was about fifty, quiet, divorced. What was he thinking? A rest stop on the parkway—what a terrible risk. Surely there was a better way now that the Stan Freemonts of NSA didn't have to worry about censure or dismissal.

Homosexuality was once a very big deal at the Agency, an immediate firing offense because of the fear of blackmail, but times had changed. Now, in fact, we had an official Agency-blessed group called GLOBE, Gay, Lesbian, or Bisexual Employees. GLOBE was described as "a professional organization made up of a diverse group of NSAers, both homosexual and heterosexual, who share a common desire to address the concerns of gay and lesbian people who work at the National Security Agency." GLOBE members had a Web site on NSA's internal, secure server and could send out messages of interest to their members over the same server.

I had no idea if GLOBE arranged social events, but perhaps they might have counseled Mr. Freemont on a different method of making new friends.

What a disaster for him. And for all of us. NSA definitely didn't need that kind of publicity. It was bad news.

But not as bad as what came next.

I should have guessed, I thought minutes later, that an arrest of an NSA employee on lewdness charges was not enough to merit a story on national television. WBAL, Baltimore's NBC affiliate, might run the story in the next day or so, but this broadcast was just hours after the fact.

The anchor was still talking. The background changed again, displaying a grainy video of a handcuffed, hunched-over man led by two Park Police into a drab government building. "Mr. Freemont is currently being held in custody at the regional Park Police lockup and is meeting with his attorney. An arraignment is scheduled in the morning at the U.S. District Courthouse in Greenbelt."

He turned to the screen behind him, which now switched to a live feed from a Park Police building. His coanchor stood ready with a microphone, her blond hair swirling in the cold night air.

"Tammie," the anchor said, "I understand there is more to this story."

I flinched and braced myself.

"Yes, Brad," the coanchor said into her mic, looking somber. "I have learned from sources inside police headquarters that Mr. Freemont had two business cards in his possession when he was arrested. The first is his own card, and it identifies him as the assistant director for special projects, National Security Agency."

Big deal, I thought. *There are a lot of special projects directors at NSA.*

"The second card belongs to Alan Sachs, director of sales for ParagonReporting, Inc.," Tammie said, "with an appointment date of three days ago written on the card."

Brad's face became concerned as he leveled his eyes at the camera.

"For those of you who may not know," he said, "ParagonReporting is a Georgia company—a data broker—which collects and sells billions of records about Americans to just about anyone who has the money to buy them. Everything from Social Security numbers, addresses, telephone numbers, assets, lawsuits, liens, criminal histories, and certificates of birth, marriage, divorce, and gun ownership, prescription drug usage, magazine subscriptions, you name it. In minutes, an investigator can know if a person has traveled abroad, bought sex toys over the Internet, or taken a course in French cooking."

Brad looked down at his notes. "Data brokers—and ParagonReporting is just one of many—began collecting personal information on Americans in a big way during the 1990s. This data is sold primarily to marketers who use behavioral profiling as a way to precisely target customers for their goods. For example, if Ford knows that you subscribe to *Off-Road Magazine*, they might send you sales brochures on their newest four-by-four trucks and accessories. If they also know you have had credit problems in the past, Ford might include a 'special offer' to finance your purchase no matter what your current financial status might be.

"Of course, most people have no idea that the minute personal details of their lives are bought and sold and scrutinized by companies out to make a buck. And what if law enforcement and government agencies buy the same information and sift through it for 'suspicious behavior'? Would you think that was an invasion of your privacy? Do you think they might even make really big mistakes that could ruin your life?"

The anchor's face went from concerned to grim. "As we understand it, the privacy Act of 1974 prohibits the federal government from secretly collecting personal information on citizens unless there is a 'proper purpose.' But, apparently, buying databases of these records from private data brokers like ParagonReporting gives government agencies a way to circumvent the law."

The anchor swiveled in his chair and faced the screen. "Tammie, do you think the NSA is planning to sidestep the privacy law and buy personal information on you and me and all our listeners from one of the largest marketers of this data?"

"I don't know for sure, Brad," she answered, nodding slowly, "but the business card makes that a possibility."

"Why would the NSA want to have all that information on U.S. citizens?" the anchor asked.

"Why indeed?" Tammie answered. "The NSA repeatedly tells us that they do not listen in on phone calls of American citizens or violate our privacy. But ParagonReporting knows if you," she pointed to the camera and all of us watching her speak, "have ever taken antidepressants, belonged to an adult-only chat group, or called telephone numbers in foreign countries." She paused ominously. "And now, the National Security Agency may soon know the same things."

Brad addressed his audience again. "CNN will have a special report about the relationship between NSA and ParagonReporting within the next two weeks. At that time we plan to include a look at how NSA might use something called data mining to discover even more information about you and me. Please join us then."

I was angered by the report. Outside of phone numbers, e-mail addresses, some ▮▮▮▮▮▮▮▮▮▮ and ▮▮▮▮▮▮▮▮▮▮▮▮ information, NSA had no need for any of that data. The FBI and police departments, perhaps, but not us. Our mission is collecting signals intelligence against foreign nationals, and we are strictly monitored to make sure we all understand that. Every six months every collector, analyst, processor, and reporter must sign an acknowledgment of the

USSID 18 rules against infringing the rights of U.S. citizens—sometimes to the point of threatening to interfere with valuable intelligence collection.

For example, if we were recording conversations of a known terrorist overseas, and he called someone in the States, we would have to stop recording until it was determined if the recipient was a "U.S. Person."

Even if bin Laden himself was on the other end of the line.

It's a result of the 1970s Church Committee crackdown on invasion of privacy of Americans by intelligence agencies. Under the same laws, I was sure searching through databases of personal information on Americans would be strictly illegal.

It would take an overwhelming national emergency, I thought, *for the executive and legislative branches to overthrow those laws and allow "data mining" of information about U.S. citizens.*

As far as I knew, none of the databases being sold had any international information in them. And even if they did, and we wanted to be able to access it, we would have a hard time finding the people to do it. Linguists, analysts, crypies, and everyone else here were running out the door so fast clutching their retirement bonuses we hardly had enough employees to plow through the actual SIGINT data we collected let alone check what kind of toothpaste someone in China used.

I thought it much more likely that Mr. Freemont was meeting with the ParagonReporting rep to discuss his own postretirement job options, but whatever the reason, this was a story that would cause much angst in Security and the Agency's Office of Media and Public Affairs. *It'll go on for months,* I thought.

I was so wrong. Stan Freemont's arrest and associa-

tions with ParagonReporting, whatever it may have
been, was about to be overcome by events so extreme
and bizarre that the whole news story and its ability to
grab the attention of the American public would fade
nearly into oblivion almost immediately.

I turned off the TV as the European weather report
started. I was very tired, but I had a few things I still
wanted to do. I was also thirsty. I reached over and
grabbed my bottle of water from the desk and swal-
lowed the last of it. I was still thirsty.

Occasionally the most ordinary of decisions, made
without much thought at all, change your life. This
would be one of those times.

I pushed myself out of the chair and walked barefoot out of my office, down the short hall between the
other executive suites, out the door, and into the main
hallway. It was empty and silent.

I walked quickly down the dimly lit corridor, past
the glass doors opening on to NSOC. There were dozens of people at work back there, but there was no clue
to their presence. A portrait of General Murray and an
American flag decorated the far wall. The mahogany
secretary's desk was deserted, as it normally would be
after the day shift ended. After downsizing began several years before, secretaries had become a very scarce
commodity at the National Security Agency.

I passed up the first watercooler I came to; the water
in that one had a strange brackish aftertaste. NSA's
designated agency safety and health official insisted
that his office had tested it and it was fine, but everyone still avoided it. After all, twenty-five years ago the
DASHO probably said asbestos was a perfectly safe
substance, too. Now the Agency was spending hundreds of thousands of dollars to remove it from walls
and ceilings. I turned left at the next corner and headed

for the watercooler on the first floor near the intersection of the north and west corridors. It was a little farther away, but from experience I knew the water was sweeter there than anywhere else. Besides, the last time I checked, the vending machines at that corner had Dove Bars. I smacked my lips.

With the turn, I left the world of the showcase hallway outside NSOC, with its wide cream-colored halls and good lighting, and entered the world of the old Operations Building 1. This building, the first constructed at Fort Meade to house NSA employees moving up from Arlington Hall in 1957, had walls of a very basic and unaesthetic cinderblock. It was an Eisenhower-era kind of thing, and it gave this part of the Agency a lingering feeling of age.

During the psychedelic 1970s, the cinderblock walls were painted all sorts of colors: pink and purple, lime green with blue trim, yellow and orange. Now they were mostly a very bland, boring tan with a reddish-brown trim, marking the progression of the Agency and its population to a more conservative age.

If, indeed, that were possible.

I pulled open the door to the stairwell and walked down the steps to the first floor. Even in the dim light I could see areas on the chocolate brown handrail where hundreds of hands had worn away the paint, revealing layers of orange, pink, and a brilliant green so bright it seemed to lift right off the rail. I stopped on the steps and looked closely. It was a kind of archeological history of NSA in paint chips, and I wondered fleetingly what kinds of things had happened during each different era of paint. The stairwell was unheated and cold, and I hurried down the rest of the steps to the hallway.

The tile floor was cool on my feet, especially in the

places where I stepped on brass rings set into the floor.
The rings could be unscrewed and removed so that
different kinds of wiring could be pulled in the area
between the current raised floor and the original one
from the 1950s. I turned left again into another hallway and passed a series of snack machines tucked into
a corner.

This part of OPS 1 was currently undergoing reha-
bilitation, an ongoing process that had resulted in
boarded-up areas, padlocked doors, and strange detour
signs. This part of the building was silent and darkened. I hadn't seen anyone or heard a sound since I
began my trip, but it never occurred to me to be frightened; you couldn't be safer than in a place protected
day and night by special police trained to keep all
threats outside the sheltered walls of the NSA complex. In here, there are:

> guards on the roof
> guards in the halls
> guards at the gates

I stopped suddenly when my path was blocked by a
yellow and black sign that read, *"This area is under
construction. Keep out."*

Everything is under construction here, I thought, as
I slipped past the sign to the snack machines. I looked
for signs of candy, chips, any kind of nourishment as I
walked by, but they were all empty and unplugged and
pulled away from the wall. That's when I heard the
noise. Or rather, sort of felt the noise, a tiny scraping
sound that might have gone unnoticed anywhere but
in this still, silent place. I looked away from the corner
and down the dimly lit hall and squinted. A blurred
form, a person of unidentifiable sex or description,

was bending over the water fountain at the end of the hallway. It straightened and began to turn my way.

I ducked quickly into the shadowed corner to avoid what I thought must be a guard patrolling the off-limits area. As I stepped back, I could see a large cut-out in the wall beside the machines and slipped into it, taking a step down into a deepening darkness. The floor was no longer cool, but curiously, and sickeningly, warm and wet. With a strong sense of revulsion, I picked up one foot and wondered what in God's name could have spilled there. The figure I had seen by the watercooler flashed by with a whoosh, and I leaned forward to step back into the hallway.

The wetness on my feet stopped me.

I turned and bent over to see what it was. It was too dark. I peered out the doorway, this time hoping to see a guard. The halls were empty in both directions. I tiptoed back and pulled the cord of an old light fixture I could dimly see hanging from the ceiling, and a thirty-year-old bulb flooded the tiny room with a blaze of light.

The next moments were burned into my brain cells as inexorably as the image on the Shroud of Turin. I was in the small kitchen area of an old snack bar, an area that had been boarded up for many years. I had heard these places used to exist in various locations in the Agency, where workers would sell bacon and eggs for breakfast and fry up hamburgers for lunch, but they had disappeared long before I was hired. Now only the two main cafeterias served food.

My God, I thought, *this is the place the intern called me about two days ago. No wonder she didn't know what to do about it.*

I had stepped through a raggedly cut entrance the workmen had made in the wall and had not yet fitted with a door and a lock. As my eyes adjusted to the flood of light, I could see that a grill with a huge vent above it still stood in the middle of the space, and outlets for a refrigerator and other appliances accented the wall.

I could also see the body on the floor, and the large spill of blood surrounding it and moving like a living, dark pool toward the corners of the room.

Blood was everywhere, splattered on the walls, dripping from the grill, sticky on my hand where I had touched the light cord. I was standing in the middle of the bloody swash, still so grotesquely warm that it felt alive. The body on the floor was definitely not alive. It was a man, in dark pants and a light-colored shirt stained with large dark blotches from the blood still oozing out of the slice across his throat. His mouth was open in a frozen grimace and his hands and arms had fallen to his sides.

It was Barry Ballard.

His briefcase, a beautiful buttery leather with a large NSA seal embossed on the front, lay bloodstained and ruined.

I froze, as if I were posing for a bizarre statue. The scene before me was so unlikely that when I finally managed to move away, it seemed very slow, a dreamlike stroll through a thick fog. I had almost reached the doorway when I stopped and turned back to the gory tableau. I took a deep breath and tiptoed around the body to the other side of the room, looking carefully at the floor as I walked.

Where was his dog? The black dog with the red kerchief. The room was not that big, and within seconds I had searched every inch of it.

Although it made no sense, Barry's dog was not there.

7

Southeastern Afghanistan
Saturday, December 2, 2000
After Midnight

Zafir lunged at the man in the hut. *I will not be the only one to die tonight,* he thought. He knocked the light away. It smashed against the wall, and the hut pitched into darkness as Zafir grabbed his attacker by his hair. The rifle clattered to the floor and the two men fought. The weeks of strenuous training paid off: Zafir wrapped his arm around the man's neck and twisted. The man sagged against a wall, his breath fading, as he whispered a few last ragged words of warning to his friend outside the hut. A shot from the man was thunderous in the cold air. It missed its target, hitting the wall above Zafir's head with a thud. The second shot did not miss. The bullet hit Zafir hard in the left shoulder and he rolled away deeper into the dark, waiting for another attempt on his life.

Another shot cracked from outside the hut, and Zafir rolled again, trying to stay alive. He landed on top of the dead man's rifle and grabbed it. He spun away to his side and pointed the rifle toward the dim light of the doorway. His own handgun, an M9 Beretta, was still in his pack, which had slipped off his back and thudded to the dirt floor.

"My friend!" A voice he had never heard, in Pashtu, added, "I have just killed a man out here and saved your life. I am Babrack. Do not shoot me, my friend." A pause, and then, "What is your name? Are you injured?"

Zafir fumbled in the dark and found a heavy flashlight, probably left over from the Russians. The glass and bulb were smashed. Gingerly, using his right hand, he fished a new one out of his pack and turned it on. He shined it at the doorway. It was empty.

"Babrack, I am Zafir. Thank God you are here. You did indeed save my life."

A tall man in pantaloons and a long coat walked into the flashlight's beam and grinned at him. "I tried to intercept you before you ran into these two, but you came so quietly I missed you. Whatever sort of bandits they are, they commandeered our hut before I got here. I have been waiting for you for nearly two hours. Are you all right?" he repeated.

Zafir answered slowly, his mouth full of dust. "I've been shot. I don't know how badly, but without your help I would be dead. Thank you." He stood slowly and walked toward the man to shake hands, but he was lightheaded and his shoulder throbbed painfully. He sat down on a sack near the door and gritted his teeth.

Babrack moved quickly to his side, removed Zafir's coat and shirt, took the flashlight and examined the wound. "It looks to me like the bullet has passed through the flesh under your shoulder," he said. He flashed the light around and lifted Zafir's arm. "I don't think you have any broken bones, and perhaps not even torn muscles, but you are bleeding badly. Do you have any bandages?"

Zafir nodded toward his pack. Babrack took out a first aid kit. "You're a lucky man," he said, "but we must get you some medical treatment. You need stitches and antibiotics so the wound does not get infected."

"No!" Zafir said. "It's much too dangerous. Besides, where would we find a doctor around here? And we can't go to a city." He nodded toward his backpack again. "There's some antiseptic salve in there. Just do the best you can and we'll get on with our job."

Babrack cleaned off the wound, smeared the ointment on it and wrapped it as tightly as he dared. "Sit still a few minutes while I see what these outlaws were up to," he ordered. "I already have a good idea what it was. Did you see the mules tied behind this miserable hut?"

Zafir shook his head while Babrack shined the flashlight around the room. There were five or six more sacks like the one Zafir was sitting on. Babrack picked one up and shook it. About fifty coffee-colored bricks wrapped in cloth, each about five inches square and two inches thick, spilled out on the dirt floor.

"Morphine blocks," Babrack said. "These two were transporting them from the opium fields where the farmers made these bricks to someplace where others will convert them into opium. They would have killed both of us without a worry except where to dispose of the bodies."

He thought a minute. "I don't think we need to concern ourselves about that. Even the Taliban is turning against the opium growers, despite the money it brings them. No one will care about these men. We will leave the bodies. But we must get out of here."

Babrack went outside and pulled the second body into the hut, cursing at its weight. He tethered his two horses to the bandits' two mounts and three mules and led the convoy around to the doorway. He threw a sack containing the bandits' rifles, bandoliers, knives, and a bag of the cloth-wrapped morphine bricks across the back of one of the mules and led Zafir out into the night air.

"Come on, friend," said Babrack. He helped Zafir mount a horse and felt his clammy skin. "Let's go find you a doctor. I happen to know one who will be pleased to treat you."

8

Where is Barry's guide dog? **Obviously the murderer couldn't leave it barking in the kitchen or let it run around the halls attracting attention. But apparently he hadn't killed it when he killed Barry.**

He? It could have been a woman, I thought. *A woman might have a harder time killing the dog. But what woman would ever kill Barry? Or what man either?*

I walked slowly back to the doorway, and that's when I heard the faint sound. A whimpering noise; the kind a dog might make if it were injured. I stopped and listened. It sounded echoey and far away. Where was it coming from?

I peered out of the snack bar opening and into the hallway again. It was deserted, dark and still. I stepped out into the corridor and started back the way I had come, then heard the whimpering again from the other direction. I turned around. To the left of the old snack bar area was a burn bag room, one of the many throughout the complex where NSAers disposed of the enormous number of paper bags we filled with classified waste each day. The rooms were very small, just big enough for a person to pull in a cart piled with burn bags and throw them down the chute to the Waste Disposal Center in the basement.

I glanced at the sign on the wall beside the door:

Classified Waste Disposal Room
Paper Only Please
Hours of Operation:
M-F: 0700–1330
1430–1600
2030–2130
Weekends: 0800–1330

I looked at my watch. Nine-eighteen, only twelve minutes until the door to the chute would automatically lock and the huge shredders in the basement would begin slicing up the accumulated burn bags and their classified contents.

I knew with a sudden surety that the dog was down in that Waste Disposal Center and I knew the horrible things that would happen if I couldn't stop the shredders. I opened the door to the burn bag room and went in. Set into one wall of the room was a small but heavy metal door that led to the chute. I pulled down on the handle and swung the door open. I didn't even have to put my head far into the chute opening before I heard the agonized whimpering from the floor below. Whoever had killed Barry had carried his guide dog over here and thrown it down the burn bag chute. There must have been enough paper-filled bags at the bottom of the one-story drop to cushion the fall and keep the animal from breaking its neck.

I didn't have time to try to imagine why anyone would do such a thing; I had to figure out what to do about it.

I looked at my watch. Nine-twenty-two. Eight minutes until the chute doors locked and the shredders started. A cardboard sign on the back wall stated in bright red letters: "Waste Disposal Center: Call 963-1124 secure."

At this time of night, the nearest gray phone was a lot more than eight minutes away. What good was just posting a damn sign? Why wasn't there a phone next to it? I wasn't sure calling would work anyhow; who would ever believe me?

The dog's whimper echoed again in the metal chute.

One half of my stunned and reeling mind said, *You must go out to Gatehouse Two and tell the guards what's happened. Tell them about Barry. Maybe they can find the killer if you report this right away.*

The other half insisted, *Alex, the killer is long gone. If you go to the gatehouse now the dog will die. Horribly.*

I chose the dog.

What could I do to save it? I had been in a burn bag room once before when it was time for the doors to lock shut. I had held the door open anyway, still tossing bags down the chute. The door couldn't lock and the destruct process couldn't begin, and because it couldn't, a clanging sound began to blare, so powerfully loud my head felt like it would explode. I had let the door slam shut immediately and ran out, my brain still ringing from the blast of sound. That was years ago, and I could still remember its awful banging.

I tore the thick cardboard sign off the back wall and jammed it between the heavy metal door and its frame. That would stop the whole shredding and slicing process until someone removed the obstacle keeping the door open. Or, a terrifying thought—unless there was a manual override procedure that could be activated by the on-duty officer. With that thought fueling me, I took off running for the Waste Control Center in the basement below.

I raced down the nearest steps, burst through the door at the bottom of the stairs and ran to the right. The corridor was narrow and dim. Piled high on one side were pallets with boxes in pink shrink-wrap labeled "Acoustic Ceiling Tiles." A forklift was parked between the stacks. It was all a part of the huge process of asbestos removal.

I began to hear the blaring noise start from behind and above me. It faded as I ran, but the clanging was good news: the destruction process had not started.

I turned another corner. Ahead of me was a glassed-in area with a sign stating it was a Classified Material Conversion Center. The sign on a pedestal in front of the door read "Do Not Advance Beyond This Point."

I ignored it, ran up to the door, and pounded on it. I couldn't see anyone behind the glass. Two desks sat empty. I twisted the doorknob—it was locked. "Crap!" I said. Where were they? What were they doing? I grabbed the sign from its pedestal and slammed it into the glass at the top of the door. It shattered and slivers of glass rained down on the floor in a shimmery stream. I cut my arm on two shards that still stuck up from the frame as I reached in and opened the door. Blood, this time my own, was running down my arm and dripping on my shorts and shirt.

A man shot out from behind a wall like he had been propelled by a canon. "What the hell do you think you're doing?" he yelled at me. He picked up the gray

phone on one of the desks and punched in the 911 signal that would bring help from the guards.

"Please," I begged him, holding up a blood-spattered
hand to stop his charge. "Please help me and then I'll
explain everything."

He narrowed his eyes and looked at me suspi-
ciously. "What do you want?"

"Just turn off the shredders. Turn them off! Please!
I know you won't believe me, but a dog's caught in
there."

"A dog?" he said, as if he knew I had just escaped
from the local mental hospital. He stared at me again
and finally looked at his watch. "It's too late to save
the dog," he said gently. "Come in and sit down and
I'll call for help."

"No," I said. "No, it isn't too late! I jammed one of
the chute doors open so the shredders couldn't start.
But that won't last forever."

The man walked to one of the empty desks and
typed a few commands into a computer. Then he stood
up, opened a black metal door and held it for me. I
walked through. He pulled back a bolt on a second
door and swung it open. We could both hear the terrible hubbub from above die away and then the cries of a
dog in pain. I ran in and knelt beside a black furry
bundle with a red kerchief around its neck. "Poor baby,
poor baby," I murmured and reached out a hand to
stroke its head. One leg looked twisted, maybe broken.

"We have to get you out of here," I told the dog. "I
sure wish I knew your name."

The man left the room shaking his head and returned with a wheeled burn bag cart. He had brought
his winter coat back with him, and wordlessly the two
of us eased the black dog onto it and then lifted the
bundle into the empty basket of the cart. I looked at the

dog's collar for identification. A brass heart-shaped disk the size of a quarter was engraved with the name Maggie. I called her by her name, and she begged me with terrified eyes to help her.

Three Federal Protective Service guards, summoned by the earlier 911 call, exploded through the doors and into the room. All three had their guns drawn. They skidded to a halt in front of us and stared. It was a sight none of us would ever forget.

"Lady, you have to come with us," one of them said to me.

"I can't," I said. "I have to stay with Maggie." I looked at the black dog curled on the coat. A tear ran down my cheek and I brushed it away with the back of my hand. I was very tired.

The guard shook his head slowly. "No," he repeated. "You have to come with us." He pointed to the man from the waste disposal room who still looked as stunned as it was possible to look. "He'll call someone to help with the dog."

I stroked Maggie's head. "Yes, all right," I told the guards. "I'll go wherever you want. But first you have to follow me. There is something you need to see."

9

Operations Building 1, National Security Agency
Friday, December 1, 2000
Late Evening

I led the three FPS guards up the steps to the old
snack bar and showed them where Barry Ballard had
been murdered. It had become surreal to me; for a few
minutes on the way I half believed there would be no
body on the floor and no blood seeping out from
Barry's neck. But nothing had changed, and the bare
lightbulb in the ceiling still blazed on the grim scene.
Two guards stayed; the third walked with me back to
NSOC, his hand at my elbow the whole way.

When we arrived, Lester sauntered out from his
glassed-in office to see what was happening. His eyes
widened and he leaned toward me when he saw the
blood on my arm and feet, and for just a second I
thought he might actually be concerned for my wel-
fare. But he quickly reverted to form.

"What's the problem, Officer?" he said, looking
away from me and sneering in disgust at my disheveled state. I did look pretty disreputable: bloody gym
clothes, barefoot, tumbled hair—and an FPS guard
holding my arm. People working at the various desks
began turning around to see what was happening.

"Sir," the guard said, well aware that Lester was

acting director of NSA in his role as senior operations officer, "I think we had better discuss this in your office."

"No, we can do it right here," Lester replied, almost certainly hoping the audience that was gathering was about to hear terrible things about me.

"Yes, Sir," the guard said. "This lady will tell you all about it."

Lester looked at me, still sneering. "About what, Alex? What have you done?"

I looked at him carefully. "Are you sure you don't want us all to go to your office?" By this time, everyone in the room was paying close attention.

"Quite sure."

I sighed. "Barry Ballard has been murdered in an abandoned area of OPS 1. Somebody cut his throat. I found the body about thirty minutes ago. This man," I pointed to the guard, "has been back to the scene with me and he can verify what I just told you."

Silence.

"Lester, I think you should call DIRNSA and send out a CRITIC right away," I said. The guard next to me nodded agreement, although there was no way he had any idea what a CRITIC was.

For a minute, I thought Lester was going to slap me.

After a long silence, Lester ordered me to sit down and followed the guard down the hall, heading toward the first floor. When they got to the snack bar, he stared at the body on the floor and tried to calm his roiling stomach. Nothing in his long career in the Agency had prepared him for this. Finally, he returned, white-faced, to start the process of reporting the murder.

The next hour was a swirling, furious tempest of activity. The NSOC conference room became a crisis

command post, filled with constantly changing groups
of people.

I sat quietly in a corner of the room with a towel
wrapped around the cuts on my arm, watching people
come, people go. Kai appeared silently and sat near me,
warning everyone away with a shake of her head. A
cup of coffee sat untouched on the long mahogany
conference table. What I really wanted was a shot of
Jameson, neat.

In my corner, I heard someone's anguished cry,
"This isn't classified! How can we transmit this Unclassified? There's no such format in our computers!"
followed by the SRO, in a frenzy of frustration, screaming, "For God's sake, send it out Secret then! Just get it
the fuck out of here!"

In a minute, the senior reporting officer ran into
the conference room clutching a copy of the message
he had prepared and came over to my corner. "Sorry,
Alex, I hate to bother you, but would you please check
this before I transmit?" I could see the effort he was
making to speak calmly. "It's just so surreal I want to
make sure it's right."

I looked at the paper:

PRECEDENCE: FLASH FLASH
CLASSIFICATION: SECRET/SPECIAL INTELLIGENCE
FM: DIRECTOR, NSA
TO: WHITE HOUSE/SECDEF/JCS/CIA/DIA/STATE/FBI/
DOE/OIS
020318Z DEC 2000
DIRNSA CRITIC 005-2000
(SECRET/SI) NSA deputy director for security, Barry Bal-
lard, was found at approximately 2130L on 1 December
2000, apparently murdered, in NSA Operations Building 1.

Classification Derived from: NSA/CSS manual 123-2, dated 24 February 1998

It was a CRITIC, a unique and rare report that is issued only in times of extreme crisis. These messages are sent to the Office of the President, the Joint Chiefs of Staff, the Defense Department, and all the other appropriate intelligence and government agencies at a startling Flash precedence, stating only the barest of facts, and then followed up by more information as it becomes available. An initial CRITIC message is intended to be on the president's desk within ten minutes of issue.

I read through it quickly, nodded, and handed it back to the SRO.

He shook his head furiously, a demon of denial at the message's content, as he walked quickly back to the NSOC floor.

Within minutes, Lester, representing DIRNSA, had convened a conference call with representatives of the message recipients at watch centers across the D.C. area. I could hear his voice, rising and falling in volume, repeating over and over the details to unbelieving ears. I heard him say, "How should I know if you should wake the president? That's not my call, thank God. I sure as hell would if it was me. What if this is some kind of attack on the National Security Agency?"

In the meantime, Lester's deputy called the NSA security officer on duty in the Support Services Operations Center. Minutes later, a new group of people, the NSA 911 Emergency Team, or Men in Black, as they've been called in-house since the movie of the same name hit the streets, thundered into the NSOC conference room, spoke to Lester, and then ran back down the hall to confirm what they also could not believe.

But they returned as believers. The security officer called the Protective Services Emergency Response Team, the Anne Arundel County Police, the Maryland State Police, and the FBI. He ordered the building shut down; no one was allowed to leave or enter without permission. Soon extra guards, brought in from the Army base on Fort Meade and all wearing camouflage and heavy boots and carrying automatic weapons, were stationed around the NSA perimeter and at the murder scene.

Each wore the same stone-faced, cold expression of armed authority and force.

I sat silently in my corner.

General Murray walked into the conference room. He held up his hand to tell everyone to stay seated and headed straight to me. I wondered fleetingly why he was still in uniform so late on a Friday night. Surely he wouldn't have bothered to put it back on to come in here for this crisis?

He sat in the chair next to mine. "Alex," he asked. "Are you all right?"

I thought about it. In some ways, I was about as all right as Jimmy Hoffa, wherever he might be. But I looked at him and nodded.

"The FBI will be here soon," he said. "They're going to have to ask you some questions. Would you like me to call someone from the General Counsel's office to be with you?"

I shook my head. "No, Sir, I'll be fine."

"Alex." He spoke again, quietly and firmly. "I know this has been terrible for you, but we'll get past it. I'll personally do anything I can to help." He put his hand over mine. "It was good that you saved the dog," he said.

"It was the only thing I could do to help," I mumbled.

"I understand," he said, "but it was a remarkable act." He stood up. "My driver is waiting. I have to go tell Barry's widow what has happened," he said. He turned and walked wearily from the room.

I sat straighter in the chair. *My God, Karen Ballard doesn't even know Barry was murdered*, I thought. *She thinks he's just fine. She doesn't know she's a widow. Her world is about to fall apart.* I couldn't keep sitting there feeling sorry for myself. Next to Karen, nothing much had happened to me at all.

I glanced around the room again at the people dashing in and out. A picture of Dick Lord, the eternally boyish founder of NSOC, hung on the far wall, and large framed photographs of sailboats in Annapolis harbor serenely decorated the others. I looked over at Kai.

"Any chance you could go back to my office and get me my sneakers and socks? I think I have some sweatpants in my gym bag, too."

Kai smiled. "Sure," she said. "I'd be delighted. How about a comb and some lipstick, too? Nothing's too good for the FBI, I've heard."

"Yep, and I'll try that coffee."

A woman standing nearby was back with hot coffee in minutes. I drank it gratefully.

Kai came back with my gym bag and walked with me out of NSOC and down the hall to the closest ladies' room. I turned on the hot water in one of the sinks and washed the blood off my feet, balancing on first one and then the other as I lifted them alternately into the sink and under the flowing facet. I looked carefully at my arm. It had stopped bleeding. I didn't see and couldn't feel any bits of glass, but tomorrow I should probably have a doctor check it out. I threw the bloodstained towel in the trash, washed my face, combed my hair, and put on a little lipstick.

"Well," Kai said, "you don't quite look like an executive yet, but it's an amazing improvement. I found you a sweatshirt, too. Actually, the senior collection officer dug this out of his locker and insisted it would be much better than that CIA T-shirt you have on."

I held up a bright orange and very large sweatshirt emblazoned with the words "Denver Broncos."

"It's not going to go with my hair," I said with a tiny attempt at humor as I pulled it over my head. It was warm and somehow comforting. "Tell the SCO I'll get it back to him soon."

I walked back to the conference room. The FBI had arrived. Special Agent Gail Huang and Special Agent Carter Giles shook my hand solemnly, and we retreated to the SOO's private office. Lester wanted to attend the interview, but the agents convinced him his team needed him much more than they did. "Okay, okay," he said as he closed the door a little too firmly behind him and went back to the NSOC floor.

Lester would have his hands full just swapping out the teams and trying to prepare the "mid" shift SOO with a synopsis of what had happened during the past few hours. It was almost ten-thirty and time for shift change; the evening or "swing" shift had been there since two-thirty that afternoon and soon would be replaced by the midnight or "mid" shift that would stay until six-thirty in the morning. For the first time since shift work started at NSA forty-five years earlier, nobody could (or even wanted to) leave. With a lockdown in place, each person departing would have to be interviewed and checked, and each person reporting for duty would have to be escorted to his or her duty station.

The two special agents soon frustrated and bored me with the repetition of their questions. It wasn't a case of "good cop, bad cop." In fact, I didn't like either of them very much. I stayed as patient as I could, and explained once again why I was working so late and why I was dressed as I was.

"I wanted to fix up my new office. I didn't have time during the day, and I was anxious to get it done."

"Don't you think wandering around the NSA with bare feet is a bit extreme?" Agent Huang asked.

You can always identify people who don't actually work at NSA because they call it "*the* NSA." None of us ever does that.

Ms. Huang looks like she probably never takes her shoes off, even during sex. If she actually ever has sex, I thought. The woman reminded me of the polygraph operators who work at the Agency. Every one I had met was grim and unfriendly and utterly humorless. "Polygraphers must be totally inbred," a friend once said after a five-year background update and lie detector ordeal. "Who else would ever touch them?"

"Tell us again about the figure you saw," said Agent Giles. "Are you sure you don't know who it could have been? Or at least if it was a man or a woman?"

The ancient voice-activated tape recorder on the desk clicked and hummed faintly whenever one of them talked. Apparently the FBI was strapped for funds like everyone else.

Agent Giles raised his voice and repeated, "Could you tell if it was a man or a woman?"

"No, it was too far away and the hall was pretty dark. I had a sense that the person was tall, but that was it. I wasn't really trying to see who it was anyhow. I just wanted to stay out of the way."

"You mean, hide?" Agent Huang again.

I ignored her.

They looked at me silently, and then at each other.

"Why didn't you report the murder immediately?" Agent Giles demanded. "Apparently you waited more than half an hour before you told anyone Mr. Ballard had been killed."

"I had to try to save his dog," I said. "I . . ."

"No!" They interrupted together. Agent Huang continued. "Your first duty was to tell the guards so they could try to find the killer, not go running off looking for a dog."

I stared at them. "Bullshit!" I said. "Barry Ballard was dead. The dog wasn't dead, and I felt that saving her was the right thing to do. I would do it again." I was exhausted and very irritable.

They looked at each other again. Agent Huang finally spoke. "Can you think of any reason anyone would want to kill Mr. Ballard?"

"Of course not," I said. "He's probably the last person here that anyone would want to kill. We all think he's wonderful."

What if he's not wonderful? What if Barry Ballard was into something evil?

"Ms. O'Malley!" Agent Huang said loudly. I was drifting, not paying attention to the questions. They had gone through everything over and over; the late hour, the dark halls, the blurred figure, the bloody crime scene.

"Sorry," I snapped back. "I'm tired."

"All right," Agent Huang said, closing her notebook and reaching for the tape recorder. "We can stop for now, but please don't discuss this with anyone else." I frowned at her. "The murderer didn't see you, right? He . . . or she . . . doesn't have any idea you were there. And you don't have any idea who it was anyway. I'm sure you're not in any danger, but I can find someone to drive you home."

"I'm not worried about being in danger," I said. "I'll be fine. I just want to go home and get some sleep. Nobody will bother me, I'm sure of it." And I was sure: who could know I was staying at my mother's house instead of my own? I looked at the two agents. "But you should think about where you are. This is the National Security Agency. The place is full of spies, for God's sake. There's been a murder inside OPS 1. By Monday, everyone will know I found the body and what time I found it. Rumors race around these hallways. Even if I don't say a thing, this will be all anybody talks about for months. Years."

We all stood up. I walked back through NSOC, smiling as best I could at the new mid shift team members who looked up at me with wide, questioning eyes. I opened the door that joined NSOC with my own organization and walked into the deserted, darkened office space.

My office looked like a strange place that I hadn't seen for years. I shoved papers, picture hangers, everything I saw into desk drawers and locked them, grabbed my coat, turned off the light, and closed the door.

Kai had stayed until the interview was over and was waiting when I reached the NSOC door. "Are you all right, Alex?" She was anxious and concerned.

"Fine," I said. "Come on, I'll drive you to your car." As a grade fifteen, I had just received an executive parking pass that allowed me to park close to the gatehouse of my choice. Everyone else, except those with medical or carpool passes, or senior executives who had numbered spaces dedicated solely to them, had to compete for parking within sight of the building.

We walked silently down the hall to Gatehouse Two, still open and filled with murmuring guards. They fell so immediately quiet when we walked into the small area that they might as well have screamed that they already had heard all about the night's events. I glanced at the large, round clock hung slightly askew on the far wall: it was almost one in the morning. I reached for my badge to swipe it into the entry/exit turnstile when I saw the sign:

The CONFIRM system is off-line. Please show your badge to the guard and proceed through the gatehouse.

I was exhausted, half numb with shock and a terrible sadness, but I knew the implications of this situation. I glanced at Kai; she was staring at the sign. CONFIRM is the name for the agency's electronic access control system. Everyone who enters any of the NSA buildings has to register electronically; each badge has a magnetic strip with identifying information, and each person is logged in and then out again when he or she leaves for the day. Or for lunch, meetings "off campus," doctors' appointments, anything. It's one of the Agency systems that has never completely recovered from last year's massive computer infrastructure crash and is still occasionally nonfunctional. Normally that wasn't critically important; tonight it was.

Without CONFIRM, there was no way to know exactly who was in the building when Barry Ballard was murdered.

10

Tsalgari, Afghanistan
Saturday, December 2, 2000
Early Morning

The string of four horses and three mules plodded
across the barren countryside, stopping often so
Babrack could check Zafir's condition and give him
water to drink. Zafir felt a little stronger as he rode,
breathing in the cold night air and watching brilliant
stars flash against a velvety black sky. He had never
seen anything like it, and despite the circumstances he
was profoundly awed by the dazzling display. *It's so
primitive here,* he thought. *So elemental, as if the universe had just been formed. I wish I could share this
with Alex. She would be amazed. Perhaps someday, if
it's ever safe here.*

Babrack and his entourage reached the tiny village
of Tsalgari an hour before sunrise, as the sky was just
beginning to glow in the east. They skirted the town,
a bleak, arid, dun-colored place with mud homes,
cracked culverts, dry streams, and worn-out vineyards,
and stopped before a high-walled courtyard at the far
end of the dusty road.

Babrack unlocked a gated entrance and led Zafir
and the animals inside the courtyard. Babrack carefully locked the gate after them. A mud-brick house

sat stolidly in the middle of the enclosure, each window covered with black cloth. A ghostly blue figure opened the door, peering at the two men outside.

"Who is that, Babrack?" the ghost whispered. "Who have you brought here? It's dangerous to have strangers in our house. And what is wrong with him?"

"Shhh, just help me get him inside. He's been shot and needs your help."

Together they led Zafir to a small bed and covered him with blankets.

"Souria, what are you doing in that burka?" Babrack asked. "I know you hate wearing it, and you never have it on inside the house." He looked at her carefully. "Sister! You have been outside again, haven't you? You promised me you would wait until I returned."

The woman pulled the burka up over her head and flung it to the floor. "I went down to the village to help Nayila deliver her baby," she said. "Her husband came and begged me to help. It was a desperate situation. I couldn't refuse. Mother and child have both survived."

"Yes, because of you," Babrack said. "But someday the mullahs will find you out there and they will hurt you. You know how they hate you. And there's the curfew—they shoot anyone outside after ten o'clock without even asking questions. You must stop this."

"Uh huh," Souria murmured, already examining her new patient. Zafir watched as the woman took his pulse, felt his skin, and looked into his eyes. She rolled a blanket and elevated his feet. "He is very pale."

She continued her appraisal. "This man has lost blood, and he is suffering from moderate hypovolemic shock, but he's lucky. Bring me my kit please, and I will dress his wound."

"Yes, Doctor, right away," Babrack answered. "Is

there anything else?" His words were sarcastic, his eyes full of pride.

He took the medical kit to his sister and watched while she cleaned the place where the bullet passed through and sutured it with a few deft stitches. Zafir's eyes widened, but he made no sound. As the woman put an antibiotic salve and clean bandages on the wound, Babrack explained her skill.

"Souria studied medicine in Paris and received a medical degree there. She was a surgical resident at Broussais University Hospital in late 1995, when she returned here to take care of our dying mother. She stayed too long. The Taliban took control of the area, and she was trapped. It has been horrible for her."

Zafir looked closely at the doctor. She was tall, nearly as tall as her brother, and strikingly beautiful. Her black, shoulder-length hair swung gracefully as she worked, catching the light from the oil lamp burning on the nightstand. She was thirty-five, perhaps, younger than Babrack, with tiny lines beginning to show around her large, dark eyes.

"Souria and I have lived together in this house ever since," Babrack continued. "The Taliban, in its own special version of religious piety, has banned women from working, going to school, even leaving the house without wearing the burka and without a male relative as escort. We must even cover our windows because a woman lives here. Last month, in the bazaar, the morality police found a woman who had red polish on her fingernails. She had raised her burka to touch the merchandise." He shuddered. "They cut off her fingertips right there, right in front of her husband. He could do nothing. The bastards would have killed them both."

He slammed his fist on the table. "No woman in

Afghanistan can visit a male doctor, and Souria is forbidden to treat women because they are not allowed to be doctors. She does it anyway, as you have seen, but someday it will be her downfall. I can't be here all the time to walk with her outside this house. The mullahs hate her because she is educated, and they are just waiting to catch her alone. Even when I am there they sometimes spit on her."

He stopped, took a deep breath. His eyes flashed with fury. "I'd like to kill them. All of them."

Souria smiled at her brother. "Don't worry, they won't catch me. Allah will protect me when you are gone. And if He doesn't, I will protect myself." She reached in her bag and picked out a steel surgical blade, cold and finely edged.

Souria took her brother by the shoulder and guided him away from the bed. "Babrack," she whispered, "something much worse than the mullahs is bothering me. I haven't heard from Bashir in days. Almost a week. Something is wrong."

Babrack looked at his sister, frowning. "No, surely not. You know Bashir; he's always involved in something that takes him away from here. He could be anywhere. Pakistan even."

"Yes, I know, but we were supposed to meet this week." She blushed. "It's been a while since we've seen each other. He would have let me know somehow if he had to be away."

Bashir was Babrack's colleague, leader of their tiny anti-Taliban network and the primary CIA contact in Afghanistan. He was the man who had coaxed Ajmal into replacing the crypto card in bin Laden's satellite phone system. Bashir and Souria had been lovers for nearly two years, a desperately dangerous situation, but one they were both prepared to live with—it meant happiness and passion and even hope in a bleak and cheerless world. It was a horrible dilemma for Babrack: he was terrified the Taliban would discover the truth and kill his sister, but he also knew she deserved what few moments of joy she could find.

"I'll try to find out what's happened," Babrack said.

"Thank you," she said. "I'm very worried."

As she spoke, a bell clanged, and they could hear the sound of someone pounding on the door to the compound.

Brother and sister looked at each other. "I'll go see who it is," Babrack said. "No one must know this man is here." He added, bitterly, "At least those blackened windows are good for something."

He came right back. "It's the new baby's father. His wife has started bleeding heavily and he is worried. He wants you to go back with him. I knew I could not keep you here, so I sent him away and told him I would take you to his house. We must hurry."

Souria packed her kit quickly and pulled the blue burka back over her head. She disappeared inside the shroudlike dress, looking out at the world from behind a mesh-covered opening. She turned to Zafir.

"You will be fine," she said, her voice muffled. "Get some rest. Just don't leave the house."

"Don't leave," Babrack echoed. "And bolt the door behind us." He put Zafir's Beretta on the bedside table. "Use this if you must." They left in a draft of cold air.

Zafir slowly got out of bed and took a small black case from his backpack. Inside was a tiny phone, a version of the Inmarsat Mini-M built specifically for CIA agents in the field. He popped up the antenna, folded into the case lid. The unit included Secure Telephone Unit Generation 3 encryption software with a mathematical keying stream that converted digitized voice into indecipherable pseudorandom bits.

The Company would be waiting to hear from him, to know he had arrived safely and was about to carry out the mission. His call was overdue. Because it involved an American agent, the Minaret mission was so sensitive his case officer would expect to hear from Zafir at least once a day.

Zafir was not getting a strong enough signal for an encrypted call. He walked slowly around the house with no luck, and then stepped outside to use his GPS device to aim the antenna at the required azimuth. A billion stars glittered in the night sky, and he briefly stopped to marvel at their brilliance. His shoulder throbbed wickedly and he felt lightheaded, but he had to make the call. Linked up with the right satellite, he went back inside and dialed. "I'm here, safe now," he told his case officer. "I've been injured—not badly— but enough to cause a slight delay." He described his wound and promised to check in the next day with a status report. "I'll be waiting," the man on the other end of the phone said.

Zafir sat on the bed and sipped the tea Babrack had made for him, thinking about white-robed figures with black turbans and Kalashnikovs patrolling the roads for people to kill or maim. He cursed. Nobody had prepared him for the enormity of this evil. His training was all about the mission, nothing about the plight of the people here in this forsaken country.

He sat up suddenly and put down the tea. An unexpected thought flashed through his mind: *Maybe they didn't warn me because they don't know.* Most of CIA's assessments, he knew, were basically impassionate compilations of data by anonymous technicians. The politically influential National Intelligence

Estimates rarely took into account personal suffering and sacrifices in the countries they examined, even if they were a major factor in the government's stability. NIEs were all about weapon caches and military might. If there were an NIE for Afghanistan, which Zafir doubted, he was sure it would discuss the collapse of the country after the war with the Soviets and the influence of "Islamic fundamentalism" and "warring tribes," without any mention of the devastating loss of hope and humanity.

Maybe CIA doesn't understand how bad it really is here, he thought again.

Maybe nobody does.

11

The doorbell rang; once, twice, three times. I pulled the covers over my head. Finally I got out of bed, wrapped a blanket around my shoulders, and called out, "I'm coming. Stop that," as I shuffled to the door.

Sleep, when I had finally found it in the early morning hours, was a plunge into a vast abyss of darkness. No dreams, no nightmares, no awareness of self at all. I thought later, looking back on that night, that I was more unconscious than asleep, as nearly death-struck as Barry Ballard but still breathing and being.

"Mike? My God, what are you doing here? What time is it?"

My ex-husband shivered in the pounding rain. "I came to make sure you're all right," he said.

"Come in out of the cold. How did you know where I was?"

"You weren't at your place, so I figured Molly and Daniel were gone again. You're always here when your mother travels, right? Watching your sister and the dog?"

"Yes," I agreed, "but . . ."

"Go take a shower and put on some warm clothes.

I'll fix coffee." He pushed me gently toward the bedroom and headed for the kitchen.

By the time I reappeared in thick sweatpants and shirt, the coffee was ready and Mike Faure had put out an assortment of doughnuts on the table. I sat and picked up a mug and looked around. Rain beat on the roof, and the gusting wind blew rivers of coursing water against the windows with such force that I couldn't see farther than the shaking panes.

It was not quite eight o'clock. Fritz, my mother's German shorthaired pointer, wandered into the room and nudged my arm. I stroked Fritz's sturdy brown face and ears and waited for Mike to speak.

He leaned close and whispered, "How in God's name did you get mixed up in this, Alex?" He sat up and shook his head. "And what can I do to help you?"

My ex and I were still friends, but until the Meridian meeting yesterday, we hadn't seen each other in weeks. Neither of us had remarried or had even a serious relationship since the breakup of our marriage three years before.

Not until Gabe, I mused. *And how serious is that?* An astonishing and scary thought flashed through my mind: *pretty damn serious.*

"How much do you know?" I asked Mike.

"Probably as much as there is. They called me in to work at two a.m. It's been a long night."

I sat back in my chair and took a sip of coffee. "It was nice of you to come over here, Mike."

His smile became apologetic. "Not just nice. I want to know how you got involved. What you might know."

I ran my hands through my damp hair. I could see red curls from the corner of my eyes. "I was thirsty," I began. "It went downhill from there."

When I finished my story, I said, "Now it's your turn. What do you know that I don't?"

Mike hesitated, gathering his thoughts. While I waited for the answer, I got up and lit a fire in the chic modern woodstove with its black enamel chimney pipe soaring up to the top of the high cathedral ceiling. I walked back to the couch and sat. Fritz turned around twice and plopped down by the stove on a rug, eyes following every move I made.

The rain hadn't slackened. Normally, from almost anywhere, you could look out the huge windows lining the back of the house and see the South River as it wound its way past Annapolis. Today, rivulets of water flowed in torrents down the panes and bursts of rainwater had turned the river into a gray, sullen chop.

This was my mother Molly's house, and it was a lovely place. The large living-dining-kitchen area looked out over miles of the river, as did two patios and a downstairs family room. In the summer, sailboats and speedboats and canoes shared the water. People swam in the river, too, except in August, when jellyfish as big as frying pans came in from the Chesapeake Bay and lurked gelatinously below the surface, stingers rising and falling with the water flow in a dead man's float.

I didn't live here. I have my own town house near downtown Annapolis on a quaint street where the tourists love to roam. But I came here to stay with my sister, Nikki, a sophomore at St. John's College, and Fritz whenever Molly and her husband, Daniel, traveled. Nikki had been sound asleep when I checked on her in the middle of the night; she was still curled tight as a fist on her bed after I got up and checked her again.

Mike cleared his throat and began talking. "Like I

said, the SOO called me in to work last night to help
sort through the wreckage. The really bad news is that
CONFIRM was down, which is a complete disaster
for the investigation." He looked at me. "But you probably already know that, don't you?"

I nodded. "Yes, it was a shock. I know the system
locks up once in a while, but it seems like an awfully
odd coincidence it would happen when it did."

"Actually," Mike said, "it was a scheduled outage
that started at six p.m. and was going to last most of
the weekend. The computer weenies are still trying to
fix that glitch the system has. Very bad timing on their
part."

"So we have to rely on the memory of the guards?
That's not going to be much help. Think about how
many faces they see going in and out during an eight-
hour shift. Although," I rubbed my chin thoughtfully,
"it was late on a Friday, and there probably weren't
many people in there. That should help."

"Unfortunately, that's not true. Remember, this is
the week of the Field Chiefs' Conference."

Twice a year, in June and December, all the heads
of the various NSA outposts from all over the world
gather at Fort Meade headquarters to discuss business, plan for the future, catch up on news and rumors,
and vote for candidates to grades fourteen and fifteen
for the next two fiscal quarters. This was the week for
that conference. It was especially critical this year
with the new plans for "Transformation." The field
chiefs—all senior executives—were in the building
all week, and a few had even attended my promotion
ceremony.

"But, Mike, those guys aren't going to work until
nine on a Friday night. You can't tell me the field
chiefs were in the building last night."

"Yes, I am," he countered. "Not because they wanted to be, but because DIRNSA made them stay. He had a meeting with them at two o'clock Friday afternoon, and all they did was argue with one another. So he made them stay late until they all agreed on his plans to modernize NSA. The whole Executive Leadership Team was there also, and so were their advisers. Including, of course, Barry Ballard. And, since the field chiefs were all there, so was Barry Ballard's ex-wife."

I put down my cup. "What? What ex-wife?" I looked closely at Mike. "I can't believe I didn't know he was married to someone before Karen."

"What's so shocking?" Mike asked. "It seems to me everyone at NSA has been married and divorced to someone else who works there. The whole place is full of exes. Just look at us."

"Yes. And Molly, too, of course." My mother, retired from the Agency, had been married three times, each time to an NSAer or someone affiliated closely with the Agency. Her first husband, my father, was a ruggedly handsome Marine who was part of the Agency's guard force in the 1960s and early 1970s. Long since replaced by the Federal Protective Service, the Marine guards were once a great benefit to working at NSA, according to Molly and her friends. They were everywhere, even at the bottom of the escalators on the first floor. They always stood at attention, and they were always gorgeous. I still have a picture of my father in his dress uniform taken shortly before he died during his second tour in Vietnam.

Except for producing my sister, Molly's second marriage was a disaster. That husband was a senior executive when they met, and as is so often true at NSA, he was not the least bit happy when Molly achieved the same high rank. I'm not sure why so many

Agency men seem to be threatened when their wives become as successful as they are, but it happens over and over. Often, after a bitter divorce, the man remarries a secretary or a much younger woman way down in the grade scale.

This time, Molly seemed to be very happy in her two-year marriage to Daniel, a Defense Intelligence Agency employee she had met when he worked as a liaison officer at the Agency.

Divorces at NSA do seem to be spectacularly acerbic, perhaps because spending so much of your life in such a secluded, guarded place sometimes breeds a high level of paranoia and distrust. And revenge. One very high-ranking senior executive will turn eighty-five soon; divorced from his wife nearly forty years ago, he refuses to retire and let her have part of his pension. Any part.

In fact, it often seems like at least half the Agency has had affairs, fallen in love with someone they shouldn't, divorced, and remarried at least once. It was bad enough at headquarters; field sites were even worse. Rumors said skinny-dipping and exchanging house keys had been commonplace at places far from home. Security clearances created strange (and varied) bedfellows.

I shook my head. "I have to say I'm stunned."

"Most people were," Mike said. "The word was that they got divorced because she wanted children and he only wanted a career. Then he ended up marrying Karen and having two kids that he went completely crazy over. You know how he always carried their pictures?"

I nodded solemnly. "Barry and his first wife must have divorced a long time ago. Who is she, anyway?"

"You're right, they have been divorced for years.

And ever since, his ex—Judy Lincoln—has stayed in the field as much as she could."

"Judy Lincoln? You mean the same woman who organized our Project Meridian group? She was involved before I was, but I've met her. She's smart, but kind of aloof. Pretty, very blond. She left, though, right? To go to England. Maybe a month ago."

"She left to become chief of Menwith Hill Station. Like I said, she never wanted to come back to the Fort unless she had to. She's worked all over for the past ten years—Germany, Hawaii, Medina, Texas. I've heard she even considered the MUSKET site, if you can believe that." Mike paused. "Apparently their divorce wasn't as amicable as ours."

Mike and I had married quickly, too quickly, in a rush of sparkling passion. When the fire cooled, we drifted apart, each becoming more and more dedicated to jobs we already pursued with an almost religious zeal. When I discovered he had begun seeing someone else, I wasn't surprised. Or even hurt. I simply spent even more time at my job. Finally, we decided to live apart, and then, to divorce.

I wondered what the story was between Barry and Judy. Any marriage that breaks up over the issue of children was probably headed for an acrimonious divorce. But murder?

"Mike," I said, "nobody thinks Judy killed him, do they? Think of all the years of hate you would have to carry around with you to do such a thing."

"It's early times, Alex. But sure, the FBI is looking at her closely." He hesitated. "But it's looking closely at you, too."

"Me! What are you talking about?"

"Take it easy," Mike said. "You know how it works.

Haven't you watched *NYPD Blue* lately? Your finger-
prints are the only ones they've discovered so far, and
in the cops' eyes the person who discovers the body is
always the first suspect. Then it always turns out to
be someone else. Someone you would never have
thought of."

"Well, what was Barry doing in the kitchen? Does
anybody have any idea?"

"DIRNSA had arranged for a driver to meet Barry
after the meeting since it was going to be so late.
Barry called the motor pool before he left his office
and told them he would be at Gatehouse Two in ten
minutes. That's why he was headed to that part of the
building," Mike answered me. "When he didn't show,
the driver called Barry's office. No answer, so he
called Security, who were, of course, still trying to
decide what to do when you found the body. But why
he ended up in the snack bar kitchen is anyone's guess
at this point."

I nodded. "I know this is a crazy idea, but I started
wondering about it last night on the way home. Is
there any chance Barry's murder is related to the Meridian failure? I can't imagine how, can you? It's just
that first Meridian goes south . . . then Barry gets
killed . . ."

"No," Mike answered slowly. "I considered it myself, but I can't make it work. Barry has the VRK
clearance, of course, but he's so high up in the Agency
chain that he hasn't really gotten as involved as the
rest of us in the project. I just don't see how it could be
related, at least not yet. But you're right; the timing is
odd, to say the least."

"Yes. I don't like it." I stood and walked to the window. The rain had finally eased, and I could see the

river and the winter-barren trees on the small island down the causeway. In the distance, tiny cars crossing a tiny bridge sprayed bright, glistening sheets of water from their wheels.

"Well, I have something else you probably won't like much either. You'd better sit back down."

I turned quickly and narrowed my eyes. "What? What else do you know, Mike?"

He pointed to the couch and I sat.

"The FBI went through everything Barry had with him when he was killed. His clothes, his briefcase."

I nodded.

"There wasn't anything in his briefcase at all, which is puzzling, and nothing much in his pockets. But they found a tiny tape recorder lying near his body. It was one of those voice-activated Sony microcassettes. It didn't have a tape in it, though. In fact, they couldn't find any tapes anywhere."

"But, Mike . . . that's impossible. Nobody is allowed to have a tape recorder in the building."

That's true. Not even blind people. Everyone knew that. Security repeatedly posted a list of things that are prohibited at NSA, and it was taken very seriously:

Recording devices
Audiocassettes
Guns
Explosives
Contraband and illegal substances
Pagers
Cameras
Personal computers
PDAs
Cell phones

"Well, what does it mean?" I asked. "Why would he have a tape recorder the night he was killed? And no tapes?"

"Sounds to me like the murderer took the tape with him," Mike said. "The FBI thinks so, too, since the recorder was open and there were bloody smudges on it. It was on the floor, pretty banged up. Like someone took the tape out of it and then threw it down. I'm surprised you didn't see it, Alex."

"No, I missed it completely," I admitted, wondering how.

"Well, the FBI is going to search the kitchen and Barry's office and house for the missing tape, but the current working theory is that the killer took it," Mike said.

"An NSA employee killed Barry Ballard to steal an illegal cassette tape from him? Doesn't that seem totally bizarre to you?"

He rubbed his eyes, yawning. "You bet. Much too bizarre to be true."

"God, you must be exhausted. You'd better go home." I hesitated. "None of what you told me is classified, is it?"

"No. Just sensitive."

"Everything at NSA is sensitive. Or, at the very least, 'For Official Use Only.'"

Mike nodded. "For Official Use Only" is a caveat NSA likes to slap on nearly everything unclassified they produce because, unbelievably, "FOUO" keeps information out of the hands of Freedom of Information Act requesters as quickly as a "TOP SECRET" classification does. It's definitely something the Agency doesn't advertise.

We stood and walked to the door. Mike put a hand

on my shoulder. "Alex, please be careful. By Monday, every single person at NSA will know you found Barry's body. Including whoever murdered him. If there's any chance at all the killer feels threatened by you . . ."

"I guess you might be right to worry," I agreed slowly, shivering a little. "Somehow I don't think this is over yet. But nobody knows I'm staying here while Molly and Daniel are gone except you. That should help keep me safe. And I suspect they'll come back from Italy for Barry's funeral. He and Molly were good friends, you know."

"When they get back, you stay here with them until this is cleared up."

"Oh, all right." I grinned at him. "You're still very bossy."

He left, and I watched him drive off. I wrapped the blanket around me and sat back on the couch, watching the rain. It bothered me, as it had so often, that two people could be so attracted to each other and then end up losing that kind of enchantment. I thought about Gabe. *God, I hope that doesn't happen again. I'm going to be very careful with my feelings.* Another thought stunned me: *I'll be careful if he makes it back here alive.* A second one made me grimace: *It's probably too late anyway. I'm already awfully fond of him.*

I frowned and shifted my thoughts to the day before. It didn't seem possible any of this could have happened: the murder, the injured black dog, the missing comms, Gabe's mission. *And the tape recorder,* I thought. *I bet that's important. Where is the missing tape? What was on it? Did the murderer really take it?*

12

Dr. Jamal Rashiq peered at his computer screen,
deep in concentration. When the pager on his hip
buzzed, he leaped to his feet, knocking over his chair.
He ran out of his office door and down the hallway to
the special CCU.

"What?" he demanded of the nurse. "What's wrong
with him?"

She held up a hand. "He's all right. I bumped the
oxygen machine and the alarm went off. Sorry."

She cowered as he glared at her. "Don't ever do that
again," he finally said in a tight voice. He reached
out and touched his patient, a small boy with a feeding tube, wrapped in blankets and hooked up to a
profusion of monitors checking his blood pressure,
electrolyte balance, fluid levels, and any sign of hy-
poxia.

"You're okay, Matthew," he said, gently stroking the
boy's face. "You're going to get better." The doctor had
been fighting for the six-year-old's life for weeks. The
first few days, he had stayed next to his patient constantly, despite the risk of infection. Even Matthew's
parents were not allowed in the room. The boy had

been flown to the secluded CDC-supported hospital and research facility in Washington, D.C., from a small medical center in Bridgeville, Missouri, where he was losing his fight for life. High fevers, exhaustion, muscle aches, and breathing problems robbed the child of his strength, and the Missouri doctors began to suspect his problem might be a viral hemorrhagic fever, such as the rare but lethal and infectious Ebola virus. They sent him, with barrier nursing in place, to the D.C. medical center as a last option. Dr. Rashiq was waiting for him when he arrived.

Rashiq knew almost immediately that Matthew was suffering from hantavirus, a deadly acute respiratory infection sometimes found in the "Four Corners" area of New Mexico, Arizona, Colorado, and Utah. The virus is transmitted by infected rodents, often the tiny deer mouse, through urine, feces, or saliva. Matthew's parents told Rashiq they had been camping in that area a month earlier, a fact the Missouri physicians apparently did not consider in their failure to diagnose. Dr. Rashiq, with his extensive background in viral research, had identified hantavirus as the most likely culprit as soon as he examined the boy and heard the constant coughing, found the fluid in his lungs, and watched as he alternately shook with chills and burned with fevers. Jamal Rashiq was a very good doctor, and children were his most cherished patients.

Jamal Rashiq had decided early, shortly after he entered medical school, to focus his studies on the pathogenic group of highly infectious viruses that produce severe disease in humans. He was intrigued, then obsessed, by hemorrhagic viruses, such as Ebola and Lassa fever, which had historically been confined to the distant areas of the world that produced them. Now, however, the increasing popularity and afford-

ability of global travel threatened to deliver any one
of them to the United States in just hours. Although
researchers published articles saying it was unlikely,
Rashiq knew the truth: it was possible for a particularly virulent virus, such as that which killed many
millions of people during the 1918 "Spanish Flu" pan-
demic, to appear at any time, spread wildly, and threaten
mankind.

He dedicated himself to learning about these viruses, which were carried by mosquitoes, rodents,
birds, or humans and which caused hemorrhaging,
nervous system malfunction, coma, delirium, and sei-
zures. At one point, he branched into parasitic disor-
ders, studying the debilitating guinea worm disease,
which produces two- to three-foot-long worms that
burst through ulcerated blisters in the skin of those
poor souls who have been infiltrated by the larvae. He
moved on to bacterial diseases, such as the plague,
Lyme disease, and tularemia and found them interesting, but he soon returned to viruses, especially those
strains that were particularly insidious and infectious.

The Centers for Disease Control and Prevention in
Atlanta, Georgia, was delighted to fund the young
man's training in this complex and often esoteric field
and to hire him after graduation from med school.
He spent two years at the Centers' Special Pathogens
Branch investigating known and recently identified
and emerging viral diseases. His work was done under
conditions of BioSafety Level 4, in a specialized facility designed to minimize the danger of exposure to
agents that could pose a high risk of life-threatening
infection. This CDC facility, specially engineered and
filled with containment equipment and one-piece ven-
tilated personnel suits, was sequestered from all other
buildings in the complex.

Rashiq became proficient, not so much in determining viral taxonomic structure or morphology or
genomic organization, as in understanding the transmission, geographic distribution, range of hosts, repli-
cation ability, and symptomatic presentation. His goal
was predictability—where and when these deadly diseases were most likely to strike and who were their
most likely victims. He published papers based on his
research on a wide range of viruses and was quickly
acknowledged as an expert in this field. Perhaps, *the*
expert.

The doctor also had a kind of sixth sense, possibly
based on long hours in the lab, when it came to diag-
nosis. It was a gift, a source of genius, which he nur-
tured and savored.

Dr. Rashiq's studies of illnesses and diseases and
their causes and preventions had consumed his life for
years. He hated the thought of failure, even when treat-
ing the most medically challenging cases. He spent
hours designing strategies to treat the sickest of his
patients. He taught himself to be supportive and caring
with those patients because he felt it was a crucial factor in finding a way to bring them back to health.

Interacting with patients, particularly adults, was his
most difficult task. He was not comfortable associat-
ing with others, even when it was critical. He could,
and did, force himself to do so, but it was stressful and
sometimes agonizing. He did not date, had no close
friends, and kept to himself whenever possible.

He was too detached, too aloof to be well-liked
among his colleagues.

He knew it, but he was too deadened to care and too
tired to make the changes that would make him appealing to others. He had made plenty of changes in
his life—most of them when he was still very young—

adjustments that simply allowed him to stay alive after
the Soviets invaded Afghanistan and eventually made
him an orphan.

Jamal had been born into a wealthy Afghan family
during the time of the monarchy of Zahir Shah. His
father was a government official; not a grand official,
but one whose position allowed the family to live in a
large house with gardens and servants in a very upscale
section of Kabul. He became used to marble floors
and rosebushes and pomegranate trees and tea served
with sweets at least twice a day.

When the king was deposed in 1973, Jamal's father
aligned himself with the new government, following an
age-old Afghan tradition of switching sides whenever
there was a new ruling faction. Their world changed
little until December 1979, when the Soviets invaded
Afghanistan. The "Christmas Invasion," they called it.
MiGs screamed over Kabul. The city was also attacked
by three divisions of ground forces and a special Soviet
assault unit of five thousand men that stormed the
Tajbeg Presidential Palace. After successfully seizing
the capital city, the invading forces began the methodical slaughter or imprisonment of everyone associated
with the overpowered Afghan government.

Jamal's uncle, who had lived next door in his own
large home, had left with his wife and overseas invest-
ments after the fall of the king and found his way to
California.

Jamal's father, who had insisted there was no reason to move away from Afghanistan when his brother
did, lost everything during the Christmas invasion. He
became a hunted man.

Jamal was twelve years old; his sister was six. His
family left their house and fled to the country, where
they lived in abandoned shacks, eating whatever they

could find or beg. His father joined what became the national resistance movement, an uneasy alliance between the modern, educated members of Afghan society who had supported government plans for the modernization of Afghanistan and the Islamic fundamentalists who wanted not only to oppose the invasion but also to reorganize the state and society on the basis of Islamic ideology, "in accordance with the Book of God and the practice of His Prophet." It was the first time Jamal heard the preaching of the fundamentalists, and he was attracted by the glory of their words and the idea of a structured, spiritual society ruled by the laws of Allah. But most of all, he learned from them that he was special, one of the chosen, not an "infidel." God's government on earth could not coexist with the infidels.

"Kill the infidels," was a mantra he began to ponder, although he wasn't exactly sure who they were.

Two years later, Jamal and his family were in a borrowed car, driving from their latest hideout to a meeting of the resistance group in a small town east of Kabul. The Soviets had put landmines on the road. When the car hit the mines, it exploded, killing everyone but Jamal. He escaped with a badly shattered left leg and nightmares that would haunt him for the rest of his life. He would often question why he had lived. He often wished he had died in that car with the others.

He lay there among the carnage of his family for several hours, until he was found by another of the men attending the secret meeting. By then, Jamal was pretty sure he knew who at least some of the "infidels" were. And now he knew why they deserved to die.

The man took Jamal to his home, where he spent weeks trying to recover from the accident. In addition to his injuries, Jamal couldn't deal emotionally with the loss of his family. He slipped into a depression that left him lethargic and leaden. The doctor who came to the house to treat him finally shook his head. "The boy needs to be in a hospital. I don't have the medicine or the skills to make him well."

The next day, the man who had rescued Jamal contacted the imam of his mosque. The two found a way to hide the boy in the back of a supply truck that rumbled slowly across the mountainous border with Pakistan. On the other side, a man met the truck and took the boy to a hospital in Peshawar. Hospital authorities called the American embassy in Islamabad and asked them to contact Jamal's uncle in America.

In six months, Jamal was living in San Diego. His leg was finally healing, but he would limp slightly for the rest of his life. The images in his mind of his family's terrible deaths tormented him. His aunt and uncle and their five-year-old daughter, Mariam, tried to make him feel like part of the family. They formally adopted him. He became an American citizen. They tried to help him fit in with his peers, but the loss of his "real" family had affected him too deeply. He wouldn't allow himself to get close to his adoptive parents and sister or go on dates or make friends; they could be torn away from him by events well outside his control. He was unwilling to take any chance that he might have to deal with feelings of loss again.

He did not adapt well to his new life.

He was very intelligent, and he worked hard during his first years of school in the States, working long hours to make up for the years of study he had missed. He became a self-imposed outcast. He loved learning and hated the opinionated, unruly, naive students he had to face every day. Sometimes they taunted him. Mostly they ignored him.

He began to excel in school, but he was an insular, troubled young man in a sea of boisterous American culture. Finally he discovered the two things that would give his life meaning: the study of medicine and, years later, complete devotion to fundamentalist Islamic principles.

His adoptive family was very proud when he received his medical degree, and he was pleased to be able to move away from them to Atlanta to work for the Centers for Disease Control and escape from the kindness and love he was unable to return. After two years in Atlanta, the CDC sent him to Paris for eight months to work with a prominent virologist at the Université Paris Descartes.

His life changed in Paris.

The first mosque Rashiq attended after he moved to France was the magnificent Mosque of Paris, constructed in 1926 as a token of French appreciation for North African assistance during the First World War. Its exquisite mosaics, stunning woodwork, and soaring minaret were inspired by the Alhambra in Spain. A café served sweet mint tea and a gift shop sold pottery and incense.

The experience was similar to the homogenized version of Islam that his adoptive family occasionally practiced. After three visits, Jamal realized he yearned to relive the fervor of the true, pure Islamic values he had been introduced to as a boy in the snowy mountains of Afghanistan. The Mosque of Paris was too embracing, too reformist.

Jamal was searching for a call to piety and devotion he had heard as a child, but he decided that that brand of Islam—which he regarded as the real, true Islam—did not exist anywhere in the West. Then, one Friday evening on his way out of the grand mosque, he saw brightly colored posters taped to nearby trees and poles. "Would you like to be a real Muslim? Come hear Imam Abdul Kahhar speak." An address followed. Dr. Rashiq smiled. *Yes, that's what he had in mind*. He wanted to be "a real Muslim," not one who prayed mechanically and lived immorally. Maybe, just maybe, there were others like him around. He decided to look for them, and nothing in his life was ever the same again.

Jamal migrated northeastward, responding to the call of the imam, into the poorer neighborhoods of Bobigny, Clichy-sous-Bois, and Montfenneil, inhabited primarily by immigrants from north or central Africa. He limped slowly past rundown public housing projects, doorways filled with menacing youths smoking cigarettes and spitting on the cracked sidewalks. Here, the elementary schools had barred windows and the few women on the streets kept their heads covered and scurried from the market to their shabby homes.

He found the mosque listed on the posters in the basement of a kebab shop and began going there for prayers. He knew a little Arabic, but he found it hard to follow most of what was said. When the imam spoke to the congregation after the ritual acts of worship, however, he switched to French, which Rashiq spoke fluently. The doctor admired the calm, deliberate sermons encouraging the mostly poor, unemployed men at the mosque to develop a sense of pride in their culture and religion and in their community. To stand up for themselves and their beliefs.

He especially liked going there on Fridays, when Imam Abdul Kahhar offered the *Salaat-ul-Jumma,* the obligatory prayers for all adult male Muslims. Each week the men of the neighborhood dressed in their best clothes and assembled in the kebab shop basement mosque for these special Friday meetings. Following the prayers and supplications, the imam spoke to the congregation on issues of the day. He interpreted the Koran and instructed them on how to live their lives. To push the government of France to recognize them as equal French citizens.

On some Fridays, Iman Abdul Kahhar slipped into a more political mode. Then, depending on the current tensions in the Middle East, he spoke of brutal Zionists who were lackeys for the American infidels and the need for a cleansing *jihad*. On those Fridays, he captured the rapt attention of Dr. Jamal Rashiq.

Rashiq knew he didn't fit in with the other men who attended the mosque. His skin was lighter, his clothes, his bearing, everything cried out that he was a stranger. He stayed in the shadows and remained quiet even when the imam led the men in discussions he desperately wanted to join. He tried to be inconspicuous. He wasn't.

After several weeks, two men appeared suddenly, one on either side of him as he walked the mile and a half from the mosque to the nearest metro station. One of the men, who introduced himself as Nazim, asked in heavily accented French, "Why do you come here, Dr. Rashiq? Are you looking for a victim to test your viruses on? Why don't you stay in the rich part of Paris, where you belong?"

"How do you know who I am?" he asked the men. They simply stared at him. "I want to learn," Rashiq said, staring back at his accusers. "I want to know more about my faith and my people. I want to be a better Muslim."

The two men looked at each other. After a moment, Nazim said, "All right, we know someone who can teach you all you need to know."

The next evening, after prayers, the men escorted Rashiq to a housing project and led him up three flights of smelly, broken steps to a tiny, disheveled apartment. A bedroom had a mattress on the floor, and the kitchen had a cracked sink full of dirty dishes and a floor of peeling linoleum. The living room held two chairs. They pointed to one of the chairs and Rashiq sat down. Imam Abdul Kahhar was in the other.

The lessons began that night. Imam Abdul Kahhar still spoke calmly, but an undercurrent of passion punctuated everything he said. He taught his new pupil his interpretation of the history of Islam, the Prophet Mohammed, and the teachings of the Koran. He talked about the persecution of the Palestinians and their displacement from their homes by the Jews. He told Jamal Rashiq stories about how the Jews tortured and then slaughtered whole villages of Palestinians, sometimes burning them alive. He talked about the discrimination the members of his mosque had suffered at the hands of the French. He told him that *all* nonbelievers were enemies of Islam and must be eliminated.

Week after week, the two men met in the apartment. Rashiq left each time in a state of anger and pride. He listened to Kahhar with the same zeal he had applied to his medical training. He began taking part in discussions. He often ate meals with Nazim and other men where the talk was all about the clash of values between Islam and the West, the power and majesty of Allah and veneration of Mohammed, His messenger ("Peace be upon him").

It paid off. Finally, Jamal Rashiq belonged; finally, he fit in. Now he knew who his friends were. Now he knew who his enemies were. At last he had something to believe in.

He began wearing *kameez partoog*, traditional Afghan clothing. He stopped drinking alcohol. His eyes blazed with a new intensity of religious fervor which impressed his new friends. After two months, the men who had taken him to the apartment drove him to a secluded villa many miles from Paris. They taught him to shoot a handgun and to defend himself. They taught him to move through the shadows like a cat and to control his breathing and his fears. He started an extreme regime of physical conditioning, working out at the gym near the university. His weak leg grew stronger, to the point where he began running as much as five miles a day. The memory of his parents' and his sister's terrible deaths lingered, but helplessness was replaced by the awareness of his increasing strength and by an ever-growing need for revenge.

As it neared the time he was to leave France, a short, squat man met with Jamal Rashiq in the apartment. His name, he told the doctor, was Abdul Majid, and he was a member of a small Afghan al Qaeda cell that was planning to change the world.

"You can be part of the change," he said, his black eyes burning holes into the doctor's soul. "You have learned your lessons well. Now it is time to decide if you are capable of putting those lessons to use for a godly purpose. I have come to recruit you for a very special mission that only you can carry out."

"Why me?" Rashiq asked.

"Because you are a respected professional person in the U.S. You are trusted there. You can go where you want and do what you want without raising any suspicions. You are the perfect inside agent for us. They think you are one of them. But you're not. Not anymore. Now, you are one of *us*. And we need you."

Jamal Rashiq looked at the dark-bearded al Qaeda

operative with the bushy eyebrows and piercing eyes and nodded his agreement. "I will do whatever you ask," he said.

Abdul Majid smiled. "Yes," he agreed, "I think you mean it. We know your background. We know you hate the infidels, especially the Russians. First, however," he said in his nearly perfect English—learned at the North Carolina university where he had earned a degree in mechanical engineering—"first we must test you to be certain you are dedicated and courageous enough to carry out this mission."

"What is the test?" Rashiq asked.

"We want you to kill someone," Abdul Majid said, handing him a sleek, black-handled knife with a perfectly balanced blade so sharp it hurt to look at it.

A thrill of excitement raced through him. *A test? Yes, I'm ready.* "Who?" Rashiq asked. "Who should I kill?"

"A Jew," Abdul Majid answered. "A highly placed expatriate Russian Jew who arranges venture capital alliances between French companies and the maggots in Israel who would kill all of us."

Dr. Jamal Rashiq took a deep breath. "Yes," he said. "I can do that."

That night Nazim drove him to a street near the Musée Rodin. A well-dressed, burly man parked his Mercedes in front of a row of upscale town houses on the Rue de Varenne and carried his briefcase into the house on the end of the row. The nameplate next to the door read "Aram Petrenko." A little girl waited for the man just inside the door, arms outstretched. *"Mon père,"* she said, hugging him tightly.

"Him," Nazim said. "You have a week."

It took only two days. Rashiq rented a car, waited outside the town house in the early morning darkness,

and followed Petrenko to his place of employment at a
large office complex in the 2ème arrondissement near
the Paris Stock Exchange. Petrenko parked in a parking garage under one of the buildings; Rashiq did the
same. He sat for hours wondering if he could take a
man's life for no reason. And then he realized he had a
reason, one better than any other: the man was a Russian. Not just a Jew, but a Russian Jew. Russians had
stolen his life, killed his family, and, for a very long
time, taken away his very wish to live.

On the second day, the Frenchman returned to his
car much later than usual. The garage was deserted
and dimly lighted. Using his best patrician French accent, Dr. Rashiq approached him and asked for directions. Petrenko pulled a map from the pocket of the
driver's door and opened it on the hood of his car. As
he bent over it with a tiny flashlight, Jamal Rashiq
buried a knife in his throat. Aram Petrenko turned
slowly to look at his attacker, stunned, his eyes wide.
He raised his hands as Rashiq struck him again in the
stomach, forcing the knife up toward his heart. The
man sagged to the concrete and died, trying to speak.
Rashiq reached in the man's pocket and took his wal-
let, scooping out the money and leaving the rest.

He drove back to his apartment, hands shaking on
the wheel. Despite his determination, he had nearly
walked away from his victim, right at the end, when
he remembered how the little girl had hugged her
father and when the oath he had taken as a doctor
flashed before his eyes: "Do no harm." He had almost
stopped at the bar near his apartment for a double
scotch. But he didn't. And after a while, he knew he
had done the right thing. He was a fighter for virtue
and honor. A Defender of Islam. He stopped shaking.
He was a new traveler on the road to glory. He had

begun his quest for revenge, and Allah was with him. He went to bed and slept like an innocent boy might sleep.

The next day the savage murder was splashed across the front page of all the city papers. The French police had no suspects. Dr. Jamal Rashiq had passed his test. He was hooked. He begged Abdul Majid to send him to Afghanistan to one of the terrorist camps to continue his training. He refused. "No, no. I told you, the Americans must think you are completely trustworthy," Majid said. "An Afghan stamp in your passport would raise immediate security alarms, and sneaking you in is too dangerous. We will give you all the training you need right here."

Majid grabbed Rashiq's shoulder, held it hard. "This is what we need you to do," he whispered, a hint of frenzy catching the edges of the words. "Sometime in the next year," Abdul Majid said, spitting out the words of hate, "we will unleash the full power of Islamic wrath to strike the corrupt world of nonbelievers." His eyes burned with the fire of madness. His voice reached a new pitch. *It will change the world. It will force every nation to acknowledge the might and glory of Allah and the courage of Muslims everywhere.*

"What can I do?" Rashiq demanded.

"The West will counterattack, almost immediately," Majid continued, a little more calmly. "My al Qaeda group is planning a secondary strike against the infidels to prove our overwhelming force and our determination to continue the divine battle for all human souls." His words intensified again. "*You*," he pointed a finger at Rashiq, *"will be the agent of Islam who will design and direct the execution of our follow-up plan, a plan so devastating and terrifying it will distract and confuse the political powers in Washington, D.C., and the U.S. military for a very long time. Long enough for us to win the world!"*

"I'm ready," Rashiq said. "What will I do?"

"Sometime after you get back to America, a man will meet you. He will give you several grams of finely processed anthrax, a small amount, but enough to kill thousands. This anthrax," Majid said, his bushy eyebrows rising and falling gleefully, "is very close to what they call 'weapons-grade.' The spores are small enough to go airborne when dispersed against a target and tiny enough to float in the air for a very long time. They are invisible floating like that. The dying will never know what hit them."

Jamal, Majid told him, had two tasks: he would use his skills and his equipment to divide the deadly bacterial spores into several packages paired with tiny timed explosive charges, and he would personally inspect a list of possible targets to determine which were most appropriate and how best to gain access to them. His job was not to deliver the poisons; al Qaeda would not risk his life when he could be so valuable to them in the future. Others would take the anthrax to the targets and plant the tiny explosive packages to release clouds of the electrostatic-free spores into the air. The men would attack the targets simultaneously, before any security precautions could be put in place. The result: nearly everyone who breathed the *Bacillus anthracis* spores would die.

"Everything must be meticulously planned and executed," Abdul Majid repeated several times. "The timing is essential. We must show the infidels that we can match their counterattack—and be assured there will be one—with an even more devastating strike of our own." He looked at Jamal Rashiq gravely. "You are

the one who will make sure our strike happens. Once
we pick the final targets, we want you to be the one to
create the anthrax packages for those targets. You will
need specialized equipment to handle this process and
a place to store the anthrax before and after the first
batch is divided. Can you do that?"

"Yes," Rashiq said slowly, thinking about the enormity of what was being asked of him. "I can do that."

"Money is not a problem," Majid replied. "We will
give you whatever you need."

"When will this happen?" Rashiq asked.

"You will most likely receive the anthrax before the
end of the year. This grade of anthrax was very difficult
to get, and we have been told there is no more available
and probably never will be. Please keep that in mind as
you work with it. You should prepare the packages right
away so they are ready as soon as they are needed, as
soon as our attack against the West happens. I can't tell
you when that will be, but you will know." The madness returned to his eyes. *"The whole world will know."*

Dr. Rashiq was impressed. He had occasionally
considered the damage that could be done to various
installations or populations using some of the hemorrhagic viruses he worked with, but designing a targeted delivery system for these dangerous and exotic
agents would be extremely challenging. They were so
infectious that hundreds of thousands might perish
before the raging epidemic was stopped. The wrong
people might die—Jamal Rashiq included.

But the inhalation form of anthrax could be dispersed in a somewhat controlled manner. It could be
used, for example, to contaminate a specific building
and deliver its deathblow primarily only to those in
that building. Because it is not contagious, its effects
could be limited to a small group. And inhaled anthrax

could be just as deadly as any hemorrhagic virus. Initial symptoms were those of the common cold, discouraging most victims from seeking immediate medical help, but severe breathing problems and shock would soon follow. As would death in most cases. A vaccine against anthrax was available in limited quantities, but almost no one, except for some in the military, had ever been given it.

Getting processed *Bacillus anthracis* spores was the challenge. Rashiq couldn't imagine how the al Qaeda cell had managed to do that. The trick to making anthrax into a bioweapon was, as Dr. Rashiq understood it, turning a wet bacterial culture into a dry powder. Initially, the dried spores, carrying a static electric charge, tended to clump together, making them too large to float fatefully through the air. It was necessary to grind the spores into a fine powder and treat them with a chemical additive that increased their buoyancy, preparations that certainly not just anyone could do. The U.S. had successfully produced this kind of "weaponized" anthrax at its biological warfare center at Fort Detrick, Maryland, but all stockpiles had been supposedly destroyed after the end of the program in 1969. The Soviet Union and Iraq had also successfully weaponized the toxic bacteria, as had several other countries. A 1972 ban on production and storage of biological weapons was signed by over a hundred countries, but nobody knew for certain that the development of "germ warfare" had completely stopped. In fact, it was a good bet that Iraq, for example, was continuing the work.

"Where did you get the anthrax spores?" he asked Abdul Majid, certain he would not get an answer.

Instead, Majid grew even more excited, his eyes wide and bright. He slowly scanned the area around

him, as if there were someone nearby who might hear
what he had to say. He leaned close to Dr. Rashiq. His
voice lowered to almost a whisper. "From a contact
inside the United States," he said, nodding his head
and smiling a conspiratorial smile. "Yes, my friend,
Allah does surely act in mysterious ways." He sat up
straight again. "But that's enough. It shouldn't matter
to you where we got them."

"No," Rashiq agreed, his mind racing. He was
shocked. *A source inside the U.S.? It had to have come
from a scientist at the Army Medical Research Institute
of Infectious Diseases at Fort Detrick. They would still
have samples left for testing. Nobody else would have
access to such highly refined anthrax, not even the CDC.
But who at USAMRIID would do such a thing?*

He stopped himself. The source really didn't matter, just the acquisition of the spores. And the man
who would disperse them. His head swam with the
delirium of self-importance. His first mission for the
glory of Islam could not be more important.

He wouldn't know the quality and virulence of the
bacteria until he received the package. Until it was
delivered, Abdul Majid told him, he was to spend his
time surveilling the list of targets the al Qaeda cell
had identified and determining which were the most
suitable—which ones would provide the highest inci-
dence of panic and death.

During his remaining time in France, Jamal Rashiq
alternated between learning the skills of medical lifesaver at the university and those of terrorist life taker
at the secluded villa. The dichotomy pleased him; it
gave his life an urgency and vitality he had never
before experienced. But it also worried him; planning
the mass murder of innocent people was confusing.

Shouldn't they be targeting those who really deserved killing—the military, the government officials, the instruments of persecution and oppression of his people? Would poisoning the Washington Monument, the Statue of Liberty, the National Cathedral, or even the Supreme Court—all of which Majid told him were on the al Qaeda list—really be the most effective use of the lethal bacteria? It struck him that there were probably excellent targets Majid had not considered.

Especially since no hope of any more anthrax meant there would never be a second chance.

There were better targets, such as the agency his adopted sister worked for, but they were well-guarded places, not open to the public like a Las Vegas casino. But, perhaps, with God's help, he could find a way.

After he had been back in the States for a month, the CDC decided to move Rashiq to a private medical center and research facility tucked away on a quiet side street in northwest D.C. to allow him to treat patients with deadly viruses as well as focus on his research.

Moving from the bustle of CDC headquarters in Atlanta to the private D.C. clinic was perfect for what Dr. Rashiq had to do. Except for occasional visiting physicians or students, Rashiq was alone in the center unless he had a patient; then nurses were brought in to help. A laboratory that was configured in accordance with the CDC's BioSafety Level 4 standards, complete with containment equipment and special ventilation quite adequate for handling anthrax spores, had been provided so he could continue his studies. When he got the anthrax packets, he could prepare them right there, in the government-funded lab, and he would have all the time and privacy he needed. He knew it was a sign that his mission was blessed.

The only thing that repeatedly disturbed him,

sometimes to the point of making him stop and consider if he could really carry out the plan, was that the
use of the poison in such public places could cause
large casualties among the children who were visiting
them. Perhaps, he reluctantly thought, he was not the
ideal American terrorist Majid thought he was. He did
not want to harm the innocents of the world. Adults,
yes—they were already contaminated and would never
change. But children were still learning, might still
see the truth. Children should not be injured. It had
happened to him, and he didn't want to cause it to happen to others.

And then the real miracle happened—the invitation
to Mariam's promotion ceremony at the National Security Agency. It was a gift from Allah. What other
explanation could there be? NSA was the perfect place
to use his one-time allocation of poisonous anthrax,
and he could kill hundreds, perhaps thousands, of the
people who worked there, and none would be children.
In addition to causing the deaths, the airborne bacteria
would poison the buildings and put NSA out of business for months, if not years. It would destroy one of
the biggest enemies of the holy warriors fighting to restore a pristine world of ancient Islamic values.

It was so much better than any of the targets on the
al Qaeda list; he knew they would forgive him when
they saw the awesome results of his actions. It was the
perfect solution to both sets of goals.

And now he knew how to make it happen. At the
visit to NSA two days ago, he had discovered everything he needed to know: where to park, how to get in
the buildings, where to go to place the deadly packages for the most cataclysmic effect, and how to get
back out of the complex. There was no need to martyr
himself, which he had to admit he liked.

He would need his sister's badge to get back inside the Agency. He would have to kill her to get it, but he could do that: she had betrayed her people by working for NSA, and she was not his real sister, after all. His real sister had perished at the hands of Russian infidels.

Beside the badge, he needed only one more thing: the delivery of the anthrax spores. If they arrived soon, it would be the final sign that God wanted him to act now, to use the bacteria against NSA rather than wait for al Qaeda's orders. His destiny would be to strike the first blow, not the last.

Rashiq smiled as he rearranged the blanket gently over his small patient. As he walked back to his lab, scowling again at the nurse, he felt a rush of excitement at what he might be able to do. *When would he get the Anthrax spores?* "Soon," he whispered, swaying a little as he walked down the hallway, "let the poison come soon."

The phone was ringing when he opened the door to the lab. He picked it up and listened to the man who was speaking.

"Yes," Rashiq said, "I will meet you there. Tomorrow at two."

He hung up, put his head in his hands, and whispered a prayer of thanksgiving, because he knew the voice on the other end of the phone had been the voice of God.

13

Zafir awoke hours later. His thoughts were clear and fresh and he was hungry. As he sat up in bed, Babrack and Souria returned.

Souria unpacked a basket filled with flat bread she called *naan* and dishes of boiled rice and lamb. Soon the delicious smell of almonds, raisins, onions, and cinnamon spice filled the room.

"She's doing well," Souria said, speaking of her patient. "The bleeding has stopped and she's resting. Her sisters are there to take care of her. They sent us this food."

"She should be in a hospital." Babrack snarled. "There can't be another country in this world where half the population can't get any medical care just because of their sex." He looked at Zafir. "We are desperate. Why doesn't anyone help us?"

"I don't think there are many out there who know what's really going on here—how the Taliban doesn't just rule this country, but rules it so brutally. I didn't, until today," Zafir said quietly.

They sat at the small wooden table and ate greedily. The walls of the house were crumbling, laying bare the mud bricks beneath. In a corner of the kitchen area, a small grate propped on blocks was layered with wood chips, ready for cooking. Oil lamps hung from hooks; electricity was erratic at best in this tiny village.

Zafir looked at Souria. "How did you manage to go to medical school in Paris? There can't be many people here who could afford it."

"Our father was a rug merchant," she said. "A very successful one. He imported beautiful handmade carpets from Iran and Turkmenistan and sold them to wealthy people in Kabul and cities throughout Pakistan. Often foreigners." She lowered her eyes. "He was killed in the war with the Soviets, but by then he had already paid for my education. Babrack stayed in the business as long as he could. Now he sells simple prayer rugs that our local women make, mostly in Pakistan. We get by."

"Where do you get the medicines you need?" Zafir asked.

"My brother gets them for me when he goes across the border. I give him a list, and he gets what he can. They are very expensive, of course, but somehow Babrack always has enough money." She looked fondly at her brother. "I don't ask him how he does it, and he doesn't burden me with things I don't need to know."

How interesting, Zafir thought, *CIA's money is keeping this extraordinary doctor in business. How many people here owe their lives to this bizarre arrangement?*

He stretched, grunted at the pain in his arm, and looked over at Babrack. "You were up all night. You must be very tired."

"Yes, I have to sleep a while," Babrack said. "Then we will leave on our trip."

Souria glanced at him and stood to check Zafir's wound. The electricity was off again and the oil lamps provided only dim light. The darkened windows added to the gloom. Babrack held the flashlight for her to see.

Finally, Souria said, "Your trip must wait, at least three days. This man has lost more than a little blood, and he needs rest and plenty of liquids. If he stresses his wound too soon he could have internal bleeding. Anything you try to do now would be disastrous for him and probably for your 'endeavor.'"

Babrack growled. "Woman, you order me around as if you were a man. You think you are in charge of this house. Perhaps the mullahs are right."

Souria had finished washing Zafir's wound and was binding it up again. She smiled placidly at her brother's teasing. "Perhaps they are."

14

Jamal Rashiq made the drive from Dupont Circle to his sister's apartment complex in Laurel, Maryland, as carefully as he had ever done anything. He did not want to get stopped by the police, especially for something as stupid as speeding or getting involved in a fender bender. He didn't want any records of this trip.

Mariam didn't know he was coming. He hadn't called because he hadn't wanted her to tell anyone her brother was going to visit. He would have to take the chance she was alone, but it was almost ten o'clock on a Sunday night, and he thought it was a good bet. If someone was there, he would leave. If she was alone, he had no doubt that she would be so pleased to see him she would let him in without question. He would simply apologize for the late hour and tell her he needed someone to talk to.

He had made a dry run of the route the evening after he had visited the Agency. He had known immediately what he might have to do, and he wanted to be prepared. When he received the phone call yesterday and discovered he was actually going to get the opportunity to attack NSA he had prayed for, he congratulated himself on his foresight.

The man on the phone had identified himself only as Dr. Giroux. "I haven't seen you in some time," he said with a French accent. "Not since Paris. Can you meet me tomorrow at the zoo, in front of the Great Apes exhibit, at two o'clock?"

Rashiq was in place well ahead of time this afternoon. A clean-shaven, well-dressed Middle Eastern man approached him a few minutes after two and offered him a bag of popcorn as they strolled along. "There's a key in the bag," he said quietly, pointing off in the distance to a group of red-crested lowland gorillas as if the two of them were discussing a mutual interest in zoological habitat and primate interactions. "Locker number 153 at Union Station. There is a letter with instructions. Be careful. Put whatever you don't use back in the locker. I have another key."

Rashiq nodded and took the bag. The two men drifted apart.

The locker contained an airtight box, which Rashiq took with him to the safety of his CDC-funded laboratory. It was there that he would spend the time he needed to divide the powdery grams of anthrax into individual packets. Although he had already assembled the tiny explosive devices, he knew it would take a few days to complete the rest of the preparations. In the meantime, he had to get Mariam's badge. It was essential; he couldn't get back inside the NSA complex without it.

Now he was on his way to make that happen. Despite his earlier practice run, tonight's darkness and slashing rain made the drive a challenge, and he missed the turn into Fox Chase Apartments the first time he drove by. He turned around, drove into the complex, navigated slowly around the squat, gray buildings to the very back of the large compound, and parked well away from the nearest street light under an overhanging tree. He sat for a moment, made sure he had everything he needed, and murmured a short prayer. He reached behind him and turned off the overhead light and opened the car door. The rain had slackened a little, but he still got soaked as he made his way to his sister's apartment on the first floor of Building 8800.

He was about to walk up the two steps to the covered entranceway when he heard a muted noise. He turned and crouched behind the shrubs as a blurred figure opened Mariam's door, peered into the darkness, and bounded quickly down the steps and across the parking lot to a car. Jamal Rashiq got a quick glance at the figure through the bushes and the rain, but it was nobody he had ever seen before. He stayed hidden until the car drove off.

He left the cover of the dripping shrubs and ran to the apartment. He knocked lightly on the door. Nothing. He knocked a bit harder. Nothing. He tried the knob. Locked. He cursed and pulled open the small bag he was carrying. He removed a slim card and worked it between the lock and the frame. After three tries, the door opened and he was inside. He closed it carefully and looked around. Lights were burning in the small living room and in the kitchen, but the rooms were empty.

"Mariam," he called softly. "It's Jamal. Are you here? Are you all right?"

He heard a faint groan. He walked down the hallway to the bathroom and looked in. Mariam was naked in the bathtub, blood pouring from her wrists into the already rusty-red water. He went in and bent down close to her. She was unconscious and her breathing was ragged and shallow. He leaned close. "Mariam!" he said sharply. She did not respond and her breathing slowed even more. "Damn it, Mariam, what are you doing? How can you do this to me?" Jamal hissed. He watched, seething, as his adopted sister died.

When he stood, he saw the paper on the floor and read what was typed on it. It was a suicide note—one he knew Mariam hadn't written. "*I am a Muslim before all else,*" he read from the note, sarcasm dripping from his lips. What fool would ever believe Mariam would write such a thing? The rest of the note was incomprehensible. He left it curling on the floor.

This was no suicide.

Think! Jamal walked out of the bathroom and looked around. He needed Mariam's blue NSA badge. It's what he had come here for. His head ached and his thoughts were swirling. *This is much too bizarre. Who came here and killed my sister? And why? What if I had arrived five minutes earlier and run into her killer? I might have been murdered, too.*

What if the murderer took the badge? What if that's why Mariam is dead? He knew that was crazy, but he was starting to panic. Everything was going so well, and now this had happened.

Think!

He walked slowly through the bedroom, the closet, the kitchen, the tiny dining alcove, and the living room, opening drawers, checking shelves, and looking in corners. He did not see a blue badge anywhere. He returned to the bathroom and knelt by his sister's body. He put his gloved hands around her head and banged it against the back of the bathtub. "Damn it," he said again. "Where is your badge?"

He got up and repeated his survey of the rooms. *Where would she keep it?*

As soon as he saw the purse hanging on the back of a kitchen chair just out of sight, he knew. He opened it and pulled out the blue-edged NSA badge dangling from a chain. A cheery picture of his sister stared out from the middle of the frame. He tucked it in his pocket, put the purse back, looked around again to make sure he hadn't disturbed anything, and slipped out the door.

Jamal Rashiq turned the radio station to soft rock and sang along quietly as he drove back to D.C.

15

We were, as usual, gathered in the Operations
Directorate Conference Room for the seven-thirty
morning meeting. It was very quiet. There were no
greetings as the group filed in, no smiles, not even a
mention of last Friday's murder that everyone obviously knew about. A few eyes shifted my way, then
looked back at the table. I was willing to bet big money
that if I hadn't been in the room the ten other people
would all have been talking about Barry Ballard.
And me.

Could they really believe I was somehow involved,
somehow guilty? I watched them not watching me.
Maybe not, but they weren't going to associate with
me until the real murderer was found.

Just in case.

At seven-thirty-five, Kathryn Ward, a senior executive and chief of the Office of Media and Public
Affairs, entered the room and sat at the head of the
polished wooden conference table. Ms. Ward was
dressed in Agency power suit attire: navy blue knee-
length skirt, matching jacket, cream colored blouse,

and an accent scarf in blue and green. She pushed aside the stack of paper piled in front of her.

"The DO chief of staff will not be joining us today," she said. "I will be running the meeting. DIRNSA has tasked us with a new action." She looked at her audience and smiled coldly. Finally, she said, "I think Alex is the right person to handle this one; after all, she's the writer in the group. But you can all help."

I smiled. *The writer? She makes it sound like something bad.*

Ms. Ward drummed her fingers on the table top. "DIRNSA wants us to prepare a press release concerning Barry Ballard's death." Her eyes scanned everyone, watching carefully for reactions, as she continued speaking. "We have been inundated with calls from the media for statements, personal appearances by the Director on every major news program and," she rolled her eyes, "requests for interviews by every rinky-dink local TV station."

I wonder, I thought, *what 9News would have to say about that.*

"Fortunately," Kathryn raised her clasped hands into a prayerful gesture of thanks, "DIRNSA has decided to decline these requests, at least for the present. But," she lowered her hands, "he does want a strong statement we can release today."

Her announcement was met by silence. Finally, Bill Jarvi, chief of the Office of Russia, asked, "What are we allowed to say? Surely we don't want to give any . . . details or speculate on who might have killed Barry?" He sat up straighter in his seat. "In fact, Kathryn, do we even want to say he was murdered? I mean, for certain? It's such terrible publicity for NSA." For all the power his position gave him, Dr. Jarvi was clearly troubled by the enormity of what we were about to do: admit a monstrous act had occurred at the National Security Agency.

Kathryn Ward rubbed her forehead and looked at us somberly. "I'm afraid we can't avoid it," she said, clearly wishing we could. "All of you," she said, "know very well he was murdered, and you've heard about most of the horror that went with it. We will have to admit he was killed, but we won't mention any of the details."

She paused and then continued carefully. "As you know, the CONFIRM system was not functioning Friday evening after about six o'clock. We know that there were still well over six hundred people in the complex at that time. I'm guessing that quite a few of those people were employees of some other agency. We don't know how many people were still here when Barry was murdered, or who might have come in after six o'clock, or which agency any of them worked for. We know only that they all had security clearances and badges that allowed them free access to the NSA buildings."

She stopped and looked at me. "When you found the body and saw the 'shadowy' figure in the hall, was there anything that convinced you it was an NSA employee? Did you see a badge? Was it a different color than blue, do you think? Could the murderer have been from an agency other than this one? Or even," she hesitated briefly, "a contractor?"

Damn, I thought. *A contractor! How ingenious of her. Wouldn't that solve everything?* Many NSAers dislike contractors and treat them poorly. Very poorly. They hate the fact that green-badged contractors often make more money than govies for the specialized, technical work they do. Contract employees are the second-class citizens of the Agency.

So much for the well-publicized NSA vision statement, "One Team, One Mission."

It's the "ruling class" syndrome and I hate it. Long ago we were taught not to discriminate against coworkers on the basis of sex, skin color, or religion. I say, "NSA wake up:

> color of skin
> color of badges
> what's the difference?"

Contractor or not, Kathryn wanted to insinuate that Barry Ballard's murderer might have been someone other than a member of the NSA workforce. She saw her primary job as protecting the Agency from the outside world, wrapping it and all its affairs in a mysterious cloak of secrecy as cryptic as the mission itself. Most people at NSA felt much the same way. It's a kind of brainwashing, with all the ubiquitous security posters and daily e-mail messages warning everyone to stay deaf, dumb, and blind to those outside the walls who might ask about the business of signals intelligence. This traditional and parochial approach disturbed me. Surely it was time to be more positive about NSA's accomplishments, more honest about its failures.

On the other hand, I, too, hated to think the murderer was an employee of the National Security Agency. *One of us.*

"Kathryn," I answered, "I could not tell even if it was a man or a woman I saw that night. I didn't see a badge or any other signs of Agency affiliation. It was too dark, too fast, too . . ."

"Frightening?" Kathryn finished my sentence flippantly.

I ignored her. *So far,* I thought, *you are living up to your reputation as a total bitch.*

The debate broke out in earnest then, most arguing

for emphasizing the large number of non-NSAers in the building who might have killed Barry. Kathryn nodded encouragement as they spoke and occasionally reminded them that they must stay somewhere within the bounds of reality. Finally I pulled out a notepad and began writing:

> *From the Office of the Director, National Security Agency, Lieutenant General John P. Murray:*
>
> *The National Security Agency and I mourn the death of Barry L. Ballard, assistant director for support services and one of my closest advisors. We send our sincerest condolences to his family and friends. Mr. Ballard was a remarkable example of integrity and dedication to all of us who worked with him, and his death leaves a terrible loss that we must struggle to overcome.*
>
> *An autopsy has revealed that Mr. Ballard died of knife wounds sometime last Friday evening. The FBI, with the full support of Agency Security, has begun an investigation of this vicious and incomprehensible crime. Several hundred people, some of whom may have been affiliated with agencies other than NSA, were in the Agency complex during the estimated time of the murder. No suspect or motive has been identified at this point, but I personally promise that everyone associated with the National Security Agency will provide whatever assistance we can in solving this horrible and cowardly crime.*

I shoved the paper to Kathryn Ward and stood. "There's my offering. You can make any changes you want. I've got work to do." I turned and left the suddenly quiet room.

I took an elevator down to the first floor and was struck as always as I passed the huge panorama on the long entrance wall just past the glass double doors leading to Gatehouse One. Painted in the late 1960s or early 1970s, the mural was about thirty feet long by nine feet high and was done primarily in colors of green, yellow, red, and purple, echoing the hallways of the time. Unique to NSA, visitors could never walk by this unusual panorama without gaping.

The wall itself was made up of tiny one-inch square ceramic tiles, giving a slightly checkered effect to the overall presentation. A blue air force jet streaked through the upper right-hand corner, flying over three different types of bright green radar antennae. Several employees, one of whom had a purple afro, leaned over a desk, conferring, no doubt, on matters of cryptologic urgency. On the left, a large green object with bright orange circles across its top represented either a 1960s-era computer or a very big washing machine.

The mural did not in any way present the typical conventional display of authority—

pictures of presidents
portraits of generals
scenes of the Capitol building
crinkly parchment replicas of the Declaration of Independence

—so common to other government buildings; it was too colorful, too cheerful, too optimistic. I worried fleetingly, as I always did when I passed this way, that someday soon a decision would be made to paint over this buoyant and winsome scene.

I stopped at the Customer Support Center to pick up a few office supplies. As I entered, the room full of people stopped talking and stared at me. When I looked back they turned away. *My God, these people think I'm a suspect, too.* I was shocked. Just four days ago, everyone was in a hurry to congratulate me. Now, the deepening silence made me feel like a pariah.

It sure is a quick trip from lord to leper in this place.

I left the room and headed up the escalator to the second floor. As I neared my own office, I saw, at the end of the hall, the outline of a large man coming toward me with long, quick strides.

"Jacks, what's wrong?"

He bent down, out of breath. He had a troubled look on his face. "Have you seen Mariam?" he asked. "I was hoping she might be with you. I know she wanted to talk to you about Lester—the way he treats her."

"No, I haven't seen her, Jacks. Why? Where is she supposed to be?"

"I worked mids last night," he said, the words spilling out in a rush. "When I do that, Mariam always comes in early, so she can see me before I leave at six-thirty. She wasn't there today."

I looked at my watch. "It's only a little after eight. Maybe she's just running late."

"No, you don't understand. She doesn't do that. She's always there by six-thirty. I called her house and her cell. There's no answer."

It finally occurred to me that Jacks and Mariam might have more going on between them than just two linguists working together at NSA. I hadn't missed the affectionate look she had given him at the Meridian meeting Friday morning, but the treasonous betrayal of the comms and Barry's murder had distracted me. To say the least.

"How about Security? Did you call them and report

her missing?" Disturbing thoughts jarred and unsettled me. *No wonder,* I thought. *Look at the atmosphere around here. Everyone's paranoid.*

"Yes, but you know they won't do anything until two hours after her shift started at seven-thirty. Two hours! Anything can happen in two hours."

The two-hour rule was instituted when two NSA code clerks, Martin and Mitchell, defected to the Soviet Union in 1961. The men were gone for days before anyone knew they were AWOL. Since then, whenever an employee unexpectedly fails to show up for duty later than two hours after their shift starts, Security springs into action. Of course, a defector could always just sign up for several weeks of annual leave, or call in sick from the Aeroflot gate at JFK, but the NSA security weenies feel much better with the two-hour rule in place.

Jacks turned, and began walking away. "Mariam was fine last night when I talked to her at nine o'clock. Now I'm afraid something is wrong. I'm going over to her place to see what's going on."

I caught his shoulder. "Wait. I'll get my coat and go with you." My adrenaline was rising fast.

16

Three men sat silently on the floor in the empty warehouse, watching a tireless figure pace across the room, white robes swirling as he strode back and forth, back and forth. The man was well over six feet tall, and he covered the ground in long, measured steps. His eyes, usually soft and deceptively messianic, were narrowed and angry.

A fifth man, Bashir, slumped in a corner. He had been beaten methodically with chains and boards and starved for days. His clothing was ripped and blood-stained, and his eyes were swollen shut. He could barely tell what was happening around him, and he didn't much care.

The building was once a thriving processing center for dried fruit, mostly raisins, that years before had been one of Afghanistan's key exports. A quarter of a century of war devastated the industry, and the warehouse was now a cavernous place with rows of wooden washing tables collapsing against each other as they rotted away.

In the middle of the room, a space had been cleared for storing weapons and ammunition during the war with the Russians; now it was empty except for a few stacks of baskets that once held the cleaned and sorted raisins.

The robed man stopped pacing and sat on the room's only chair. An oil lamp flickered nearby, catching the rage in his dark eyes. The Americans had outwitted him; an unbelievable feat, and he had been betrayed by Ajmal, one of his own; an unforgivable act.

The tall man was the Arab al Qaeda leader Usama bin Laden, sometimes called *Sher*, "The Lion," by his Afghan followers. He had learned six days earlier that his satellite phone system had been compromised again and the infidels were listening in on *al-Buraq*, the plan he was making to destroy them. He had led his *jihadists* to victories in the past, but *al-Buraq* would be the biggest. It would be a holy attack that would awaken the Muslim world from its deep sleep, a victory that would convince his followers that they had as much power as the decadent warmongers in the West. It would change everything.

He couldn't let Ajmal's treasonous act stop him.

A boy of about eleven brought him tea and sugared almonds, and he ate quietly, his eyes focused on a far-away place. He took a last drink of tea and wiped his lips on a towel.

"He hasn't told you *anything*?" he demanded of the three terrified men. "I thought you could do this by yourselves. I never guessed I would have to come here myself." He glared at them. "You have had that man," he pointed accusingly at Bashir curled up in the corner, "since we caught him coming back from Pakistan. We searched his house and found medical supplies and bags of money. Ajmal spoke the truth—Bashir was his contact. The maggot knows it all, and he must tell us.

And what have you found out from him? Nothing! Have you?"

They shook their heads. "He has said nothing, *Sher*, although we beat him until we were afraid he would die."

One of the men gathered his courage and spoke. "One of my neighbors tells me things he has heard. In return for small favors." He looked at the robed man nervously.

"What has he told you?" bin Laden demanded. "Something about Bashir?"

"Yes . . . he told me Bashir has a special relationship with a doctor in Tsalgari. A woman doctor named Souria who lives with her brother. She and Bashir are, he said, very 'good friends.' He heard it from his wife whose cousin . . ."

The tall man held up his hand. "That's good enough. Go get her." He thought a minute. "It will take you until sometime tomorrow to get to Tsalgari. Wait until night to take her, and do it quietly. Kill her brother if you must, and bring his body back with you. It will look like they ran away and disappeared like so many others."

He stroked his beard and smirked. "Bring her here and we will see if her lover talks when we beat her instead of him."

In the corner, Bashir forced his eyes shut tighter, biting his tongue and wondering what to do before the men came back with Souria. He could never stand it if they hurt her. He was afraid he would tell them whatever they wanted to know.

The man they called *Sher* stood and walked out the door to the vehicle that his bodyguards had waiting. His dark eyes flared. Ajmal's betrayal posed serious challenges to his plan. He would cope with them; although he was often aggressive and audacious, he was never reckless. But it made him very angry. And paranoid. His al Qaeda cells had already switched to microwave communications, and he was terrified that the Americans would find a way to intercept them, too.

Bashir's refusal to talk infuriated the Arab. He was sure it meant something was going on, something he badly needed to know about.

At least, bin Laden thought, *we still have the American girl. Kidnapping her has proven to be more valuable than we could ever have hoped. It's good that we forced her to make another tape recording last week. When the courier gets back from Quetta, we'll know if this recording worked as well as the last one.*

He looked at his watch. His messenger should be returning at any time. Too bad the man had to drive all the way to Pakistan to make an international phone call, but the call they needed to make was impossible from Afghanistan now that they couldn't use satellite phones.

Bin Laden frowned and entered the vehicle in a flourish of white robes.

17

Fox Chase Apartments, Laurel, Maryland
Monday, December 4, 2000
Morning

Ten minutes later we were in my car heading to-ward Laurel. I was driving too fast on the rain-slicked road, dodging pools of standing water near the berm, my hands sweaty on the wheel. Jacks sat beside me, his large body crammed into the passenger seat of the red Integra.

The drive down Maryland Rt. 198 was as dreary as always. Trash lined the road, and out-of-business gas stations and restaurants competed with a junkyard, several auto dealers, four or five motels, and old shopping centers. The infamous 602 Club ("The Deuce"), frequented by NSAers in the 1960s and 1970s, had become a Korean liquor store and hangout called Utopia. A supermarket sat darkened, empty, and abandoned. A liquor store near the Laurel Race Track called the Starting Gate was busy as usual, its parking lot filled even at eight-thirty in the morning.

"Jacks, please tell me what's going on," I said softly. "Why do you think there's something wrong?"

He clenched his fists. "We . . . Mariam and me . . . we've been together for six months now." He looked over at me. "As a couple, you know?" I nodded. "It's never happened to me before; this kind of thing. I didn't think it ever would." A tendril of fear crept into his voice. "I love her. And she loves me." He looked at me again. "I'm worried. She would never have not showed up this morning. Not called."

He took a deep breath and changed his position in the seat so he could sit up straighter. "Maybe I'm only upset because of what's happened at the Agency. The murder. It's made all of us half crazy," he said, echoing my own thoughts of paranoia.

"Well, that's the truth," I agreed. "And no wonder." I reached out my hand and touched his arm. "Maybe Mariam forgot her cell phone, or she overslept and was in the shower when you called." *That has to be it,* I thought. *It can't be anything else.*

He glanced at me. "Sure," he said. "Something like that. You're probably right."

I turned left at the intersection with Rt. 197, where the area's only "high rise" apartment building, Steward Towers, loomed with all the power of its eleven stories, paint peeling on its sides. A quarter of a mile later, I turned right. A sign at the entrance stated, "Fox Chase Apartments, a Beautiful Place to Live." On the right, a brightly lighted 7-11 seemed starkly out of place. Several teenagers, unaffected by the raw, biting cold and rain, leaned on cars outside the convenience store, laughing and gesturing excitedly.

Jacks pointed the way through the maze of buildings. Mariam's building, 8800, was in the back, set off obliquely from the others, and across the street a thick field of trees dripped rain from their bare branches.

I parked and we ran through the rain to the door. Jacks pushed a key in the lock and swung the door open, shouting for Mariam as he raced inside. No answer. I followed slowly, dreading what we might find and how this big, gentle man would survive it.

It didn't take long to find out.

I was still in the living room when I heard Jack's anguished cry. I ran down the hall and found him standing in the middle of the bathroom, holding his head in his hands and moaning. I walked in beside him and looked down. Mariam lay in the bath, her dark hair floating in a tub full of bloody water. Her face was drained of all color, her lips were blue. She looked as if she had been dead for some time. Beside the bathtub, on the floor, was a wicked-looking bone-handled knife.

Instinctively, I put an arm around Jacks's shoulders and pulled him to me. He moaned again and dropped his head. Still speechless, he pointed to a corner of the bathroom. I followed his gaze. A piece of paper, computer-sized, lay on the floor, rolled up from the dampness. I picked it up by two corners and unfolded it.

"Jesus, Jacks, it's a suicide note."

"No." He shook his head.

"Come on, come out of here now."

The big man shuddered and looked back at the body. He leaned toward the tub, hand outstretched.

"No, Jacks, don't touch anything, okay? It will just make it harder to sort it all out."

He nodded slowly and we left the bathroom and sat on the couch in the living room. Still holding the paper by two corners, I read the words out loud.

Please forgive me for what I have done. I told them about the Meridian comms. I am a Muslim before all else, and I thought it was my duty. Then Mr. Ballard found out and I had to kill him. It was wrong. I know that now. I can't go on living with this any longer.

Jacks exploded, a fireball of furious denial. "No! That's a lie. Mariam would never have betrayed us. She was so proud, so happy to be working on something that might save this country—her country—from whatever those terrorists are planning to do. And she might have been born a Muslim, but she isn't one now and she hasn't been for years. She has problems with that way of life for a lot of reasons. That note is a damn lie!"

He slammed his hand against the couch's armrest. "And kill Barry Ballard? Never! She would never kill anyone. Not for any reason. Besides, the man was blind. How could he have 'found out' anything so fast without help? And I was with Mariam yesterday, and she was fine. She wasn't upset at all. For God's sake, Alex, what is happening here? What?"

"I don't know, Jacks," I said quietly, "but we'd better call the police."

While we waited for them to arrive, I wandered through the small apartment, looking but not touching anything. It was a standard boxy place, but Mariam had hung pale blue curtains at the windows and on her bed was a matching blue quilt garnished with a trellis of flowers and leaves. Over the dresser was a framed certificate stating that Mariam Rashiq had been granted the title of "Senior" in the Language Analysis Technical Track Program. The official seal of the National Security Agency glittered in the corner of the certificate, an eagle standing proudly against a blue background. On top of the dresser was a variety of pictures, mostly of her family. I recognized her mother and father from the promotion ceremony. There was only one picture of her brother, taken some time ago, when he was much younger. One large framed picture stood in the middle, a formal photograph of Mariam and

Jacks smiling at each other against a background of green trees and a cloudless blue sky. He was wearing his dress uniform, she a long skirt and white blouse that set off her black hair and eyes perfectly.

I had just reached the neat, tiny kitchen when two Prince George's County policemen burst in, followed quickly by a contingent of detectives and NSA Security officers. I went back to the living room and sat beside Jacks while he answered questions. It was obvious they didn't know yet which way to lean: believe the note and declare Mariam's death a suicide or treat the large black man as the prime suspect in a murder. Two detectives continued the questioning, while several officers took pictures of the bathroom and made notes. Finally the medical examiner arrived and took out the body.

After several hours of questioning, the front door opened again and Mike Faure entered the apartment. He stopped, stunned, when he saw me. "What in the bloody hell are you doing here, Alex? How did you manage to show up at another NSA death?"

Without waiting for an answer, he turned to Jacks. "I know who you are. You're one of the linguists in the Meridian project, right? That's why Security finally got around to calling me in on this—they discovered the dead woman was one of the Meridian linguists." He sat down in a chair facing them. "The woman who killed herself," he looked at a notepad, "Mariam Rashiq, she was the other linguist, wasn't she?"

Jacks nodded. "Yes, but she didn't kill herself. That note is a setup. Mariam was murdered . . ."

Mike cut him off. "Maybe, but not likely. The medical examiner told me he's already looked at the knife she used to cut her wrists, the size and type and serrations, and he thinks it could be the same knife

used to kill Barry Ballard. Apparently there was something unusual about it."

"That doesn't prove anything," Jacks said. "Maybe
the same person killed them both and used the same
knife."

"Who would that be, Sergeant? And why? The police will consider murder, I'm sure, but suicide makes
a lot more sense. And besides, there's one more thing."

"What," Jacks demanded. "What else?"

"There were bloodstains on some shoes in Mariam's closet. We already know it's the same type as
Barry's—the lab can do that test in minutes. When the
DNA results come back in a day or so, I'll bet you they
confirm the match."

18

By Tuesday, Zafir was not just rested but restless.
It was time to move. His wound was still slightly swollen and inflamed but otherwise was healing nicely.
Souria, the surgeon, pronounced him fit to travel.

"I'll pack some of this *pillau* and *naan* for you to
take," she said to Babrack. She didn't ask where they
were going.

Well after the sun set, when they knew the village
streets would be still and deserted, the two men left,
each on a horse carrying equipment and weapons and
bags of water and food. They slipped silently to the
back of the village and stayed in the dark shadows of
the courtyards. Finally the houses vanished from sight,
and they urged their horses into a faster pace. They
had miles to go and a long night ahead.

They did not follow roads, even the dirt ones that
barely qualified as goat trails. They crossed frozen
brown fields, mud holes in the spring and dried up
dusty earth in the rainless summertime. Again the
fiery stars danced in the sky in an Old Testament scene
of fierce innocence. Zafir was spellbound, not at all

surprised by his thought that God Himself might appear at any time.

As they rode, Babrack talked about his country and its years of war. "See there," he pointed through the darkness to the barren miles of dirt surrounding them, "those fields were once full of grapes. And there were pomegranates and apricots and apple trees and corn and grain. We had an irrigation system so good that water was plentiful. But the Soviet soldiers filled in the ditches so the *mujaheddin* couldn't hide in them. Then they cut down the trees so the resistance fighters couldn't hide behind them. And then the drought came. Now there is nothing."

He sighed. "The cities are rubble, filled with legless beggars and starving children. Our women are locked away, the Talibs have forbidden any kind of happiness, even laughter. They will beat you or throw you in jail for laughing in public."

"How did they ever get control?" Zafir asked. "I would think everyone would fight them to the death."

Babrack laughed. "You are beginning to sound like a real Afghan. Fights, feuds, revenge; that's been our way of life forever." He paused, gathering his thoughts. "After the Soviets left, we thought there might be some hope of peace. But there was not. In some ways it was even worse. Tribal warfare was so brutal that rockets fell on the cities every day. Kabul is a ruin and Kandahar is not far behind. Rival commanders and their men pillaged whole villages and raped the women. The lawlessness was so terrible that for a while we thought the Taliban would save us. We welcomed them at first."

Zafir shook his head. "My God."

"Yes, in retrospect you are correct. We all know it now. But then things were so bad we were desperate for help. We had no idea of the evil that would follow.

Now there are pockets of resistance everywhere, but the Taliban has a stranglehold on most of the country."

After a few hours they reached their destination: a huge steel microwave relay tower springing incongruously from the monotonous brown landscape.

The two men unpacked the equipment Zafir would need. It was very quiet and very dark. Even the horses were still, their breathing hushed.

Okay, here we go, Zafir thought as he gathered his tools. With Babrack's help, he erected a small, fiberglass parabolic antenna from the kit in his pack. They were both pleased to finally be doing their job.

"Just like playing with Legos, right Babrack?"

Babrack snickered. "Sure. Whatever you say. Someday you must tell me what they are."

Zafir had assembled the parts—feed horn, preamp, modulator, GPS tracking system, and all the others— so many times he could do it blindfolded. In fact, he had. He looked up at the tower, one hundred sixty feet high, and grinned. *Now the fun starts.*

Zafir fitted a miner's lamp on his head, its beam bright and fixed, put his arms through his backpack, and started climbing.

The huge tower, fixed to a concrete pad and steadied by heavy guy wires, swayed gently as Zafir ascended the metal rungs of the maintenance ladder. He could not turn off the power or switch to a backup source while he worked; an interruption in transmission could be noticed if anyone was monitoring the system. He would be working "hot," definitely not recommended. He would have to be careful to protect his eyes by not looking directly at parts of the microwave transmitting system, especially waveguides and feed horns. He didn't see any stationary monitors that would alert him to high radiation levels, but they could be inside an equipment room somewhere away from the tower. He would have to cross his fingers on this one.

He maneuvered carefully around the antenna arrays mounted near the top of the tower. A microwave system requires precise aiming of the antennas at each end of the link. If one antenna moves out of position slightly, even just a few degrees of arc, it can cause problems with synchronization of signals and require maintenance, a circumstance most unwelcome for Zafir's purposes. He stood on the small platform at the very top, clipped his safety belt to the metal structure, and unfolded the dish antenna he had assembled on the ground. Methodically he attached it to the tower and began the slow and dangerous process of tapping into the power source—a wire strung from the electric poles running along the nearby potholed road. His legs began to ache. His injured arm had been throbbing since he started the climb. He would be glad when he was finished.

Far below, Babrack suddenly whistled, one quick shrill signal for "trouble." Zafir heard him ride off. He put out his headlamp as the sound of the horses faded away.

19

A blustery, raw wind whipped through the ceme-
tery, spinning up funnels of icy snowflakes, and the gray
sky was puffy with shroud-shaped clouds. The tented
structure positioned over Barry Ballard's gravesite
snapped sharply with each strong gust.

All but one of the Project Meridian members attending the funeral huddled together near the grave,
despite the contentious meeting we had had just that
morning. We had gathered in the Director's suite at
ten o'clock at his request. Judy Lincoln was included
in the group, as she still had the VRK clearance and
was not allowed to return to England until Barry's
murder investigation was officially closed.

We had been seated around the long mahogany
conference table for about ten minutes before General
Murray entered the room, three silver stars shining on
each squared shoulder. We stood up quickly, and he
motioned to us to sit back down. He scanned each of
our faces quietly for a moment, and said, "I have some
good news for all of you. You will be pleased to learn
that steps have been taken to establish a substitute for
the lost Meridian comms, and I am optimistic that

will happen. Sorry, but I can't give you any more details at this time."

Gabe is safe. Thank God! was my first thought.
He's safe so far, was my second. I tried to picture him
in the strange country so far away, climbing microwave towers and hiding from al Qaeda.

DIRNSA's eyes focused on Jacks. "Sergeant Jackson, if the project is restarted, much of the responsibility for its success will be up to you. You are now
the only remaining Pashtu linguist the National Security Agency has, and it will not be easy to find others
quickly." He sighed. "We should have hired a variety
of linguists over the past few years, but our priorities
have not always been as clearly thought-out as they
should have been. And, of course, our budget has been
cut to shreds by Congress."

*Well, this Director is certainly the honest face-the-
facts guy everyone said he was,* I thought. *Maybe NSA
will get back on track after all.* I couldn't imagine a
previous Director who would speak so candidly to his
subordinates.

Jacks nodded, his large body a commanding presence in the room despite the hollow look in his eyes.
"Yes, Sir," he said. "I'll work twenty-four hours a day
if I need to."

"Thank you, Sergeant."

DIRNSA searched our faces again. "I'm sure you
have heard about Mariam Rashiq's death on Monday.
I have the most recent information to give you on the
status of the case. I prefer that you not discuss it beyond this room."

We all murmured our agreement.

"The autopsy showed that death occurred from the
wounds on her wrists. There was a blow to the back of
the head, but the coroner thinks it could have been

caused by Ms. Rashiq herself when she passed out and hit her head on the bathtub. Also," he paused and looked at some notes in his hand, "DNA results prove conclusively that the knife had Barry Ballard's blood on it as well as Mariam's and was certainly the same one that killed them both. DNA also proved that blood found on the shoes in her closet was Barry's." He put the notes on the table and said, "The medical examiner has declared this case a suicide, and the FBI is going to release a statement tomorrow that they believe Ms. Rashiq was responsible for Barry Ballard's death. I know . . ."

"They're wrong!" Jacks knuckles were white where they clutched the edge of the table. His eyes blazed. "She didn't do it. She didn't kill Barry. She was framed. Mariam was murdered."

The room filled with a stunned silence. Captain Kip McColloh, the OCMC chief, stared at Jacks, mouth open. Judy Lincoln put her head in her hands. Enlisted men did not argue with officers. Never. And especially not with three-star generals. It was career suicide. Generals do not like to be questioned.

But this general was different. He simply shook his head and held up a hand. "I was about to say, Sergeant, that I knew you would disagree with this assessment and that I personally am sorry for the situation you find yourself in, but . . ."

"Jacks is right, Sir," I interrupted DIRNSA again. The roomful of people rocked in their chairs, open-mouthed and eyes wide. "Mariam didn't kill anyone, including herself. I believe that and I think we can prove it."

"How the hell can you do that?" the DDO, Paul Eckerd, asked impatiently.

"She can't," sneered Lester Krebbs. "She's just being a drama queen."

DIRNSA glared. "Quiet," he said.

We were.

He looked at me. "What are you talking about?"

"We have to find the tape, Sir. I believe it will have all the answers on it."

"What tape is that, Ms. O'Malley? I don't remember hearing about a tape."

"The cassette tape that was missing from the recorder Barry had with him when he was killed. Everyone's forgotten about it now that we have such a convenient suspect, but it exists, it's out there somewhere, and if nobody else is going to look for it, I am. And I will find it." I hoped I was as confident as I sounded.

All eyes clicked back and forth throughout the exchange; now they focused on the table, waiting for DIRNSA to explode. To tell me to leave the room. He didn't.

He rubbed his chin, deep in thought. "Yes, I do remember talk about a missing tape now. The FBI searched for it, though, and didn't find it, and I'm sure they won't be in a hurry to search again. But," he said slowly, "I will ask them about it." He looked at me and Jacks. "I'll let you know what they say."

He stood up. "In the meantime, we must go to the funeral this afternoon and then get back to work."

The meeting was over. Each person filed silently out of the office. We were all attending Barry's funeral, and when we arrived at the cemetery, we banded together automatically despite the acrimony of the morning. The urgency of our mission was a tighter bond than most of us had ever known. Only Judy Lincoln was missing from the group.

The hearse carrying Barry's body drove up and the pallbearers slid the coffin from the vehicle, carried it

slowly to the grave site, and placed it on the shiny
brass bier. A priest in swirling dark vestments stood
solemnly to one side, bracketed by altar boys in white
tunics topped by warm winter jackets. One held a
Bible, the other a scepter and container of holy water.

Karen Ballard stepped out of the long, black limou-
sine leading the cortege and held her children's hands
as they walked up the slope to say their last good-byes
to their adoring father. Behind them, the funeral director helped an elderly woman into a wheelchair and
positioned her near the casket.

I bet that's Barry's mother. I had heard somewhere
she was still alive and living in the area. Others joined
them, standing quietly in small groups. General Murray and his wife, a striking woman wearing a black
coat and matching Coach hat with a cream band, had
placed themselves slightly away from the group and
looked inclined to stay there.

Every important person in the Agency, both military and civilian, appeared to be present. Most had
their spouses with them. They clustered together, trying to stay warm, waiting for the final rites.

I watched the mourners as the priest began his last
readings. Over a hundred people stood on the windy
hillside. Most were as close to expressionless as it was
possible to be, but some were visibly shaken. Like
Paul Eckerd: tears began running down his face and
dripping off his chin. From time to time, he wiped the
tears away with the back of his wrist and looked away,
embarrassed by his display of grief.

I had heard that Paul and Barry had been friends for
a long time, since college, and that for the past several
years they had shared an office suite on the ninth floor
of the Headquarters Building. I had often seen them

walking together down the hall, laughing and talking, or eating together in one of the cafeterias. I wondered briefly why Paul's wife, an NSA employee herself, wasn't with him at the funeral of his friend.

Off to the side, close to a stand of pines, was the solitary figure of a woman. Her head was bowed and she hugged herself against the cold wind. It was Judy Lincoln, alone with the terrible emotions that must have driven her to attend this ceremony for her ex-husband.

The priest took the scepter from the altar boy and dipped it into the vessel of holy water. He held the scepter high and blessed the casket, shaking holy water over it as he spoke. The wind blew the water over the huddled mourners, and several crossed themselves quickly when it struck them.

Katie Ballard, four years old, left her mother's side and walked slowly to her father's casket. She reached out and touched the smooth, rich wood, leaned over and kissed a corner of the coffin, walked back and took her mother's hand. Her brother, two years older, watched quietly without moving.

The woman at the edge of the trees turned suddenly and walked down the hill to her car. She got in without a backward look and drove away.

When the funeral services ended, I left the Meridian group and walked over to where my mother and Daniel were standing. They had indeed returned from Italy to pay their last respects to Barry, and I was glad to have them home. As we stood on the hillside and talked in low voices, Karen Ballard slipped away from her family and joined us.

"Alex," she said quietly, "I am so sorry you had to go through what you did. But thank you so much for saving Maggie. The children and I are very grateful to have Barry's dog back home." She held up her hands. "She's all we have left and she's very important to us."

I had made it all the way through the funeral cere-mony without crying, but this pushed me over the edge. I hugged Karen and, choking on my tears, walked away quickly.

20

Brookview Medical Center
Tuesday, December 5, 2000
Afternoon

Dr. Rashiq opened the door to the clinic's small waiting room and greeted the man and woman seated there. They both stood and shook his hand and silently waited for the doctor to speak.

"Matthew is going to get well," he told them. "I wasn't sure of that for some time, but now I am confident he will recover completely. He's responding to the treatments and this morning I ordered the feeding tube removed. He sat up in bed and ate Jell-O with whipped cream and asked for more."

Matthew's mother collapsed in the chair. She covered her face with her hands and sobbed. His father reached out and touched the doctor's shoulder. "We can never thank you enough," he said.

"It's going to be a while before he can leave," Jamal Rashiq said. "He's very weak and needs to get back on his feet slowly. He still needs a lot more care." He looked out the window, surprised and embarrassed by the sudden swell of tears in his eyes. "The boy very nearly died," he said in a low voice. "I must tell you an act of God has happened here."

"You are God's act," the woman said, wiping her face.

Rashiq smiled at her and went back to work. He was tired. He had spent most of the last two days gowned and masked in the center's special laboratory. His precautions with the *Bacillus anthracis* spores were so meticulous he might have been back at the CDC complex in Atlanta. Over and over, he whispered thanks to the U.S. government for teaching him the techniques he needed for this work.

When he wasn't in the lab, he spent his time either monitoring Matthew at the clinic or reviewing his notes and going over his plans. He had had to take time out to speak to the police about Mariam's death, but they had not seemed suspicious that he was involved. He told them he thought she had been under a great deal of stress at work and that perhaps that had been the reason for her suicide. He had talked with his adoptive parents, too, consoling them about Mariam's death and planning a memorial service for her back in San Diego. They had stayed in D.C. for a few days after the promotion ceremony at NSA to visit tourist sites, and they had still been in town when Mariam's body was discovered.

But most of the time he was in his lab. He was working quickly now, afraid the Agency might take Mariam's badge ID out of the CONFIRM system before he tried to use it. He could only pray it hadn't already happened. Dr. Rashiq didn't know he had plenty of time to act, that clearing CONFIRM of retired, resigned, or dead employees occurs only on the last working day of each month. He wanted to have everything ready to take into the NSA complex the next night after midnight when Gatehouse 2 opened for the early shift workers.

The lab was cool and quiet and he was focused completely on his methodical preparations. Thoughts of what he had done to prepare himself personally and what he was soon going to do to fulfill his destiny made him shiver with anticipation. Every day he felt himself changing, becoming a newly born man of action. His body was thrilled, roused. Not in a sexual way, really, but with the fervent passion of the righteous.

21

Molly and Daniel walked with me down the hill of graves to my car.

We parted ways at the small parking area. They drove off toward Riverside Drive in their pale gold Lexus, and I turned my comparatively utilitarian red Integra toward downtown Annapolis and my town house to get more clothes. It was nearly four o'clock and the light, already low, was beginning to fade quickly. It seemed to me that we hadn't seen the sun, even a thin winter sun, for weeks.

I found a parking space two blocks from my house and walked briskly up the sidewalk, clasping my coat tightly around my throat to keep out the chill. The cold wind blasted down the street and swirled dirt and debris around my feet as I walked.

It was good to be home, back in my own space. I switched on every light on the first floor, and soon the rooms glowed. Upstairs, I packed a bag with shoes, clothes, and a few pieces of jewelry, wishing I could just stay. As I packed, I thought about what the events of the past few days had done, not just to me, but to all of NSA.

Barry's murder and the shock of Mariam's death had

pretty much destroyed what little was left of morale after the financial cuts over the past ten years had brought the Agency to its knees. Work was, for the moment, secondary to concerns for personal safety and outright paranoia and had been since Friday night. The FBI had not yet announced its decision that Mariam had killed Barry and then herself, and until they did, neatly resolving the catastrophic series of events, almost no one at the Agency was fighting the SIGINT wars.

This afternoon, before the funeral, I saw that DIRNSA had already announced a series of new security measures and instructions to the workforce:

1. Additional Federal Protective Service guards will be hired and will be posted throughout the complex.
2. Special Forces from the Fort Meade Command Group will augment FPS forces indefinitely.
3. FBI investigators may question some of you; please cooperate fully.
4. Security has set up a "hotline" for those of you who may have any information, questions, or reflections on this crisis. Please call x7474 (secure) with your concerns.
5. A more rigorous entry process will be put in place, including metal detectors and random hand searches of belongings.
6. All walkways through the security fence surrounding the parking lots will be closed.
7. Cameras will be mounted throughout the hallways of the OPS 1, 2A, 2B, and Headquarters buildings.

All of these precautions were scheduled to be completed in the next two weeks, apparently with the money that often magically appears during a government crisis.

None of it made anyone feel any better.

NSA was no longer a safe haven. Despite the presence of extra guards, people walked the halls with wide, suspicious eyes and neatly skirted areas of the buildings not clearly lit or easily observed by others. Stairwells were unpopular. No one, it seemed, wanted to get in an elevator with just one other person. The secluded Meditation Room tucked in a corner behind the Friedman Auditorium, once the site of a lurid sexual tryst discovered by a cleaning crew after hours, was avoided even by those in need of spiritual comfort. Some people just stayed home.

The NSA workforce was an extraordinary group of people, many with advanced degrees and brilliant minds. We were respected and rewarded: year 2000 statistics said the average NSAer made over $63,000 a year. We weren't nervous, fearful people. We were hired, in large part, for our balanced, rational behavior.

On the other hand, of course, we were not hired to be bold and courageous in the face of violent crime that threatens our universe. NSA employees faced the world of "Evil Empires" every day, but anonymously and at a distance. This was different: a threat so personal that it intimidated us all.

Above all, in a world where anything could happen at any time, the NSA complex had always been considered safe. NSA employees might not make as much money as those in the private sector, but we have never had to worry about being physically secure.

That had changed in a sudden, electrifying moment with the murder of Barry Ballard, a respected senior executive, in a deserted old kitchen, by someone with a badge. Someone who still had access to the buildings and who could kill again. It was terrifying. Employees, banded together in small groups, drifted to the area to peer at the "Police Line Do Not Cross" tapes. They murmured to each other, still in shock at the macabre event.

Almost nobody thought it was over. I didn't. I just wanted to stay here in my own home and wait until the nightmare ended.

I could stay for a little while, I decided. I lit a fire in the living room fireplace and sat in front of it for some time and examined the accumulation of mail I had tossed on the coffee table. I sipped a glass of red wine while I sorted through the envelopes. It was very peaceful.

I looked up at my father's picture on the mantle. He had that stern, martial look that only a Marine could project so perfectly. It must have been a shock to her friends when my mother, a free spirit and "peacenik" in the 1960s, married a soldier. I was glad she had—where would I be without him?—but it surprised me, too, whenever I thought about it. By NSA standards, Molly had always been a nonconformist, another ENTP who survived the rigid conservatism of the Agency; a Marine didn't seem like a great match for her. But she told me often about the breathtaking love they had shared.

I sat back on the couch and thought about my mother. I've called her Molly since I started working at NSA, where we occasionally interacted. "Mother" just didn't seem like the appropriate way to address a senior executive. It was certainly unusual. The National Security Agency has had many father-son teams, and even a few father-daughter combinations, many of whom were in positions of power and influence. As far as I knew, Molly and I were the only mother-daughter pair who had been in that kind of situation at NSA.

There were lots of Molly stories still floating around
the Agency. Maybe the best one was about the time a
few years back when she filed a formal EEO complaint on behalf of all the women in the Agency. She
was on the eighth floor of OPS 2B when she passed a
series of bronze plaques engraved with the names of
those NSAers who had been awarded the Presidential
Rank Awards. The awards, which recognized things
like *"sustained extraordinary accomplishments in
management of programs for the United States government"* or *"major contributions to the Intelligence
Community's foreign intelligence mission,"* often were
accompanied by large sums of money: $10,000 or
more. Molly did a quick count: of the three hundred
seventy awards given since 1956, a grand total of
thirty-nine had gone to women. She was outraged by
the disproportionate reward ratio. After she filed her
complaint, she was told by the inspector general, a
large pompous woman with a hint of facial hair, to
drop it or "risk your career." Molly never backed
down, but EEO refused to consider the suit. However,
a lot more women have gotten the awards since then,
and we all know why.

Molly adored working at NSA from the very beginning, when she was an analyst, like almost everyone
else, working on the Soviet problem. And my sister
and I still pay the price: we were named for the last
Czar and Czarina of Russia. ("They weren't the most
sensitive rulers around, but they weren't any worse
than Stalin and his bunch," my mother said.) I was
born first and got Alexandra. Poor Nikki turned out to
be a girl, too, and was named Nickolass by our pertina-
cious mother.

Molly retired early because Agency politics had
burned her out, but she loved NSA and its mission so

much she still worked there occasionally as a consul-
tant, one of a small group of purple-badged retirees
who advised the Agency on special projects for the
heady sum of a dollar a year.

I was still deep into my recollections when I heard a
noise on the back porch. As I turned my head I saw a
shadowy figure pass by the kitchen window. Someone tried to turn the knob on the door, then knocked
lightly when it wouldn't turn.

Someone at the back door? My heart thumped and
I stood up, unsure what to do next. I got up and picked up
the poker from the set of fireplace tools and started to
walk toward the kitchen.

Someone knocked on the front door.

I turned around and raised the poker. *There's more
than one of them and they've surrounded the house,* I
thought wildly. My heart was racing now.

The front doorknob turned, then caught. Thank
heavens I had locked the door when I got here.

"Who's there?" I choked out.

"Alex, it's Daniel. Are you all right? Can I come in
please?"

I lowered the poker, opened the door, and gasped,
"My God, Daniel, are you trying to scare me to death?"

"What do you mean?"

Confused, I told him about the back door and he ran
to the kitchen and opened it, stepping onto the porch.

He was back in a few minutes. "I didn't see anyone,
Alex, but I believe you. And it wasn't me. Molly was
right to send me over here to check on you, wasn't
she?"

I nodded and hugged him. "Thank God for both of
you."

22

Near Qalat, Afghanistan
Tuesday, December 5, 2000
Night

Zafir leaned on a beam at the top of the tower, muscles quivering, and tried to relax. His shoulder throbbed. A shooting star blazed across the sky, but his eyes were focused on the ground below, straining to see what Babrack had seen. Or heard. In a few minutes, a vehicle bumped along the road, the beams of its headlights jerking wildly. Zafir curled himself into the smallest shape he could manage. Below him, the vehicle pulled off the road and stopped near the bottom of the tower. A man got out and started climbing the structure, up toward Zafir.

Zafir took his gun out of his coat pocket and waited.

About twenty feet up the tower, the man stopped and pulled something out of his pack. Zafir could hear rustling and clanging as metal touched metal, but he couldn't tell what the man was doing. Was he a resistance fighter, trying to disrupt the Taliban's microwave network? A bomb would do that nicely; blow up this tower and it would take months to restore the system. Wouldn't they wonder whose body was blown to pieces along with it?

Fuck, Zafir thought. *I can't possibly be that unlucky.*

There was more rustling, then silence. In a few minutes, the man climbed back down, got in his vehicle, and roared off.

Zafir took a deep breath, turned his light back on, and continued his delicate and precarious work. *Finish what you're doing and get the hell out of here.*

By the time Babrack returned with the horses, Zafir had completed his splice and checked signal-to-noise levels on the array. Everything was in place and working smoothly. Nobody would notice the additional antenna; it looked just like three of the others. He descended as fast as he could, stopping twenty feet from the bottom to see what the stranger had placed on the tower.

It was a large poster, taped securely to the rungs, and would be visible for some distance in the daylight. Across the top, in several languages, it read, "Join us in the struggle against the Taliban." Under the writing was a picture of General Ahmad Shah Massoud, military commander of the Northern Alliance guerilla forces. He stared proudly and defiantly from the picture, his dark hair a stark contrast to his pale skin.

Reluctantly, Zafir cut the signboard down and took it with him. He didn't want the attention it would bring to the tower.

Babrack convulsed with laughter at the poster. "If that man had only known what was going on here, he would have peed his pants," he said, choking. Zafir merely shook his head.

They rode back to Tsalgari, reaching the village as the sky began to lighten in the east, gray deepening to an intense blue as the dawn gathered strength. Despite the bright beauty of the new day, both men felt oddly uneasy as they approached the town.

Before they dismounted inside the walled courtyard surrounding Babrack's house, they knew something was terribly wrong. Dark patches stained the dirt walkway, and the door to the house was open wide.

Inside, the rooms were empty. Souria was gone.

The house was in shambles. A chair and a lamp lay broken; scraps of cloth littered the floor. Souria's shiny scalpel was dark with blood, and more blood stained the rugs throughout the room. Zafir could almost hear echoes of the fight.

The fight that Souria had lost.

Babrack fell to his knees and picked up the scalpel. "She tried. She said she would and she did. But they got her, didn't they?" He threw the knife across the room. "Damn them all."

"Who took her, Babrack? The Taliban? The terrorists? Where would they take her?"

Babrack shrugged. "I don't know. My first guess is the mullahs came and dragged her out of here like they've been threatening to do for years."

He put his head in his hands and muttered, "But it could be the others. Al Qaeda." He looked up at Zafir. "I haven't told you everything about my sister. For the past two years she's been close to a man named Bashir. Sometimes he stays here with her when I'm gone. It's dangerous, but damn it, she deserves some happiness."

"And who is Bashir?" Zafir asked. "Certainly not al Qaeda?"

Babrack snorted. "No, my friend. Bashir is one of us. In fact, he's the most important man in the resistance. Our leader. He's the one your agency contacts most of the time. He seems to have gone missing several days ago." Babrack made a fist and punched it into his other hand. "I'd like to think it's a coincidence, but such things are hard to believe in."

"But the terrorists wouldn't know about him and Souria, would they?"

"Hard to tell. People here are so terrified of the Taliban that some of them repeat rumors they have heard. They betray their own neighbors to escape punishment or to get more food or better jobs. The Taliban and al Qaeda are like this." He put his hands together and gripped hard.

He stood and walked to the door. "First, I have to go see if she is in the prison the Taliban has near the soccer field. If she is, they are almost certainly planning to stone her to death with the others they have decided did something 'unholy.' There are a few other places I can check. Stay here."

He whirled out the door and back onto his horse. Zafir watched him ride away into the magical light, a light unlike any other he had seen outside this strange and ancient country.

Babrack did not return until after dark. He was exhausted. His face was stony and bleak. "She's not in the prison. I talked to my neighbors. One of them said a truck woke him up in the middle of the night last night. He looked out and saw Souria in the back. Two men up front. He didn't recognize them. I don't know who they are or where they took her. I looked everywhere, even in all the towns near this one." His face crumpled and he held out his hands. "I don't know what to do or how to help her." His words were full of pain. "It's hopeless."

Zafir led Babrack to a chair and pushed him gently into it. He righted the one other unbroken chair and sat beside him. "I have an idea," he said.

23

Operations Building 1, National Security Agency
Wednesday, December 6, 2000
Morning

I sat in the darkened conference room and frowned
at the scenario before me. A group of intelligence analysts who had formed a self-directed committee to
improve the health of Agency reporting was giving a
seminar, "Switching Verb Tenses: When Is It Appropriate?" As the new Agency reporting chief, my presence was, if not compulsory, at least expected. I wanted
to be out there, somewhere, looking for the tape instead of stuck in this briefing, but I did have a job to
do—a job that included attending potentially influential reporting conferences. And I didn't have a plan to
find the cassette yet anyway. I knew it was possible
that the killer had actually taken it away after Barry
died, but I didn't think so. Especially after the mysterious visitor at my house the day before.

I wanted to *do something*.

And, most of all, I wanted to know what was happening to Gabe.

But here I was, trapped in the conference room. The
briefer at this seminar was Jacqui Simpson-Trent, an
intelligence analysis technical track master much
impressed with a sense of her own knowledge and

prominence at the Agency. Of course, reaching a "Master" level in any career field at NSA was indeed an achievement, somewhat like getting PhD in your field of study. Others in the Better Reporting group filled the ten chairs around the large conference table. The viewgraph currently projected on the large screen at the front of the room read:

When Is It Acceptable to Switch Tenses in the Middle of a Sentence or Paragraph?

Traditionalists: "Never."

Pragmatists:"When a sense of timeliness is necessary."

Jacqui was telling her audience what an extremely important topic this was and how it had captured the attention of some "heavyweights of the Agency reporting scene." They had, she said, been grappling with the issue for over six months. I groaned.

The next viewgraph presented the idea that there could be:

EXCEPTION TO THE RULES

The verb in the subordinate clause should remain in the present tense if it expresses a general truth or describes habitual or regular actions.

Jacqui, however, was not in favor of bending rules this way, even if the *College Writer's Reference* said it was acceptable. "The dominant tense of a piece of writing is its governing tense, which affects the choice of tense for every other verb," explained Ms. Simpson-Trent.

Jacqui continued speaking. "Listen carefully to the difference between these two sentences and you will see what I mean:

'Lawrence told me that he works for Unisys, but the company has no record of him.'
'Lawrence told me that he worked for Unisys, but the company has no record of him.'

Do you see the difference? Changing the tense of any verb can change the meaning of a piece."

It was probably the tension of the past few days, I thought later. The murders, the funeral, and worry about Gabe's perilous mission had all taken their toll. Normally I would not have criticized a briefer in public; today was not normal. I stood and firmly said, "Stop."

Jacqui stopped. Someone near the door flipped on the lights. Jacqui said, a tinge of anxiety in her voice, "Ms. O'Malley, thank you for coming." She definitely recognized me as her new boss. "Can I answer a question for you?"

"Perhaps you can. Why are you—all of you— wasting time on this? It's not important. We have plenty of critical reporting issues to fix. Things like timeliness, over-classification, redundancy, lack of interpretation, understandable English, and just plain willingness to share information. Half our analysts don't use Intelink or collateral sources because they don't think putting SIGINT in any kind of context is their job. And it definitely is!" I looked over the room full of people. "Fixing things like that—that's important!"

For the second time in two days, I had shocked a roomful of people into stunned silence.

"But," Jacqui stammered, "a lot of senior people . . ."

"If any 'heavyweights' at NSA spent more than five seconds on this issue, they should be fired." I took a deep breath. "We need priorities here, and I mean priorities that don't include worrying about dependent and independent clausal relationships. For heaven's sake, think about it. This agency is supposed to collect intelligence and send it to the people who need it. Fast. Verb tenses are about the last damn thing we need to focus our precious time and attention on."

Everyone stared at me, mouths open. Jacqui sat down, visibly shaken.

The door to the conference room opened and a woman from the outer office came in. One glance at the roomful of people, heads turned, gaping at me stopped her so quickly she had to put out a hand to steady herself. Fifty pairs of eyes turned to look her way, and she finally managed to say, "Ms. O'Malley, I just spoke with your secretary. You have a STU III call in your office. The caller said he was phoning from outside the country and it was critical that he talk to you right away. I promised to send you back immediately."

The eyes returned to me, still standing in the midst of the crowd. I nodded. "Thank you. I'm coming." I addressed the crowded conference room once more. "Please, put aside this presentation and talk about the things I said. How to make real changes here. You are all very smart people. Use your abilities to fix the multitude of things that actually need fixing. Make me a list, prioritized, of the five most critical reporting problems you think we have and some ways to correct them." I looked at Jacqui. "I'll call you in a few days for a report."

I walked down the steps and out the door, leaving a silence as deep as a black hole behind me.

I practically ran down the long corridor. It always seemed like a trek; today it was interminable, but I made it to my office in record time. Obviously something important was going on.

Only the White House, embassies, S&TI Centers, military commands, and a few prominent private contractors use STUs to talk to NSA. They don't have gray phones like most of the Intelligence Community, and the secure telephone unit with its code-excited linear prediction voice protection gives them the ability to speak securely over unprotected lines. Created by the OPSEC element of NSA, the system's terminals are designed to operate as both ordinary telephones and secure instruments over the dial-up public switched telephone network.

An international STU III call is unusual and almost always urgent because, unlike most organizations who use STUs, outside the country calls can be from collectors or deployed troops or collaborating agencies such as GCHQ, the British equivalent of NSA. I really had no idea who might be calling. I thought of Gabe, of course, but that was just too outrageous. He could do it with his satellite phone, but calling me, or anyone except his CIA case officer, would be strictly against the rules.

I picked up the STU III phone in my office, checked to be sure the Fortezza encryption card was inserted, and pressed the button to "go secure" as requested by the message on the screen.

"Yes," I said, a bit out of breath. "This is Alexandra O'Malley."

A slight hesitation, and then, as clearly as if he were calling from Langley, Gabe's voice came over the line. "Alex," he said, "I need your help. It's going to be a little . . . unorthodox."

"Hold on." I got up and closed the door. "Gabe, is it really you? Are you all right?" I wanted to say so much more, tell him how ecstatic I was to hear his voice and know he was alive. But not on an STU.

"Yes, it's me, and I'm fine, but I need you to help me. You know the new phone tap I just put in place over here? You should be intercepting calls on that link by now. I need you to listen in on all those calls and try to find someone for me."

He told me about Souria's disappearance, the man named Bashir, and Babrack's fears for his sister. "We think al Qaeda has her, and, if they do, they might be talking about her on the microwave link. I know this is pushing the envelope, but I have nowhere else to turn." He explained he couldn't go through formal channels to get the information—if indeed it was there—because this was definitely not part of his mission. CIA would tell him to get the hell out of the country and leave the family to solve their own problems. Besides, calling CIA and having them request priority tasking on the link could very well take much too long to be useful.

I bit my lip. "Jesus, Gabe, what you're doing sounds so dangerous. I would do anything in the world to help you, you know that, but I feel like doing this will just help you get killed."

"These people saved my life, Alex. At considerable risk to themselves. I know the chances of us finding Souria are slim, but you are absolutely the only hope we have. And you have to hurry; if they are talking about her it's probably happening on the microwave links right now."

I didn't hesitate again. "Of course, I'll do everything I can. And I have a friend here who will be happy to help, even under these circumstances. When will I hear from you?"

"I'll set up my satellite phone and call you again on your STU about noon your time. Say, in about two hours?"

When we hung up, I sat in my chair and stared at the phone. I was the new head of NSA reporting, and I had just agreed to break two of the Agency's major rules: never circumvent normal collection procedures and never give unanalyzed and unpublished "raw SIGINT" to a customer.

Well, hell, lives are at stake, I thought. *And hopefully no one will ever know. Except, of course, it will probably come up on my next poly.* I sighed. *I'll worry about it later.*

And at least I wouldn't be breaking any USSID 18 laws by listening to a call about a U.S. citizen without permission. This was all about Afghans.

I picked up the gray phone and called Jacks.

24

West of Kandahar, Afghanistan
Wednesday, December 6, 2000
Evening

The pickup truck bumped over the pitted roads
between Tsalgari and the warehouse, jolting and shaking the two men and the nearly unconscious woman in
the backseat. The operation to seize Souria had not
gone well; she was moaning from the pain of several
broken ribs and both men were bleeding from nasty
cuts.

The men cursed their bad luck. They had never expected a woman to put up such a fight, and their mascu-
linity was as damaged as their bodies. At least, they
thought, they had succeeded in abducting the woman
from her home and they would be able to deliver her to
The Lion. Anything less would have meant their death.

The drive over the deteriorated roads took most of the
day and included a stop at an al Qaeda camp, where the
men phoned ahead to the raisin factory to report their
"successful" mission of capturing the doctor. Once,
the driver nearly flipped the truck when he veered too
far to the right to avoid a huge rock and slipped into a
ditch. It took what seemed like forever to get it out. When
they finally pulled up outside the warehouse, the men
sat a few minutes in the darkness before they picked up

Souria and pushed their way through the door. It was cold, and they were exhausted, injured, and starving, but they knew the night had just begun.

Inside the cavernous warehouse were seven men, two of them dead. The bodies were bloody and entangled. One of the dead men was Bashir; the other was the man left to guard him.

Bin Laden was back at the warehouse, pacing again near the center of the room, waiting for the two men he had sent to get Souria. They bowed their heads and dropped the woman in the ripped, blue burka at his feet. The Arab's face was fierce in the dim light, a controlled wrath that terrified both men. "Somehow," bin Laden said, "despite his injuries, Bashir managed to kill his guard and then turned the weapon on himself so we couldn't use that woman to make him talk." He kicked Souria in the side as he spoke, and she gasped at the pain.

"We will see if Souria knows anything herself, but your dead friend who was supposed to be guarding Bashir took away our best hope when he allowed himself to be tricked." He frowned. "We will not wait for my courier to return from Pakistan. We will try another way to find out what the Americans are doing."

He waved to the four other men in the room, his constant bodyguards, and they approached catlike and smiling. "Take these two away from me," the Arab said, pointing to the men who had brought Souria, "then come back and help with the woman."

While they were gone, he dragged Souria over to the body of her lover. "He died for you," he said. "You must have made him very happy when you were with him. Perhaps you can do the same for us."

Souria lifted her burka over her head and spat in his face.

Operations Building 1, National Security Agency
Wednesday, December 6, 2000
Noon

I was waiting by the STU III when it rang again,
my office door already closed. When the phone's secure light blinked, I spoke to Gabe.

"Give me two more hours," I said. "We have tapes
of new intercepts from the microwave links you tapped
into. Many of them are in Pashtu, but we have only one
linguist to review them. He thinks he might have a lead
for you, but he has to wade through a lot of garbles
and irrelevant calls. And there are several strange calls
about packages and deliveries and 'the fruit' and
things you would never understand unless you had
some idea of what it's about. Also," my voice was
heavy with worry, "we have a major problem. Forwarding of intercepts on this network ended nearly an
hour ago. It isn't scheduled to resume until morning
your time. You know how it is here—we're sucking up
so many links all over the world that all the data can't
get sent back to NSA at the same time. Everything is
prioritized. I have to think of some way to get the Afghan al Qaeda comms forwarding restarted even if it
bumps something else."

"Yes, you do." Gabe spoke quietly but firmly. The

digital voice signal made it sound as if he were just next door. "You know, don't you, that every minute of these guys talking is one we can't afford to lose?"

"Yes, I know that. And so does Sergeant Jackson. Our linguist. If anyone can figure out what these people are blabbing about, it's him. I'll take care of the collection forwarding problem."

"Thank you, Alex. We're counting on you. I'll call back in two more hours."

"Right," I said. I read off a different STU III number. "Call on that line, please. It's in the Meridian office. I'm moving down there to stay with Jacks while we work on this."

I called Captain McColloh, the OCMC chief, to discuss the collection problem and then spent the next two hours sorting through the intercepts with Jacks. I was ready when Gabe called back.

"Gabe, we just listened to a recording made a few hours ago of a couple of men on the link discussing *two* women. You were talking about just one, right? And," I paused, shaking my head, "is there any chance at all Souria is a doctor? That's what these guys seem to be saying." My voice reflected my skepticism. "Could there be a woman doctor in Afghanistan?"

"Yes!" Gabe's excitement surged through the line. "Yes, she is a doctor! Sorry, I should have told you that. What did they say about her?"

"My linguist says the men were calling ahead to a place they referred to as 'the old raisin factory' and said they were taking a woman doctor there. They said they would arrive sometime this evening. Does 'the old raisin factory' mean anything to you?"

I heard mumbling as Gabe turned to the side to ask Babrack my question. The two men spoke rapidly in Pashtu, then Gabe said into the phone, "Alex, he knows where it is! By God, you've found her." He spoke over his shoulder to Babrack again, then returned. "This place is not too far west of Kandahar, near where some grape orchards used to be. We'll leave now, but it will take many hours to get there. It's almost ten o'clock here, so the men are probably at the factory with Souria already." He hesitated. "Alex, did they say anything about why they took her there?"

"Well, the whole conversation was very curious. And confusing. They didn't say anything directly, but one speaker said that someone he called The Lion wanted to use her to 'take control.' Do you know what that could mean?"

"No, I don't. I'll ask Babrack if he can figure it out. But it doesn't sound good."

"One other thing. The people talking, they mentioned something else. Something very puzzling. Back to the 'two women' thing. They said the woman doctor would be joining 'the other one.' 'The one with pale hair.' And then something about mud. Several references to mud."

"Okay," Gabe said slowly. "Well, we'll leave you to try to figure that one out while we travel." He paused. "What about the collection problem? How did you solve it?" He didn't doubt for a minute that I had.

"I lied," I said calmly. "I told the OCMC we had indications in the Afghan comms that the terrorists might be planning an attack on an American, and that I would personally be staying here all night to help Jacks figure it out. Besides, it's not entirely untrue if we count you as the American."

"Good Lord, Alex. You are something. Yep, that'll make sure we get ironclad coverage as long as we need it. But try not to get in trouble, okay?"

"I won't. Jacks is on our side, believe me, and who

else in this place is going to translate Pashtu? He's our only linguist since Mariam was murdered."

"What! What murder?"

"My God, Gabe, you don't have any idea what's been going on back here, do you?"

"No . . . nobody's told me anything. What's happened?"

I summarized, as concisely as possible, the grim series of disasters. When I finished, a weighty silence filled the line.

"It sounds as dangerous back there as it is here," Gabe finally managed. "Watch yourself."

"Yes," I agreed. "I will."

"One more thing. Can you keep listening to those bastards' chatter and tell me if you can find out anything else if I call you again, say, in the morning when we get close to Kandahar? We need to know how many men are at the raisin factory. How well the building is fortified. Anything they say that might help us."

I glanced up at the clock on my office wall. It was after two. "Yes," I said. "Call back when you're there. I'll be waiting. We'll do our best to have information for you."

26

Brookview Medical Clinic
Wednesday, December 6, 2000
Afternoon

Dr. Rashiq sat quietly beside the hospital bed of his young hantavirus patient. Matthew was gaining strength by the day. He was eating, watching television, walking around the halls, and talking about going home. His parents had just left after visiting him for most of the morning. They were increasingly anxious for their son to leave the facility and get back to his life.

"Perhaps next week," the doctor said. "As long as there are no unexpected complications."

Matthew was still chattering away, talking about going back to school, playing baseball, and riding his bike. Dr. Rashiq sighed, a deep, long sigh. Much as he hated to admit it, he had grown quite fond of the boy. Even when Matthew was still too sick to talk, the child's eyes, full of trust and adoration, had followed the doctor's every move. Rashiq truly wanted to cure Matthew, not just, as usual, for his own self-satisfaction, but because he had started to care about his patient as a person. Sometimes he wondered if he saw something of himself in the slightly built, defenseless child.

He sighed again, almost a groan. The questions

came again, flitting through his mind. How could he pride himself on saving this small boy's life—on being a physician who took an oath to value all lives—and still carry out his mission of death? He put his head in his hands and prayed. Slowly, very slowly, he regained his focus, his determination. For about the thousandth time, he reviewed his plans.

Very early tomorrow morning Rashiq would plant his deadly poisons inside the National Security Agency. He had finished his preparations and packed up everything he needed. He had to act now before he had to fly back to San Diego for Mariam's memorial service on Friday.

He had been given more anthrax than he needed for the mission he had chosen, and early this morning he had carefully divided the leftover powdery spores into seven envelopes which he returned in the airtight box to locker number 153 at Union Station. He included a letter, which read, in part, *"If you are reading this, I am dead, in jail, or in hiding and I will no longer be able to help you. However, I have placed anthrax spores in these envelopes which I have addressed to people or places whose contamination will arouse terror in the American populace. Write letters of warning to put in the envelopes (I suggest phrases like, 'Death to America. Death to Israel. Allah is Great.') and mail them when you judge the time is right. HANDLE THEM CAREFULLY."*

The first two envelopes Dr. Rashiq addressed to "Tom Brokaw" and "Editor, *New York Post*." On the second two he carefully printed return labels of an elementary school in Franklin Park, New Jersey, and just as carefully addressed them to "Senator Leahy" and "Senator Daschle." One more was targeted for American Media in Florida, which printed a tabloid that Rashiq hated for its attacks on Islam and a particularly demeaning article speculating about the size of Usama bin Laden's "private parts," and two others to the New York offices of ABC and CBS. He was pleased with this selection; it was, he thought, an effective mix of victim types.

In a sudden act that took him by surprise, Dr. Rashiq kissed the tousled curls on Matthew's head. He turned quickly and left the room.

27

Office of the Director of Central Intelligence
Wednesday, December 6, 2000
Afternoon

General Murray was angry, an emotion he rarely allowed himself. He had discovered many years ago as a young first lieutenant in Vietnam that anger was not only pointless but destructive; half his platoon was killed when the air cover he had requested never arrived, and he had wasted precious minutes cursing the pilots instead of solving the problem. It was a miracle that he and most of the remaining men survived.

He never let anger play a significant part in his life again. Until now.

He knew when he accepted the position of NSA Director there would be challenges unlike any he had ever faced. His background did not include much exposure to SIGINT, for example, but he learned the basics quickly. Leading a workforce of thousands of civilians was an eye-opener for a man who was rarely questioned when he gave orders. And he knew the Agency was in the throes of despair, battered by the press and by Congress. But he didn't know until he took over the eighth floor Director's suite in Ops 2B how bad it really was.

The Meridian project had been hugely important to

this DIRNSA. He knew intercepting the al Qaeda comms was critical, not just for the country, but for the morale and reputation of his agency. The information in the comms had been so promising, and then it all just disappeared.

And now, murder? Someone had killed Barry Ballard, the man whose judgment he had come to trust more than any other senior executive. Had an NSA linguist really killed Barry? The murder/suicide had never rung quite true; it was too easy a way out. General Murray didn't believe there were many easy ways out in life, and after listening to Alex O'Malley's comments about the missing tape he had significant doubts about blaming Mariam Rashiq so quickly.

He got up and paced across the waiting room. He had already been there for twenty minutes and it wasn't helping his mood. He had been summoned—again—by the DCI and had made the long trip from Fort Meade to Langley in silence. His driver and his aide were silent, too. They recognized anger when they saw it, even though they had never seen any evidence of it before in the general.

The door to the office of the DCI opened, and Louis Hahn himself came out to welcome General Murray. The men shook hands, entered the handsomely appointed office, and sat in soft leather chairs, a coffee table between them with an assortment of drinks and pastries. "Thank you for coming back, John," Hahn said. "I have to brief the president tomorrow morning, and NSA's problems are definitely the first order of business."

General Murray's eyes narrowed. "They should be, Lou. I don't care what you might say about CIA, NSA's SIGINT is the most reliable source of intelligence information there is. And, in my opinion, the Agency is slowly falling apart."

The DCI sighed and nodded his head slowly. "Yes, I've heard that story before, of course, but I was hoping you would tell me it wasn't true. Or not entirely true."

"True? Oh, it's true all right," DIRNSA growled. "What else could you expect? We've lost a third of our workforce in the past ten years, we can't hire more than a few replacements, our infrastructure is crumbling, and nobody seems to care. Nobody. All we get are budget and billets cuts." He stared out the window at the snowy landscape. "And, Lou, the managers left in the Agency, the ones who haven't taken an early retirement, many of them are astonishingly bad. The workforce is carrying the place on its back—has been for a long time—and it can't keep it up much longer without help."

He stood and walked toward the window, hands clasped behind his back. The DCI watched him quietly, waiting to hear the rest.

DIRNSA continued, "The intelligence business is fundamentally about skills and expertise, and that means people. A wide variety of people who can cope with the damn global telecommunications revolution that's been going on out there while we've been paying our most experienced analysts large bonuses to retire. Our newest supercomputer is far from state of the art, our Goddamn computer networks are still precarious, and now we find ourselves in the ridiculous position of having only one," he held up a finger, "one Pashtu linguist to transcribe and translate the Taliban and al Qaeda comms. And now Security wants to take his clearances away until they prove he wasn't involved with his girlfriend in betraying the Meridian comms and killing Barry. What would we do then? Drag some Pashtu speaker off the streets of D.C., send him to the Columbia office, and trust him to read the comms for us without telling anyone he's doing it?"

The DCI poured himself a cup of coffee and sipped it. General Murray sat back down and rubbed his eyes. "Tell you the truth," he said, "I think Usama bin Laden has a better communications network than we do. All these damn agencies running around, half of them have information they haven't told anyone else about, the other half don't know what the hell they have. This has got to change."

He gritted his teeth. "You know what else? We had all better start taking the terrorist threat seriously. We'd better recognize these people are religious fanatics—hell, they're Goddamn fascists—who want to destroy us. I think we should have drawn the line at the *Cole*, gone in and cleared out the whole bloody mess of them wherever they were. But, no, the politicians don't want to risk losing oil, the FBI is still so damn focused on organized crime it hardly knows what a damn terrorist is, and half the Intelligence Community is still hoping the Soviets will come back. They were a threat we could all understand."

The DCI started to speak, but DIRNSA held up his hand. "One more thing, Lou. Think about this. Congress has tied our hands so completely that if bin Laden, or someone like him, crossed the bridge from Niagara Falls, Ontario, to Niagara Falls, New York, our laws would force us to stop copying his comms as long as he was in the States unless a judge gives us permission. And then we'd have to turn the operation over to the FBI. No matter what the bastard was saying. How long do you think that would take? We must reevaluate our priorities and decide what the line between security and liberty should really be."

DIRNSA paused, then added, "I don't want to sound melodramatic, Lou, but in my opinion it's five minutes to midnight, not just for NSA, but for the whole country, and we'd damn well better do something about it."

Louis Hahn looked at the general grimly. "I assume you would prefer this conversation stays between us for now?"

General Murray nodded reluctantly. "I guess it will have to. Nobody is ready for these issues yet, are they?"

"I know you have a lot of concerns, John. I have them, too. But the president," Louis Hahn said firmly, "wants to know several specific things tomorrow. He wants to know how the NSA workforce has held up under the added stress of the murder and suicide. He wants to know what we can reasonably expect from these new al Qaeda comms now that we have them back. And, most of all, he wants me to reassure him that the IC will be able to give appropriate warning if the terrorists are really planning a major operation. Especially against the U.S."

"Speaking for NSA, the answer to the last question is no. I can't guarantee you—in fact, I would refuse to guarantee you—that even if we were at the top of our game, which we clearly aren't, we could stop all the bad things that can happen to Americans. The people we have work very hard, and most would work twenty-four hours a day if you ask them to, but it's not enough. The bad guys work very hard, too."

"Yes," Hahn agreed, "that's the only reasonable answer we can give. What about the other two questions?"

"You can tell him that I expect a lot of excellent information from the new comms links we just started intercepting. But it's too early to know for sure just what kind of details we will get. Hopefully, al Qaeda will continue talking about the *al-Buraq* operation on these links just as they did on their satellite phones. And we will find out what they are planning." DIRNSA stopped and shook his head. "If we have enough linguists to tell us what they say."

The general filled a glass of water, drank half of it, and continued, "As far as NSA workforce morale goes, I'm afraid that's not the most relevant question concerning the murder." He braced himself for the DCI's reaction to the bombshell he was about to drop. "Lou, I'm beginning to have doubts that Mariam Rashiq either gave away the comms or killed Barry. Or herself." He explained why.

The DCI put his coffee cup back on the table. "Jesus Christ, John, you can't be serious. How can I tell the president of the United States that the FBI is wrong and there still might be a killer running around the National Security Agency?"

DIRNSA turned and looked at his boss, the head of the entire Intelligence Community as well as the Central Intelligence Agency. "Lou, the man trusts you. He must know the truth. How can you not tell him?" He hesitated, and added, "And you might want to remind him what the Israelis say."

"What's that, John?" Hahn asked softly.

General Murray leveled his gaze. "They say, 'The further we are from the last crisis, the closer we are to the next.'"

28

Tsalgari, Afghanistan
Thursday, December 7, 2000
Just Past Midnight

The jeep was packed with as much as it could carry. The back seat was full of rugs, which hid the Kalashnikovs, two carbines, and several bundles of morphine blocks. "Good for bribes," Babrack explained. Two large cans of petrol were strapped to the back, and several containers of water and food were stuffed beside the rugs. Zafir had two money belts with both Afghanis and U.S. dollars fastened under his clothes. He kept his Beretta close.

Their journey from Tsalgari to the raisin factory west of Kandahar was not more than a hundred fifty miles, but they knew it would take many hours. The roads were spectacularly abominable, in some places little more than interwoven braided ruts, in others, merely craters blasted by bombs and rockets during the war with the Soviets. They knew, also, that they might have to go cross-country at times to avoid Taliban checkpoints. Driving in darkness, with the nightly curfew, was not the best, but daylight travel could be equally dangerous. And they couldn't afford to wait. They would have to take their chances.

The first part of the trip was slow, almost snaillike.

It was difficult to see where they were going by the moon's light, but they couldn't risk headlights. Occasionally Zafir had to walk in front of the jeep to make sure the "road" was navigable. Twice they spotted lights ahead and cut across the guttered fields to avoid the checkpoints. They were terrifying detours: the Soviets had planted mines across much of the country; in some estimates, well over a million. Their favorite was a "butterfly" mine, which they dropped in huge quantities from helicopters. Its explosive charge was set low enough to maim, not kill, accounting for the large number of *mujaheddin* and others—including many children—who were without legs or arms. It was a tactic designed to make the war not just deadly but excruciatingly cruel; so cruel that the *mujaheddin* would stop fighting. It didn't work.

Each mile off-road for Babrack and Zafir was not just dangerous but fiercely unnerving. The hair on Zafir's arms stood on end as he gripped the handholds on the jeep, jerking wildly in the frozen ruts. When the delicate light of dawn filled the skies again, they had barely driven past the town of Qalat.

"We can go faster now," Babrack said. "But there will be new challenges." He pointed to a line of over-packed trucks piled high with animal hides, timber, foodstuffs, and passengers crowded together like cattle. In the back of one truck were wild-eyed, bleating sheep racing back and forth across the mounded cargo. "It will not be easy to share the road with those."

At least we don't have to drive through minefields now, Zafir thought. Occasionally he could see the debris of war off in the distance: bomb craters, upended and unexploded rockets, the carcass of a tank. One large piece of metal, unrecognizable as a component part, still had bits of shiny black Cyrillic writing on the side.

He tried to envision green fields the color of malachite and blossoms of hundreds of fruit trees floating like pink clouds in the spring skies. He could not. The ruins of the landscape, brown and bleak, overpowered his senses.

He tried to imagine what it would be like to live here, to be unable to go back to the comfort and freedom he had always known. He couldn't.

"Babrack," Zafir finally said, "do you know who the terrorists are talking about when they say 'The Lion'? My friend who's helping us says she heard that name in the phone calls here she's been listening to."

Babrack looked over at his passenger. "Yes, I know who that is. I'm surprised you don't." He thought a moment. "Afghans have a tradition of calling an especially strong leader by that name. Like General Massoud, leader of the Northern Alliance—we call him The Lion of the Panjshir."

Zafir nodded. "But who is the new Lion?" he asked.

"It's bin Laden, the Arab who came in and helped the Taliban destroy Afghanistan. He pays for half of what they do. *Sher* is the Pashtu term for 'The Lion' and 'Usama' actually means 'The Lion' in Arabic."

"Really?" Zafir's voice was incredulous. "I considered that, of course, but I thought it was very unlikely that Usama bin Laden is at some old raisin factory waiting for your sister. I thought The Lion must be one of his aides."

Babrack's brow furrowed. "It would certainly be unusual for bin Laden himself to do the dirty work. He must be very angry about something." Babrack scowled. "They must have Bashir, and bin Laden is almost certainly going to use Souria to get Bashir to talk, to tell him all the names of those who work against him and what you and I have done to the microwave towers. We must get there soon." He stepped harder on the gas pedal for emphasis and the jeep bucked and jolted. He looked at Zafir again. "You must not tell your agency he could be there. They will bomb the warehouse and kill everyone inside. Including Souria."

"No," Zafir agreed. He knew it wouldn't do any good anyway. It would take CIA days, if not weeks, to arrange such a strike. First they would order imagery, then study it, ask NSA for any COMINT to support the claim that UBL was really there, then coordinate with the air force. The terrorist would be long gone. "I won't do that. But we must try to kill him ourselves."

Zafir rubbed his chin, thinking. "My God, Babrack, if Usama bin Laden is actually involved, the place will be crawling with bodyguards. This is a suicide mission."

"Backing out, my friend?"

Zafir grinned. "No, *Sher*, I will follow you into this valley of death. And we will come out of it alive."

Aside from saving Souria, he thought, *having a chance to kill bin Laden is worth all the risks we're taking.*

29

Project Meridian Office, NSA
Wednesday, December 6, 2000
Late Evening

I was nibbling a bag of stale pretzels, and Jacks was asleep on a dilapidated chair we had dragged in from a nearby ladies' room when the STU III rang. I grabbed it. "Gabe?"

"It's me. We're getting close to Kandahar and the raisin factory. Do you have any updates for me?"

"I wish I did," I said. "But there's been very little traffic on the lines we're intercepting, and nothing about what you need to know." I looked at my watch. "Probably because it's been night over there." I added, firmly, "But, Gabe, don't go into that place without checking with me again, do you understand? Call me again."

He laughed. "You are a pushy woman, Alex, just like Souria. I guess that's why I like you both so much."

"Yeah, well, whatever. Call me."

"I will, I promise."

Two hours later, I was idly paging through an English-Pashtu dictionary. I looked up the word *mud*, which was *khátti* in Pashtu. I yawned. Jacks was still asleep, a blessing, I thought. The man was anguished and exhausted. It was hard for me to bear seeing the sorrow in his eyes. The office was still and silent. When a knock came at the door, I jumped out of the chair, flipping the book across the desk. Jacks sat up and growled, "Who the hell is that?"

It was Kai.

"What are you doing here?" I asked her. "How did you know I was here, and how did you ever find this place? I can't let you in, you know." I slipped out the door and we walked down the hall together. The basement was even spookier at night than in the daytime. A shadowy underworld of dim lights, even in the afternoons when there were people around; at night its long hallways were deserted and ghostly.

"Someone in NSOC heard you were here from the duty officer in the OCMC, and he told me you were working on some urgent project. Then all I had to do was wander around the basement for half an hour to actually find this office." Kai took my arm. "Listen, I have to show you something. I think it could be important. Maybe as important as what we did last year."

I was wide awake now. "What? Show me."

"It has to be in the ELINT lab. Meet me there at eleven? My watch is over at ten-thirty and that will give me time to hang the tape. Although," Kai sniffed, "for once it's not really a tape that I had to wait weeks for. This is a digitized sample of an intercept sent over the Buff Line from the field site. But it's enough." She sniffed again. "The line was designed for COMINT and telemetry, of course, but if you find the right person and beg hard enough they might stoop to sending ELINT over it, too."

"The 'ELINT-is-a-step-child' whining is getting old, you know."

"Yeah, so you say." Kai grinned. "Just wait 'til you see this. And Alex," she said, seriously, "it has to do with Afghanistan. Do you know where that is? Better check a map before you meet me."

I laughed, amazed at the thought of Kai talking about some ELINT discovery in a little-known target I had been immersed in for weeks. "All right, Kai, I'll try to read up on it a little."

Privately I thought, *I didn't even know there were any radars in Afghanistan.*

30

W9D ELINT Lab, Operations Building 1,
National Security Agency
Wednesday, December 6, 2000
Night

At eleven sharp, I rang the bell outside the ELINT
lab. The Meridian comms had been either silent or
contained only irrelevant chatter for the past few
hours. Jacks would call me if he needed me or if Gabe
called.

Kai was ready with an oscilloscope display and a
map of Afghanistan. "See here?" She pointed to the
Kabul area. "We know the Taliban forces have SA-2s
in this area, left over from the Russians. They're old
surface-to-air missiles, but the system has good reli-
ability and great range to knock down aircraft. Just
ask Gary Powers. These babies could still be very
dangerous if they've managed to keep them in working order. They turn on the radars from time to time
and track an aircraft or two, probably old Antonov
passenger planes that used to be part of Ariana Airlines, so it looks like they might be a factor if anyone
decided to attack Kabul by air. That is, if the missiles
still work, of course. I can't tell that from just the
radar tracks."

"How do you know Afghanistan has an airline, let

alone what it was called and what kind of planes they have?" I had done little more than think about Afghanistan for several weeks, and I didn't know anything about that.

"Last night, after I got home from my swing shift, I looked it up on the 'net. I couldn't do it at work, of course, because the ELINT Watch Officer doesn't have an Internet terminal. I wonder if even the SOO has one."

I nodded. I wondered, too.

Many NSA offices have no Internet connectivity at all; those that did might have one terminal for a hundred people. Why? Two reasons:

Management is afraid people will waste time surfing.

It isn't SIGINT anyway. How important can it be?

NSA is an astonishingly SIGINT-centric place. Internet access at the desktop just doesn't fit with the Agency's ways of doing things. Even in the new millennium.

Kai shrugged. She was used to researching background material at home. She pointed back to the map and moved her finger to the south, to an area just west of Kandahar. "This is what I want to tell you about. Apparently the Taliban has brought in more SA-2s and situated them to defend the area down here. They must have gotten them from Pakistan, since nobody else would sell them weapons like that." She rolled her eyes. "Well, maybe the French would. God knows what they might do. But in this case it's surely Pakistan. I noticed a couple of nights ago on my NSOC shift that these radars were popping up in a place I'd never seen before, so I called the collector and asked them to Buff back a sample of the ELINT data."

"That's not really your job anymore, is it?" I asked, smiling.

"Well, no, but I knew nobody else was going to get excited about this for quite a while. I think it's very significant."

"Why?

"Hold on, let me tell the whole story. Then you'll know."

She put the map away and pushed the power button on the oscilloscope. In the dim light, a series of bright green dots danced across the screen. "See that? Right there?" She touched the screen, backed up the tape, and ran it again.

"Mmmm." *Looks like green worms,* I thought. *At least to me.*

"That's the intercept of the radar data, probably tracking an aircraft like I said before. You can tell from looking at the modulation on the pulse that this is the Chinese version of the system, called the HQ-2. Not surprising; that's what the Pakis have and what they would sell. The Chinese have upgraded the SA-2 with modern electronics, improved warheads, and more maneuverability, but it's still vulnerable to sophisticated electronic countermeasures. Jamming."

She looked at me to make sure I understood. I nodded. I knew from experience that if I didn't agree, Kai would launch into a lecture on things like pulse compression techniques, polyphase intrapulse modulation, or, worst of all, 13-bit Barker codes as an example of time-bandwidth product.

"Now look at this." Kai's voice was higher pitched, excited. She pointed to the green dots again. "See those dropouts in the track data? They happen at the same time in each scenario."

I narrowed my eyes and peered at the screen. "Right," I said. "I see them. What do they mean?"

"I can't prove it from just this sample, but I think someone has changed the way this system attacks its targets. It could use an optical camera like some of the newer Russian versions. But maybe it's something really new, something we haven't seen before in this system. Maybe it uses a passive radar target seeker to detect the specific electromagnetic signals emanating from its target. Basically that would mean it uses its target's own jamming frequencies to home in on and destroy it. It wouldn't need the fire control radar all the time, and it would be much more resistant to ECM."

Kai snorted. "Of course, it's highly unlikely that a bunch of Afghans made these tracking upgrades. It had to be the Chinese."

I sat back in my chair. "So . . . you're really telling me two things, right? First, that for some reason the Taliban suddenly think they need air defense systems near Kandahar as well as at Kabul." Kai nodded vigorously. "And, second, that these aren't just the old Soviet-based SA-2s but a new variant that makes them much more deadly."

"Exactly!" Kai smiled and nodded as if I were a prize student. "But what I don't understand, and maybe you can help me out, is why this is happening. Why would this decrepit old country that nobody really cares about think they need to get more and better air defense? Could they possibly think someone is going to attack them?"

"Yes," I said slowly. "I believe they think exactly

that is going to happen." I grabbed Kai's arm. "You have no idea what you've discovered here. It's more than important, it's astounding." I hesitated. "Any chance you ordered imagery?"

"I didn't have to," Kai said. "I called my buddy Agnes down at NIMA, and she checked what had been already snapped. Bingo! She has the radars and missile launchers on film. She's going to write it up."

I grinned. "Great. And Kai . . . did you call our favorite S&T Center?"

Kai wrinkled her nose. "Yep," she said. "And they acted just like they did when we published our infamous missile report. 'Don't do anything until we order the tapes and look at them. We have to verify what you're saying.'" She pounded the table. "Shoot, Alex, that'll take weeks. At least."

"Well, we're not going to wait for them. People need to know this and know what the heck it means. People like the DCI, the secretary of defense, maybe even the president."

"You mean, of the United States? Are you sure?" Kai was shocked at the intensity of my reaction.

"I'm sure enough to bet a paycheck on it. I think this means al Qaeda is planning an attack on a country that will retaliate with modern aircraft and weapons. Almost certainly the U.S. And it would have to be something very big. I'm going to try to get you the clearances I have so you can hear the whole story. In the meantime, let's get a report out of here tonight. Stress the location of the radars; that's fact. But mention the system changes, too, so other analysts can start looking into them. We can use the requisite number of 'possibles' and 'probables' our editors love so much since it's so new, but please start writing. Call me when you have a draft. Let me go back to the Meridian office and write my own version of this to put out in VRK channels."

The gray phone rang, echoing loudly in the empty lab. I picked up the receiver. "Better get back here now," Jacks said. "Those bastards are talking again and you're not gonna like what they're saying."

31

By the middle of the morning, Babrack and Zafir were driving through the provincial capital of Kandahar. The city, like Kabul, was in ruins. Buildings that had not been completely destroyed were mere facades, crumbling away to piles of mud bricks behind their bullet-scarred fronts. Men wrapped in blankets huddled near the streets; many were missing arms or legs. A few women in light blue or mustard-colored burkas, accompanied by a male relative, walked quickly along what was once a sidewalk, holding the hands of thin children. The town was gripped by fear and desperation.

Near the center of the city, a pickup truck filled with the Taliban's ubiquitous morality police stopped and grabbed a shrouded woman. They screamed at her, ignoring her elderly husband who cowered in the shadows, and finally beat her across the shoulders with clubs. Her crime? She was wearing white shoes, a color reserved for the Taliban.

As the two men left Kandahar behind, the sky turned from icy blue to white to a sinister brown. The wind picked up strength and raced moaning through the scattered buildings on the outskirts of the city. "Just what we need," said Babrack, wrapping a scarf around his head. "A winter sandstorm."

The wind swirled across the barren fields, blowing brown particles of dirt and debris across the road. It was impossible to see more than a few feet in front of the jeep, and Babrack drove slowly behind some shacks and stopped in their meager shelter. Both men hunched over and covered their heads.

After about twenty minutes, the wind died down and the sandstorm began to dissipate. Zafir wiped the dirt from his eyes and looked around. Suddenly, he gripped Babrack's arm and shouted over the wind, "What is that?" He pointed to a structure barely visible in the whirling dust.

Off in the distance, a huge walled compound rose ominously from the flat, brown landscape. Just in front of its entrance, several brightly colored plastic palm trees, each about four feet high, bent with the wind. Lights of red, yellow, and blue twinkled incongruously from their branches, flickering and dancing with each gust.

"Hah!" said Babrack. "I have heard of this, but I never saw it before. This house belongs to a man called Mullah Omar. Have you heard of him?"

"Yes," said Zafir, scratching his head. "Yes, I remember seeing that name on a briefing board. He's one of the religious extremists, right? Is he deranged? Those palm trees are very weird."

"Some say he is, but he's also quite clever. He's the leader of the Taliban; has been since 1994. The rumor is that he has only one eye, that the other was blinded by a Soviet rocket during the *jihad*, and that he clawed it out himself in anger. He's very reclusive and very pious. A religious zealot. And he has declared himself

'Commander of the Faithful,' which means he is the spiritual leader of all Muslims in Afghanistan. He and his advisers make the rules—like the ones against laughing—and everyone must follow them."

"How does he get away with that?" Zafir asked.

"People are afraid of him. If someone doesn't agree with him, he just orders his men to kill him."

"The place is immense." Zafir pointed again to the compound, which loomed even more forbiddingly as the sky began to lighten.

"Yes," Babrack agreed. "There's supposed to be a guesthouse, stables for his Arabian horses, even a mosque inside the walls. Along with his own villa, of course, and probably separate houses for each of his wives. Bin Laden built the whole thing for him three years ago. Bin Laden has sworn allegiance to the Mullah as the leader of the faithful and Omar lets the Arab operate his training camps and al Qaeda cells throughout the country. They are very close. In fact, bin Laden's own compound is supposed to be around here someplace."

Zafir shook his head. "Religious extremists and terrorists. Not a good combination, is it?"

"No, it's not. It's an evil partnership."

The two men sat in the jeep and chewed on *naan* as the sky continued to clear. Stale as it was, the bread was delicious, and the warm water they washed it down with made them feel like kings. "As long as we're stopped," Zafir said, "I'll make my last phone call."

"Good idea," Babrack said. "See what you can find out about what we're getting into."

As Zafir opened the Mini Inmarsat case and set up the antenna, a shiny black Land Cruiser with tinted windows raced past them, driving recklessly toward the compound. Two cars followed closely, barely visible in the cloud of dust spun up by the Cruiser.

"Let's get out of here," said Babrack. "You can make the call a little farther down the road." He glanced at his passenger. "I've also heard our friend bin Laden makes his visits here in a black Land Cruiser with his bodyguards following behind."

They stopped two miles away, in view of the raisin factory. It appeared to be deserted. Not a car was there and there was no sign that anyone had been in the place in months. Zafir set up the satellite phone again and placed his call.

"Alex," he said when I picked up on the first ring, "we're here. Do you have any idea what's going on? The place looks like it's vacant."

"It's not," I answered, speaking rapidly. "From what we've heard, Souria is in there but I don't know if she's still alive. Bashir is dead. Apparently he managed to kill the one guard they left with him, and then he killed himself so the terrorists couldn't use Souria to make him talk."

I took a deep breath and continued. "According to our intercepts, they beat up Souria anyway, but if she knew anything she didn't say. Not even that you are there, or that her brother could be involved in the resistance. They gave up. But then, according to the phone conversation, a courier arrived from Pakistan with some kind of news that changed everything. Bin Laden is beyond furious. Before he left, he tied up Souria and his men set a dynamite charge to blow up the warehouse. I don't know what time it's set for, but soon I would guess. Apparently the place is falling down and they were going to destroy it anyway—now they're angry enough to do it with Souria alive inside. And

Gabe, they mentioned 'the other one' again, and said the Pashtu word for 'mud' a couple of times."

"All right, we're going in."

"Wait! There's more—another intercept. Not about this, but it's important."

"No time. I'll call you later."

He flung down the phone. The two men grabbed their weapons and ran toward the building. The blast came when they were getting close, and it slammed them both to the ground. Flames shot out from the roof and black smoke filled the sky.

32

W9D ELINT Lab, Operations Building 1,
National Security Agency
Thursday, December 7, 2000
Midnight

Kai printed out the report and bent over it with
a red pen to make changes. She would have to make
certain it was all accurate and concise; no editors were
around to help her in the middle of the night, and after
what I told her she wasn't going to wait until morning
to publish.

She scanned what she had written:

Subject: Taliban Forces Deploy Upgraded Version of SA-2
near Kandahar, Possibly in Anticipation of Foreign Attack
(TS-TKZ)

Well, that will get everyone's attention, Kai thought.
*Not many tech ELINT reports leave NSA with that kind
of title.*

She read on:

(TS-TKZ) By 4 December 2000, Taliban forces had deployed at least two HQ-2 surface-to-air missile batteries
to an area west of Kandahar (31.608N 65.705E), Afghanistan's second largest city and the spiritual center of

the Taliban government. The HQ-2 is an enhanced model of the Chinese version of the Russian SA-2 SAM system already in place near Kabul.

The rest of the report went on to describe the testing of the radars, the threat of such missile systems and the possibility that the command guidance features could have been changed to make them less vulnerable to electronic countermeasures.

Kai hesitated, then turned back to the computer and added the optional "Comments" section, despite the risk that she might Get in Trouble.

She squared her shoulders and wrote it anyway.

(TS-TKZ) Comments: The presence of the recently deployed air defense systems outside Kandahar and the concentrated testing of the radars suggest that the Taliban forces may anticipate an attack on the area in the near future. The possible new missile guidance upgrades indicate they think this attack will be made by an air force that employs modern jamming techniques, such as the United States.

When Kai called to read me the report, exciting as it was, I found it hard to concentrate on what she was saying. I was frantically worried about what was happening in a raisin warehouse halfway around the world.

"That's good, Kai. Sorry if I sound distracted. People I care about are in terrible danger, and I don't know how in God's name to help them. Give me an hour and I'll hand-carry your report to NSOC and make sure the SRO puts it out tonight. E-mail it to me, okay?"

I hung up the phone and turned to Jacks. "They've got to get out of this. Gabe has to be okay."

"Yeah," Jacks agreed. "He has to get back alive. We

can't both be this miserable." His eyes had the cheerless, dull look of the bereaved.

"What about the other conversation you just heard on the live intercept?" I said. "Tell me again what you heard bin Laden say. And are you certain it was really UBL himself?" I pictured the al Qaeda leader, wind whipping his white robes, holding his phone in some remote area of Afghanistan and growling out the warning we listened to through the tapped microwave phone lines.

He nodded. "I know his voice, and he has a way of clipping a few vowels that makes him unmistakable. Besides, we have this voice recognition software hooked up, and it agrees with me. Not," he snickered, "that I always agree with it."

I nodded. "I believe you. What did he say?"

"Well, a couple of guys were chattering about Souria and the raisin warehouse and all that kind of thing. Suddenly they stopped, and UBL came on the line and told everyone on the network, *'Stop using the phones.'* Then he waited a few seconds and said, *'You will pay for this,'* just like he was talking right to me. It gave me a chill, Alex, I swear it did. Then the comms went silent again. Haven't heard a thing since."

"He knows we're listening to him again, doesn't he?"

"I'd bet on it. But how?"

"I don't know, Jacks." I was so tired I felt like my body was shrinking, melting toward the floor. This was a blow I didn't need. Up until now we were helping Gabe every step of the way; now that would be impossible. We were completely in the dark.

"Gabe is not going to like it when we tell him the comms are gone again," I said wearily.

"No," Jacks agreed. "He's not. All that work and all that danger. All for nothing. But, at least if we get to tell him it means he's still alive."

33

Outside Kandahar, Afghanistan
Thursday, December 7, 2000
Mid-Morning

Babrack and Zafir leaped to their feet and raced toward the burning factory. Flames licked at the rooftop and a wall of heat met them at the door. Through the billowing smoke, they could see the bodies of two men, both in grotesque positions of violent death.

At the back of the large room, invisible in the gloom, a woman coughed and moaned. The men covered their mouths and made their way toward the sounds. At the far end of the room, still surprisingly smoke-free, Souria was on the floor, leaning against a wall, hands tied to a post behind her. Babrack went to his sister and cut her free. He sat on the floor beside her. She lifted her face. One eye was swollen shut and bruises rose darkly from her cheeks and lips. She was unrecognizable.

"How badly are you hurt?" Babrack asked quietly, gently stroking her arm. She winced at even this slight touch. "What happened in here?"

She sat up a little straighter, holding her side. "They came for me a few hours after you left the house," she said. "They tied me up and threw me in a truck and drove me to this horrible place." She coughed again.

"They were going to torture me to make Bashir talk." She closed her eyes. "But he outsmarted them, as you can see."

"Souria, besides what I can see happened to your face, where else are you injured?"

"So much of me hurts it's hard to tell yet. I think several ribs are fractured; perhaps my left wrist is broken. A few other things perhaps. I could use a doctor."

The smoke was creeping toward them. Suddenly, part of the roof shuddered and cracked, raining sparks down on the floor of the room. Most of the warehouse was made of corrugated steel sheets, but the roof and the tables once used to wash grapes were wooden, and there were plenty of them to create a huge bonfire. The sides of the building were bending outward, and the heat inside was rising fast.

"Babrack, for God's sake man, pick her up and let's get out of here. This whole place will collapse soon." Zafir reached down to help.

"Wait," Souria said. "You must bring her along." She pointed to a heap of clothes in a corner. "It's a blond girl, an American. Her name is Katie."

Zafir stared. *Katie? Of course, Katie. That's what they were saying on the phones. Katie, not "mud," not "khátti."*

Zafir cut the rope binding the unconscious girl and put her over his shoulder. He ran with her behind Babrack and Souria from the burning building to their vehicle. Ten minutes later, Babrack pulled over and parked the jeep behind some large rocks. In the distance, the two men and the women could hear thunderous crashing noises, the last of the warehouse burning and falling in on itself.

The girl Katie had awakened from her stupor, but she could not stop shaking. They gave her water and a piece of bread, but she only stared at them. She was pale and thin, and she looked very young. Zafir switched to English, feeling like he hadn't spoken it in years.

"You are safe now, but who are you, child? How did you get here?"

Katie bowed her head. Souria reached out and put a hand on her shoulder, a quiet moment of comfort that touched the girl. After a few minutes of gathering her thoughts, Katie started talking.

34

The STU III rang shrilly in the small space. I
picked it up. "Please tell me you're all right."

"I'm fine. So is Babrack. We got his sister out of the
building before it collapsed. She's hurt pretty badly,
but I think she'll be okay if we can get her out of this
damn country to a doctor." Gabe's voice sounded
weary, dejected.

"But . . . that's all good news. What else is there?
What's wrong?"

"There was another person in the warehouse. A girl.
She says she's twenty years old, but she looks much
younger. We brought her out, too. She's an American.
This is going to be very hard to believe, Alex, but I'm
sure she's telling the truth."

He hesitated and then went on. "Here's the executive
summary: a group of al Qaeda members kidnapped
this girl about two weeks ago from the private school
in Switzerland she was going to and managed to smuggle her into Afghanistan. Some kind of fantastic and
terrifying plane flight that landed somewhere on the
Arabian Peninsula and then another to Kandahar. The
girl said the aircraft was full of weapons. It's going to

take a long time to get all the details, but apparently
she was very upset by her parents' recent separation.
She told a new Saudi friend in Zurich that her father
had deserted her mother and ruined her life because
she would have to leave Switzerland and return home
soon to continue school. That her father thought he
could treat people that way because he was a big deal
executive for some government agency. Then she told
him which agency. Apparently the guy passed that information to someone who passed it on to someone
else who knew immediately how valuable she could be.
She's not in very good shape, physically or emotionally."

Silence. Finally, I choked out, "What?" I tried again.
"What are you talking about, Gabe? That is way too
bizarre to believe!"

"Bizarre or not, Alex, I'm afraid this is not going to
be good news. Not for NSA, not for any of us. They
captured this girl and used her to force her father to
tell al Qaeda about the Meridian intercepts. Her name
is Katie Eckerd."

I closed my eyes. Jacks looked at me in alarm and
touched my shoulder. I shook my head. "Jesus, Gabe,
how did they do that?"

But I already knew the answer.

"They forced her to make a tape to send to her father. An audiocassette tape that they mailed to him at
NSA, along with a small tape player. Katie told her father on the tape that she had been kidnapped and taken
out of Switzerland. She told him her kidnappers would
kill her if he didn't do exactly what they wanted. And
what they wanted was to know if NSA was listening to
their satellite communications." Gabe paused. "Obviously, they managed to trick him into believing that
they already knew they had been compromised and

just needed the details from him. Or frighten him so badly with their threats that he simply caved in. In any case, he told them the truth. Katie told me her father adored her. He must have gone crazy over this."

I bowed my head and tried to believe what I was hearing.

Gabe was still talking. "I've got more bad news. The worst."

I gripped the phone and said nothing, waiting. I knew what it was going to be, and I didn't want to hear it.

Gabe's voice sank to almost a whisper. "Last week, they forced Katie to record another tape. She was terrified, and of course she did it. This time she told her father that her captors wanted to know what NSA was doing to recover the lost intercepts. That they already knew something was in the works and they would kill her if he didn't tell them the truth and that they would fly her home if he did. This time, they couriered the recording to someone in Pakistan who apparently called Paul and played it to him over the phone. I'm afraid Paul might tell them what we've done, Alex. All of this will be for nothing."

"That's what I tried to say to you the last time you called. I think you're right. The courier must have returned from Pakistan with Paul's answer. It looks like Paul told them you're in country and what you're doing there. We intercepted a call about an hour ago. Bin Laden's own voice." I told him what UBL had said. "There's been nothing since."

Neither of us spoke for a moment. Then Gabe said, "Look, I know this is a case of a father trying to save his daughter by any means, but apparently in doing that your DDO has already killed at least one person and may have risked the lives of thousands of Americans.

The only way to redeem anything from this is to make sure Paul Eckerd goes to jail for the rest of his life. I'm going to try my best to get Katie out of this country, where people can talk to her. She won't say a word on the STU. Not to anyone. Hell, she wouldn't talk to the president right now. Not a chance. She's our only proof of what happened except for that damn tape."

"How hard is getting out of there going to be, Gabe?"

"Hard. Pakistan is seventy miles southeast of here and now there are several of us to get across the border. I have to find someplace to get gasoline. The Taliban patrol the roads, and if the comms have gone silent again it means you can't help me anymore." His voice hardened. "Alex, I'm getting us out or I'll die trying just like they say. In the meantime . . ."

"Find the missing tape?"

"Just in case I can't get Katie back there. You need proof of all of this."

"Yes," I agreed, heart pounding.

"Listen to me, Alex, I plan to make it. I will see you in a few days. I'll call you again when we're safe in Pakistan."

"I'll be waiting."

I had to be professional now, no emotions. It wouldn't help Gabe at all, not in this situation. But I added in a low voice, "Please come back to me."

As I hung up the phone, I had another shocking thought: *Now I really have collected SIGINT on a U.S. citizen without a court order. Great NSA reporting chief I am.*

I shrugged. *I'll ask forgiveness later.*

35

Outside Kandahar, Afghanistan
Thursday, December 7, 2000
About Noon

Zafir folded the Inmarsat antenna and packed the phone away in its case. "Well, Babrack, we have some decisions to make."

Babrack sat in the driver's seat of the jeep and stared at the man from America he had so recently met. "Zafir, I am going to tell you what we must do next. We have to hurry and not spend time arguing. I have all the necessary papers to travel to Pakistan. I do it all the time, and I was going to drive you there, as you know. I wouldn't have stayed there though. I would never have left my sister. Now I have to. You must take her out instead of me. She can use my papers. They are perfect. Priceless. They will guarantee her safety."

The men left the jeep and drifted out of range of the two women. "Babrack, I have to take Katie back with me. We don't have papers for both of them."

Babrack took Zafir by the shoulders. "We don't have papers for *either* of them. But think about it: Souria is the only one who can reasonably pass for an Afghan male if we cover her properly. That other child's blue eyes and pale skin will get you killed in a second. We can hide her under the rugs. If the border guards get that far, you're all dead anyway. More papers wouldn't do any good."

Zafir was quiet, thinking, calculating the chances.

"Is it the mission? It must come first, ahead of lives? It's completed, done, and no one will ever make me tell about it." Babrack was pleading. "Souria will die unless you help her. There's nothing, nothing I can do. She must get out of here."

More silence. Neither man spoke for a long time. "All right," Zafir said quietly. "I will do my best." He looked into Babrack's eyes. "What about you, my friend. I will give you plenty of money, but where will you go?" He pulled the money belt from under his shirt and handed Babrack half the Afghanis, worth almost ten thousand dollars and a near fortune in that country.

Babrack pointed to a rundown farm not too far away. A corral held several horses; a couple of them looked to be in fairly good shape. "I will go over there and buy a horse." He grinned. "A good one, maybe a mule or two, and food if they have it to sell. Too bad," he mused, "that I can't just use my own horses and mules, but my neighbors will be happy to take them when I don't return home. I have money, this Kalashnikov, lots of ammunition, a pistol, and these morphine blocks." He reached in the jeep and pulled out the poster they had taken from the microwave tower. "I'm going north, to the Alliance."

They put Souria, dressed in a spare coat with her hair tucked up under a flat wool hat, in the passenger seat. Zafir wrapped her face turbanlike with bands of cloth and braced her bruised body with blankets. The back of the jeep was filled with the prayer rugs he was supposedly crossing into Pakistan to sell. Underneath the rugs was the blond girl Katie, instructed to stay silent no matter what. No crying, no moaning, no movement.

She nodded. "I won't make a sound," she whispered.

"Don't let them stop you at the border except to show your papers," Babrack said. "There should be no problems—give them money if you must—but don't get out of the jeep."

He kissed his sister and murmured something to her. She nodded groggily. Tears welled in Babrack's eyes as he clasped Zafir's shoulders again. "Thank you for giving Souria this chance to live," he said. "If it is the will of Allah that peace ever comes to this land, perhaps I will see her again some day."

He disappeared into the shimmering Afghan daylight, plodding through dusty fields to the farm.

36

Swann Street, Washington, D.C.
Thursday, December 7, 2000
Very Early Morning

The alarm clock rang, a loud and piercing noise in the quiet apartment. Jamal Rashiq reached over and silenced it with a sense of relief. He was awake anyway and had been for some time. It was time to get up and get moving. He showered, dressed in warm, dark clothes, and drank a little tea. He didn't think he should eat anything until he got back home; his stomach was edgy and his whole body zinged with the tension of what he was about to do. He wasn't jittery, exactly, just not as relaxed as he might have wished.

He opened his briefcase and carefully checked its contents. Everything was there, in its designated place; the packets of anthrax with their explosive charges, Mariam's badge, a knife, and the pistol he had bought years ago in San Diego. He shouldn't have a problem getting the briefcase into the NSA complex; when he attended the promotion ceremony he had observed that the guards did not examine anything anyone was carrying as they *entered* the buildings, only what they were carrying as they *exited*. *What a mistake*, he had thought at the time. Now, he only hoped that process hadn't changed.

Rashiq had rehearsed his mission over and over in his head, planning the minute details of where to park, exactly what time to enter the gatehouse, how to stand on the mat in front of the CONFIRM machine, swipe Mariam's badge and enter her PIN, and stay just far enough away from the others who would be going in the building with him so that nobody spoke to him. He was also well aware he might have to improvise at any time. He rocked a little in his chair, going over his plans one more time and taking deep breaths. Finally his heartbeat slowed and a peaceful sense of calm swept over him.

He was doing the right thing, he knew that. This one act would bring the National Security Agency to its knees and destroy half the intelligence gathering capability of the U.S. government for a very long time. Whatever Abdul Majid and his men were planning to do, this would be a huge help to them. They would forgive him for selecting a target that was not on their list. They would be grateful to him forever.

He finished his tea and put the cup in the sink. He would wash it when he got back.

37

I looked at my watch. Two a.m., still hours before the early workers arrived. I was tired and, I suddenly realized, hungry, but it was time, past time, to look for the tape that al Qaeda had used to blackmail Paul. It was around here somewhere, I was sure of that, and it seemed possible to me that Barry might have listened to it somehow and stashed it away someplace before he was killed. If the FBI hadn't found it in the kitchen, the only logical possibility was that it was hidden somewhere in Barry's office. An audacious plan was half-formed in my mind; it was, I knew, the only possible way to search the office. And I had to do it before the halls filled up with people.

I hadn't told Jacks about Paul yet. He would instantly realize that it was Paul who had killed Barry to get the tape and then killed Mariam to cover up his crime—to make sure he wouldn't have to take a polygraph. Jacks would go out right now and find Paul, wherever he was, and strangle him. *Not that he doesn't deserve it,* I thought. But I didn't want Jacks to go to jail.

In one small way, I felt sorry for Paul: his daughter's life was at stake under the worst of circumstances. But there were other ways he could have handled it, none of which involved treason and the murder of two people. Of course, without the blackmail tape, there was no real proof he had done any of it unless Gabe got back safely with Katie. I couldn't count on that, no matter how much I wanted to. I had to find the damn tape; it was the only way I could help.

I printed out Kai's ELINT report and put it in an envelope. "Jacks, I'm taking this down to NSOC. It must go out tonight." He nodded, too tired to talk.

The senior reporting officer read through the report, looked at me, and said, "You're going to cause trouble with this one, I'll bet. Look at that subject line. You might as well attach fireworks to it. Can't you just be obscure like everyone else here is with their titles?" I rolled my eyes and he grinned at me. "It'll be out of here in ten minutes. NSA Alpha distribution, immediate precedence. And you," he grinned again, "you'd better take cover."

I laughed and headed toward the back door but turned just before I reached it and wound my way through what looked like acres of cubicles to the rear of the NSOC area. I rummaged through their emergency toolbox, which they had considerately stored in a back room well out of sight of any curious shift workers. I borrowed a medium-sized, sturdy screwdriver, flat-headed with a black handle, and a small pair of needle-nose pliers. I slipped through the back door adjoining my own organization and walked through the dark to my office. In five minutes I had changed into jeans, a black sweatshirt, and sneakers, always packed in my gym bag in case of emergency. And this was an emergency. I put the screwdriver, pliers, and a small flash-light from the gym bag in my pocket and stepped carefully into the main hallway. It was deserted.

I walked quickly past the main NSOC door and down the hall to a stairway that I knew went to the basement. I stayed close to the walls and weaved quickly in and out of ceiling tile skids, turned two corners, and found the Headquarters Building elevators. At the ninth floor, the doors opened silently and I stepped out. Nobody was around. Just what you would expect in the middle of the night.

I glanced at the towering arrangement of pictures on the wall at the end of the elevator bay. Twenty-seven large and somewhat dated scenes of the National Security Agency filled the space; each set off by a brass-colored frame and mounted on a dark-paneled wall. These were mostly pictures of people listening on earphones, greeting one another in conference rooms, smiling, and cheerfully doing the work of protecting the country. The collage had been placed there years ago to greet visitors when the Director's office was still on this floor of the Headquarters Building. Some of the pictures were old enough to be in black and white, but the arrangement was still oddly appealing, even in the dim light.

Because the ninth floor, the highest in this building, had housed DIRNSA's office before OPS 2B was built, it was decorated differently from any other floor in the Agency. The walls were covered in light brown and cream-colored waffle-textured wallpaper, probably *de rigueur* for the times. The wallpaper had faded a bit, but was still shockingly sophisticated for an NSA hallway.

The raised hallway floor was made up of two-by-two-feet square tiles found in many of the NSA corridors, even the "new" buildings. The flooring supports on the ninth floor were hardly typical, however, since they were covered with squares of reddish-brown tweed carpet instead of regulation off-white vinyl. Some had frayed edges or worn spots, but the combination of dated carpet and shabby wallpaper hinted at a much grander time.

The squares on every floor, whether carpeted or not, were designed to be popped out to provide instant access to the thousands of feet of electrical wiring that ran everywhere under the floors. This type of flooring, called under-floor raceway, is typically installed in a series of parallel steel grids to provide a flexible arrangement for power and communication cables. It is a common installation in office buildings everywhere, allowing easy access to electrical wiring. Pry a square up with a screwdriver and you had access to the entire subfloor grid.

I had often glanced down at the hole left by a pulled tile, gleefully called engineer traps by those analysts without actual engineering degrees, when contractors were pulling or pushing wiring through the space below. I knew there was probably enough room down there for a person to fit, should anyone really want to do so, but I didn't know how difficult it would be to actually move from place to place. And, most important, I didn't know if there were any kind of steel grates or other barriers to delineate and shield office spaces.

I would soon find out. I could think of no other way to get into Barry Ballard's office to search for the missing tape. I certainly wasn't on the authorized key list for this space. I would pry up a hallway tile and crawl through the underground raceway into the suite of rooms Barry had shared with Paul Eckerd, then search quickly and crawl back out.

This is so risky, I thought for the hundredth time. *But not nearly as risky as what Gabe is trying to do.*

I walked quickly down the darkened ninth-floor hallway, passing doorways with signs that read "Visitors'

Dining Room" (a leftover from the old days when
DIRNSA occupied the ninth floor), "DO Intelligence
Staff" (where we hold our daily seven-thirty meetings),
and "Messenger Mail Only Slot" (another outdated
sign). Finally, so curious that I stopped for a moment
to stare, 9A162's office title was posted in a neatly
handwritten script:

> *Not Much of Anything, Really*

In stark contrast, the door at the very end of the corridor had a dignified brass plaque that read:

> SUITE 9A138
> DEPUTY DIRECTOR FOR OPERATIONS
> MR. PAUL ECKERD
> DEPUTY DIRECTOR FOR SECURITY
> MR. BARRY BALLARD

I knew that inside the entrance was a six-foot alcove
with two more doors, one straight ahead to Paul's office
space and one on the right to Barry's. It seemed about a
hundred years ago that I had ruled out Paul Eckerd as a
suspect because he and Barry were longtime friends.

And because I saw the bastard crying at the funeral.

I pulled my hair into a ponytail so it wouldn't get
caught on steel gridwork or loose wiring. I looked
around, saw no one in the quiet corridor, pulled out the
screwdriver, and knelt on the hallway floor. The tile
popped out neatly when I pried it up, and I took a deep
breath and slid into the dark space below. I pulled the
carpet tile back over the opening and found several

holes on its underside that allowed me to grip it and pull it silently back in place. In seconds, I had disappeared completely from the world above me.

Much as I had wished several times that there had been cameras in the halls the night Barry was murdered, I was sure glad right now there weren't any. No one had ever imagined there would be a time when cameras inside the complex would be necessary. *Soon they'll be everywhere,* I thought, *even in the elevators, Las Vegas–style.* I snickered a little, shaking my head in the dark. *Cameras will certainly cut back on all the sex that goes on in here.*

I was entombed in a small, pitch-black space. I hoped I was alone. I had heard the stories of rodents chewing on wiring under the floors in several areas at NSA, but I didn't hear any hint of tiny feet scurrying or tiny teeth munching.

I turned on the small flashlight and moved its beam in a semicircle. Dust balls the size of grapefruit lurked in the distance, and a brown, gritty substance covered most of the subfloor. I estimated the raceway to be about fourteen inches high, enough room for me to wriggle through fairly easily if I was careful. Cables and wires snaked everywhere, challenging my route with tangled traps. But, hallelujah! The underfloor ducting was open as far as I could see, with no security grates marking the office perimeters.

I listened carefully for footsteps as I began to crawl through the open doorframe into the alcove. I doubted if my pencil-beam light would shine through the carpet tiles, but I did not want to take any chances. I flicked off the light and slid across the grit and the grids, bent my body to the right between steel supports, and moved cautiously through the darkness into the area under Barry's office. About six feet in, I turned the light back

on and carefully scanned the surrounding area for a
very small, plastic audiocassette. I spent several minutes in this search, knowing it could spare me considerable time and agony if I could spot it quickly. It wasn't
there. Two things were clear: Barry hadn't hidden the
tape under his office floor, and the undisturbed dirt and
grime betrayed the FBI's failure to search here. Finally,
I turned off the light and lay still, listening for any hint
of activity above me.

Silence.

I pushed up on a tile. It didn't move. I pushed harder.
Nothing. Suddenly a small furry body scuttled past
my face, just brushing my lips. I panicked, banging
my head against the tile above me and biting my
tongue. Finally I lay quietly, wiping my mouth over
and over with the back of my hand.

When my breathing returned to normal, I slithered a
few more feet and tried pushing upward again. This
time the tile popped right out, and I followed it as
quickly as I could manage. I stood up over the opening
and brushed myself off, and then replaced the floor covering. The tiny flashlight showed I was in the right area,
and that I had tried first to move a tile that supported a
large, heavy file cabinet with a combination dial lock.
The door to the cabinet was open, the space inside empty.
Nearby were Barry's wooden executive desk and an arrangement of chairs around a small coffee table. Framed
pictures of his family were everywhere.

It took about thirty minutes to search every square
inch of the office. Under chairs, in the radiators, desk
drawers and trays, window sills, pictures. I checked to
see if a cassette was taped behind the toilet tank in the
small shared bathroom, as in *The Godfather*. I
searched the small conference room between the two
offices, tipping over the table to look for hollow legs or

other possible hiding places. I looked anywhere a tiny cassette might be hidden, even tipping each ceiling tile to be sure it wasn't up there. It wasn't.

I walked to the office door and opened it slowly. Ahead of me was a visitors' waiting area with a secretary's desk and a couch and another door to the hall. I crossed this vestibule and tried the knob on the door to Paul Eckerd's adjoining office. It wasn't locked and I went in. Dim light from the security lights outside filtered through blinds on a large window, and I could see the outlines of a desk and a bookcase. I flipped on my flashlight again and moved the beam over the bookcase.

Paul's taste in books was eclectic, to say the least, varying from *The History of Fiber Optics* to *Managing Projects, Leading People* and *Special Features of the Contact Interaction of a Gun Bore with a Shell Obturating Band*. I shook my head and wondered if Paul had read them all. Or—a sudden thought—written them all. He was, I knew, supposed to be one of the most brilliant people who had ever worked at NSA.

I searched this office, too, not quite so intensely. I wasn't really sure what I was looking for. I didn't believe for a minute that Paul had taken the tape from Barry after he killed him. If he had, he wouldn't have needed to come to my house to stop me from looking for it. But as long as I was here, I could look around.

I played my flashlight beam across the office. A vanity wall held framed diplomas, certificates, letters of appreciation and thanks from government officials from several agencies. In the middle was a picture of Paul and his wife, obviously preseparation, with President Reagan, whose autograph was scrawled across the top.

On Paul's desk was a large framed photograph of him with his arm around a young blonde girl, presumably his daughter Katie. The drawers were locked, but under the desk was a leather briefcase, identical to the one I had seen lying near Barry's body. I pulled it out, fingering the soft leather and the raised NSA seal, and looked at it carefully. What had happened to the bloodstains? Why would Paul have Barry's briefcase? Surely the FBI had taken it away for evidence. It was unlocked and empty except for a handful of business cards inscribed with Paul's name and title. I shook my head. This wasn't Barry's briefcase; it was Paul's. Apparently theirs were identical.

A sudden thought jolted my heart into a thumping beat: *Maybe that's how Barry got the tape to begin with—he and Paul were at a meeting together and Barry picked up Paul's briefcase by mistake and thought it was his. He must have found the cassette Katie made inside the briefcase and listened to it. But then what?*

I checked my watch: almost three a.m. It was time to leave. I got my bearings and planned my escape route back under the underground raceway, prying up a tile directly in front of the door to the suite so that I wouldn't have to wriggle around through any more ninety-degree turns. I slipped under the floor, stretched out my legs, and reached up to pull the carpet tile back into place. Just as it popped back into its space, I heard the door above me open, missing the tile by a space the thickness of a shadow.

Footsteps, heavy over my head, marched into the office and stopped. A man coughed, dropped something metal, cursed. I stopped breathing. It was Paul. *God above, what's he doing here? It's three o'clock in the morning. If he finds me, he'll kill me.*

38

This was supposed to be the easy part, Zafir thought as he bumped along the road back to Kandahar. He should be winding down, relaxing beside Babrack as he drove the two of them along what the Afghans quaintly referred to as a "highway." Instead, without Babrack's help, he was smuggling two women out of the country—one, unbelievably, an American—and trying not to get lost or break down. Babrack had assured him several times that the jeep was fitted out with a rugged suspension system, and so far it seemed to be working well. That reassured him somewhat, but he knew the rickety bridges, crumbling tunnels, and washed-out road that lay ahead would be a challenge. *At least it's easy to stay awake.*

Souria slept peacefully beside him, occasionally stirring and opening her eyes. Near Kandahar, she awoke and sat up.

"You are a brave man," she said. He thought she was smiling at him, but her face was covered and he could only tell by the tiny lines that crinkled at the corners of her eyes. Her right eye was still swollen shut, turning black and purple. He squeezed her hand and smiled back.

"I know a shortcut around the city," she said, "if you would like to try it."

"Yes, please," Zafir replied. "A dirt road can't be any worse than this, and we're picking up a lot of truck traffic."

She pointed out a hard-packed shingle road just west of Kandahar and Zafir turned onto it gratefully. Soon it deteriorated into a fractured, crumbling track, but it was empty of other vehicles. The landscape was dreary, scattered here and there with low brushwood and thorny plants. A few tiny villages dotted the countryside, but no one came out of the crumbling mud-brick houses to watch them drive by. The going was slow, but safer than the main road. They stopped for an hour out of sight of any curious eyes to rest and eat some of the dried food Zafir had brought with him. He dug Katie out of the heap of rugs and offered her food, but she refused to eat. He forced her to drink water, and then Souria kept watch while Zafir napped.

After another hour they had bypassed Kandahar and rejoined the main thoroughfare to Spin Boldak. It was difficult in many places to tell that the road had once been paved. Erosion carved huge ruts through the worn and pitted blacktop, and holes of every size lurked dangerously. In some places, the surface was sunken; in others, ridged. Trucks rumbled along in both directions, slowing the traffic to a crawl in several areas. A few men on wobbly bicycles rode down the sides of the road, risking injury with every truck that passed them. Donkey carts piled high with goods joined in as well, plodding along unconcernedly as vehicles swished by.

Occasionally, a pickup truck full of armed Taliban

forced everyone off what was left of the pavement as they pushed their way through the mass of vehicles. Zafir worried each time the militia appeared. He knew the Taliban military arm patrolled the major roads and restored order by force, which included many on-the-spot executions. But none of them gave his jeep a second glance.

"My goal is to get to the border at Spin Boldak before dark," Zafir told Souria. "I thought this trip might take as long as four hours. Now I must admit it may be longer. Even so, I'm hopeful we will be there before nightfall." He had made an Inmarsat call to the consulate at Karachi before he and Souria left their resting place south of Kandahar. His contact there told him the Company was very angry they hadn't heard from him for so long, but the man promised Zafir an escort would be waiting for him at dusk just on the Pakistan side of the border. It was a necessary escort: the route through Baluchistan from the border town of Chaman to Quetta was notorious for bandits and anarchy. Even Afghan highways were safer.

At Quetta, Zafir and the two women would board a plane and fly away to safety in Karachi—although "safe" was not a word normally used to describe Karachi, one of the world's most lawless cities.

Then I'll go back to Langley and listen to them tell me how irresponsible I was, Zafir thought. *That nothing, nothing, must ever interfere with a mission. Even rescuing an American will not make up for my sins. They will probably stick me back behind a desk for the rest of my "career."* He sighed. Life had gotten complicated. He had anticipated problems, injury, perhaps even his own death, but not this entanglement. *Don't think about it now.*

He drove on at a sluggish pace, only occasionally

able to pick up enough speed to feel very optimistic about their escape. Fuel was a problem; the gauge had registered empty for some time. His extra petrol tanks, both small, were dry. About ten miles from the border at Spin Boldak the jeep began shuddering, running on fumes. Zafir managed to pull off the road behind a tumbled down shack and into the filtered shade of a solitary olive tree. He set up his satellite antenna and dialed Alex's STU number. She needed to know what was happening.

A few seconds later, two pickup trucks of armed Taliban militia pulled up beside them. The men in the truck beds glared with dark, hard eyes at Zafir and Souria.

39

I carefully eased out a breath and slowly drew one in. Blood had rushed to my head and was pounding in heartbeat time in my ears, obscuring the sounds from above. I shut my eyes and concentrated on staying statue-still. *Please,* I prayed, *no more furry creatures under here with me.*

The footsteps receded, moving, I thought, toward the back of the office. *What if he stays there until morning? Until the halls fill up with people and I can't get out?*

I inched forward and stopped. What if I make a noise? Sneeze? My eyes flicked from side to side, searching the darkness. My underfloor compartment was cold and tomblike.

Off in the distance, I heard a toilet flushing and water running. A few minutes later, Paul started pacing back and forth over my hiding place.

Then, suddenly, he stopped and stood silently, as if he were listening for something. An icy hush filled the air, seeping down through the tiles into my hiding place. Goose bumps raised chillingly on my arms.

He knows I'm here, I thought, panic rising in my throat.

I waited, terrified, for him to start pulling up tiles; to reach down and grab me by the neck. I started to choke as this irrational fear charged through my body.

Paul started pacing again. My breathing eased. I closed my eyes tight. *Go away,* I prayed. *Just go away.*

Finally, he did just that. He opened the door and walked out, carefully locking it behind him. I heard him walk away down the hall, oblivious to the incredible scene he had just missed. I lay there exhausted for several minutes and finally slithered under the doorframe and into the main corridor. I listened again for several minutes. Then I pushed up on a floor tile and peeked out at the hallway. It was silent, darkened, and deserted, and Paul was not waiting to grab me as I emerged from my underworld journey.

I exited the raceway, put the tile back into place, and nearly jumped the four steps to the stairwell. I had to get away from the ninth floor and Paul's office quickly, and I knew I could probably run down the steps faster and safer than walking back to the elevators that had brought me there. I beat at my clothes to wipe off the filth as I raced down the stairs. It was cold there; the stairwell was an unheated fire exit of old, dull gray cinderblock, but I barely noticed.

At the bottom of the steps, I slammed to a stop, feet tangled and eyes wide. On the floor, a memorial plaque and silk flowers marked the place where, two years before at Christmas, a lonely and troubled Airman First Class had thrown himself off the top of the stairwell and fallen nine floors to end his life.

God, is there nothing in this agency but death? I bowed my head and hurried away.

Within minutes I was walking through the basement, retracing my earlier path toward OPS 1. I kept moving until I reached the Meridian office, wiping my dirty face with my sleeve as I punched in the code and opened the door. My glow of relief drained away as I looked at Jacks, sitting on the cot, head in his hands.

He looked up at me and snapped, "Where the hell have you been? You've been gone for over an hour. You and I both know there's a murderer in this building, maybe even now." He stood up and put his hands on his hips. "Damn it Alex, we're not dealing with a car thief. We've got a killer here. If you're going to wander around this place in the middle of the night, at least take me with you."

"Okay, okay. I'm sorry I worried you."

Jacks shook his head. "You didn't just worry me, damn it, you terrified me. Now, stay here while I go down the hall and get a Coke. Promise me."

"Yes, I promise. Get me one, too, please. And a candy bar if there is one."

Five seconds after he left, the STU III rang. I answered slowly, still vibrating from the narrow escape from Paul.

"Alex," Gabe said, breathless, "listen to me. You have to find the tape Katie made. You might need it. I'm not sure we're going to get out of here. We're boxed in by two vehicles full of Taliban militia and they don't look happy to see us."

I heard the roar of truck engines in the background before the phone went dead.

40

Southeastern Afghanistan
Thursday, December 7, 2000
Afternoon

The trucks spun around in a swirling cloud of dust
until they were facing the jeep. Zafir and Souria sat
and watched as two bearded, black-turbaned men
climbed out of the cab of the closest truck and walked
toward them, waving automatic weapons and ordering
them to get out of their vehicle. Three men remained
in the truck bed, and several more were in the other
pickup. All had weapons.

Zafir passed a Kalashnikov to Souria and took one
of the assault rifles for himself. Between them, he figured, they had plenty of firepower. But so did the Taliban, and there were a lot more of them.

"The only way out of this is to kill them," he whispered to Souria. "I'll get the two walking toward us
and the ones in the truck behind them. When I start to
fire I want you to empty your weapon into the other
truck. Just press on the trigger until you run out of
bullets. Can you do that?"

"I can," she said through gritted teeth.

Zafir opened his door and stepped out of the jeep.
He held up a hand and spoke to the two Talibs walk-

ing toward him. "We ran out of gas," he said. "Can you help us? My brother and I are driving to Pakistan to sell rugs."

The two men lowered their weapons. "Walk away from the jeep," they said. "Let us see you."

Zafir picked up the AK-47 from the driver's seat with his right hand and aimed it through the open window of the driver's side door. He killed both the Talibs with the same burst and they fell several yards from the jeep.

Souria pushed her rifle out the passenger window, balanced it on the frame to keep the weight off her injured wrist, and aimed it at the men in the other truck. Her cap fell off her head and her long, dark hair spilled out over the shoulders as she began firing.

Zafir turned his AK-47 toward the truck bed on his side. Two of the men fell immediately; the third ducked behind the side panel of the truck and waved his arm. "Stop firing!" he begged.

Bullets pinged against the jeep as Zafir turned his attention to the right. Souria had blown out the front window of the other pickup and silenced all the men, except one standing in the back, firing at them with a sweeping motion of her weapon. Zafir stepped away from the jeep, raised his rifle, and shot the man through the chest.

Suddenly silence returned to a world that had been thundering with gunshots and screaming. Only the huddled man in the truck bed made any noise, still begging for his life. "Shut up!" Zafir said in Pashtu, then repeated in Dari. The man raised his arms and stood. "*Bandi*," he said, pointing to himself. Prisoner. Zafir nodded and motioned him out of the truck.

Souria sank back in the passenger seat. She looked

at Zafir and smiled. "There's an Afghan proverb," she said, "that might apply here: 'Cage a cat and get a tiger.'"

"You truly are a tiger, Souria," he agreed. "Perhaps you'd like to come home with me and be my body-guard?"

She nodded wearily. "Perhaps. You seem to need one from time to time."

Zafir walked away from the jeep. He kept his rifle trained on the man standing by the truck as he checked the others. They were all dead. *"Teel?"* he asked the man. The man nodded vigorously and pointed to the truck. Two large black and yellow jerry cans full of gasoline were strapped to a rack. "Get them," Zafir ordered. He watched as the man unloaded the cans and filled the jeep with gas. When he was finished, Zafir tied the man to the olive tree and turned to leave. "Please," the man pleaded, "you can't just leave me here. There's no water. No one can see me. I will die."

Zafir glanced at him with contempt. "It won't be long at all before someone shows up to see why those pickups are parked out there," he said. "Although it's hard to say just who that might be. But you have a bet-ter chance than you were going to give us." He glanced at Souria. "What do you think?"

Souria looked at the man, then at Zafir. She shrugged. "Let's go," she said. "Let's get out of this miserable country."

Zafir pulled back the pile of rugs in the back of the jeep. Katie was awake and uninjured. She looked up at him with huge, solemn eyes. Zafir gave her water and covered her again and got back in the jeep. They re-joined the line of vehicles on the pitted road, headed for Pakistan and freedom. It would not take very long to get there.

Souria fell back into a deep sleep, stirring only occasionally. As they approached the border crossing, Zafir gently shook her awake. She moaned and sat up, holding her side. She adjusted her headpiece and face wrapping until only her eyes showed, the bruise grown blacker and even more noticeable. Zafir whispered over his shoulder to Katie to stay still and silent. A muffled answer signaled her agreement.

They drove up to the checkpoint behind a long line of trucks. The border guard, bored and indifferent, looked at their papers. "What happened to him?" he asked, nodding at Souria.

"A fight with his uncle," Zafir said. "You should see the uncle."

The guard laughed, waved them on. A tinny phone rang in the guard shack, and a man ran out as the jeep pulled forward.

"Stop them! Don't let them through!"

Zafir gunned the jeep, glancing off the iron security bar as it began to drop in front of them. As they barreled across the border into Pakistan, automatic weapons began to fire from behind them. Bullets banged off the sides of the vehicle and whistled through the back window to smash into the windshield. He and Souria both slid down in their seats.

Waiting for Zafir on the Pakistan side was the escort the consulate had sent to protect him on his way to Quetta. Two of the escort vehicles were big SUVs, roofs cut off and fitted with their own automatic weapons much like the old Somali "technicals" Zafir had seen on the news. The escort surrounded the jeep, firing back at the Taliban guards, and then driving off to the east with Zafir's jeep in the middle of the pack. The vehicles were filled with rough-looking men, laughing and jeering and driving fast.

Zafir felt like he could finally breathe again. They had escaped. Unbelievably, they had gotten out of Afghanistan. Only three more hours to Quetta.

"We made it, Souria. We're in Pakistan. We'll find you a doctor and soon you'll be back in Paris." Zafir glanced over at the woman beside him, hoping for a smile. She was slumped against the door of the jeep. He looked again, sharply. A bullet had hit her in the back of the head, flowering out in a crimson hole just above her eyes.

Souria would not smile again.

41

Near Chaman, Pakistan
Thursday, December 7, 2000
Afternoon

Five years ago, Mubashar had two hundred goats, as many sheep, and fifty camels. He was the leader of a caravan of *Kuchis*, the Dari term for Afghanistan's nomads. Severe drought and ethnic hostility from landholding warlords had gradually extinguished his way of life. His animals died, his caravan scattered, and his family was starving when he moved them to a refugee camp in Pakistan near Chaman. Conditions were dangerous and unsanitary. There was never enough food or water. But it was better than their existence inside Afghanistan. Mubashar hired himself out as a day laborer whenever he could to buy something for his wife and children to eat.

He had just finished working on his job for the day, digging drainage channels and filling potholes in the sunken tracks of the road, when a convoy of vehicles coming from the direction of Spin Boldak pulled to the side of the highway and stopped. He leaned on his shovel and watched as the man in the driver's seat of a jeep put his arms around the shoulders of a motionless woman in the passenger seat. The man stayed like that for several minutes, head bowed.

He's holding a dead woman, Mubashar thought.

When a girl with blond hair crawled out from under a pile of rugs in the back of the jeep, Mubashar's eyes opened wide in amazement. He had never seen hair that color before. *Inglestan,* he thought. *Perhaps American. What is she doing here?*

Finally, the driver got out of the jeep and walked to the vehicle behind him, a banged-up Land Cruiser with two men in the front. He spoke to them for some time, then handed them what looked to the *Kuchi* like a great deal of money. The men got out of the Land Cruiser and carried the body in the jeep's passenger seat to the back of the Cruiser, covering it gently with a blanket. They drove off on a dirt road to the south, clouds of dust swirling high into the air.

The man stood beside the jeep and watched them leave until they were out of sight and then slowly got back in the driver's seat. The blond girl was already in the seat on the passenger side. It looked to Mubashar like she was crying. The jeep left with the remainder of the convoy, driving quickly in the direction of Quetta.

Mubashar shrugged and began his long walk to the camp.

42

I hung up the STU and raced out of the Meridian office and up the steps to the first floor. I had to move, go out and do something. I couldn't just sit around and worry that Gabe was dead. I would go look for the tape again.

The cassette was still at the murder scene. It had to be there; I was certain it was; it was the only place left. Barry must have been able to hide it or somehow tossed it away as he was being killed. I could only imagine his desperation and terror.

I headed for the old kitchen, walking fast. It wasn't even a week since I had discovered Barry's body there, but the darkened halls seemed unfamiliar and foreboding. Finally, down long corridors and around the corner, was the snack bar area, cordoned off by the police "Do Not Cross" tape, but the guard was gone. I slipped past the tape, ignored the "No Trespassing" signs stuck to the kitchen's boarded-up entrance and pulled the creaking plywood open far enough so I could squeeze through.

I stepped down inside the tiny deserted kitchen, an ink-black and eerie place. I could smell the coppery odor of blood. No one had cleaned away the remnants of brutal death.

I flicked on my tiny flashlight, half expecting that Barry's corpse would still be sprawled on the ancient green tile floor. It wasn't, of course, but a thick yellow chalk mark traced its ghostly outline.

I moved the light around the room slowly, looking again at the bare hanging light bulb and the large rusty grill abandoned when the area was boarded off years ago. In the far corner stood a rack of metal shelves I hadn't noticed before. On the wall facing the hallway, a green linoleum countertop covered with more than two decades of dust was obscured from imaginary customers by a huge corrugated metal pull-down grate. I could almost hear the echo of its last rackety ride down the side rails, slamming shut forever.

I moved around the perimeter of the small kitchen, shining the light at the baseboards as I walked. The outside hallway was about ten inches higher than the kitchen floor. Someone had nailed sturdy pieces of plywood all around the bottom opening where the green tiles did not meet the flooring outside the kitchen. Perhaps plans to close the snack bars were in place when the raised hallway flooring was installed, and no one wanted to bother to raise the level of the kitchen because soon it wouldn't be necessary.

After my circuit trip, I stood near the doorway where I guessed Barry must have stood in his last few seconds of life and tossed the screwdriver from the NSOC tool chest backward with my right hand. I turned quickly and watched where it hit the plywood before ricocheting away into the middle of the room.

I picked up the screwdriver and, kneeling on the dirty tiles, pried away the boards at the bottom of the wall where the impact had occurred. In this area, as in most of the rest of the kitchen, the boards did not quite touch the floor. Enough space existed for an object slightly thinner than the round-handled screwdriver to slide underneath. A tiny cassette, for example. When I finished pulling off all the plywood from that side of the room, I lay flat on the tiles and reached my hand holding the flashlight into the newly visible opening at the kitchen boundary.

Just inside was an ancient frying pan, cast iron, blackened with age and grime. A few feet away, a carving fork caught the light with a dull reflection, its two long tines nearly smothered in dust. Wires snaked here and there with the nonchalance of a child's design, and the green tiles were blackened with grease and dirt. For the first time, a hint of doubt crept into my brain. Even if the tape were here, I'd never be able to see it.

But I did.

The pencil beam swept slowly over the debris and power cords. I strained my eyes so hard I nearly missed the miniature cassette, its tiny plastic body finally catching and faintly reflecting my light. It lay well beyond my reach, a priceless gem, waiting serenely, patiently, for its discovery.

I wondered why the FBI hadn't pried the boards loose in their search for the tape the night Barry was killed. Were they convinced that the murderer must have taken it? Or maybe they pulled up the flooring around the outside of the kitchen instead. It would have been much easier than what I was doing and potentially more productive. But if they tried it, the cassette must have been so hidden by the wires and filth that they missed it. Or maybe by the time they got to that, Mariam's death made further searching unnecessary in their minds.

Apparently Paul didn't know Barry had flung the cassette away and that it had skidded under the boards and into its underground tomb. Was the throw intentional? It must have happened in the struggle, when Paul was too distracted to notice. He might even have accidentally kicked it under the board himself. Imagine his fury when he discovered the recorder and not the tape with all its damning evidence. The evidence he had killed Barry to get.

I reached into the darkness and stretched my arm farther, farther, pushing my shoulders under the flooring until I could grasp the carving fork. I buried my mouth in my sleeve and took a deep, nearly dust-free breath, and twisted and writhed until I finally forced my shoulders into the small under-floor space. Connectors and rivets and rough edges snagged my clothes, and I had to stop frequently and detach myself from their snarling grip. I was filthy and getting more disgustingly so every second. *I'll never get the damn tape out of there,* I thought.

But I did.

My head and shoulders were all the way under the floor before I could reach the cassette with the outstretched utensil. I scraped it back with the prongs, making several tries before I succeeded, and finally it skittered back into my waiting hand. I put my head down with a sigh.

Extricating myself from my underground enclosure was nearly as difficult as entering it. I was repulsively dirty and smelled of rancid cooking oil, but my exuberance trumped it all. I clawed and crawled my way back into the kitchen, turned off my penlight, and sat in the dark, smiling in the silence.

His voice came quietly out of the darkness, floating

like a specter's might, as he took hold of my arm and sat down beside me.

"You found it, didn't you?" His voice was exhausted, almost indifferent. "Just like I thought you would."

I jumped and tried to pull away, but his grip was strong. "How did you know I was here?" I whispered.

"I've been in the building since after midnight," Paul said. "I don't sleep much anymore. I had some things to do here anyway. I was on my way to NSOC when I saw you come up the steps from the basement a while ago, and I followed you. I thought you might be going back to my office. It felt different in there, like someone had been looking through my things. You were there tonight, weren't you?"

I nodded in the darkness. Paul kept talking. "I can't even imagine how you got in," he said. "You are certainly one resourceful person. You move around NSA like a panther."

He stirred a bit, changing his position. "After you left the basement, I followed you all the way down the long hall, but you never noticed. Clearly you were on a mission, and I knew just what it was. You found the damn tape like you said you would. And now you're going to give it to me."

43

The darkness expanded and thickened. It pulsed against my chest and face and choked me as I breathed in its urgent warning of certain death.

I moved slightly and Paul's grip firmed. "Stay still, Alex, or I will have to kill you."

"You're planning to kill me anyway, whether I stay still or not, Paul. I know you came to my house this week to stop me from finding the tape. I know everything. I know you gave up the Meridian comms. I know you just told them we tapped into their microwave links. And I know you murdered Barry. Barry picked up your briefcase instead of his, didn't he? They were so much alike they probably felt just the same to him. He must have listened to the tape and wondered what was going on. But he made the mistake of asking you about it, didn't he? And you brought him here to kill him. And then," I took a breath, "then you killed Mariam so you wouldn't have to take a polygraph that would certainly show you were the one who betrayed us and murdered Barry."

"You're good, Alex. That fucking briefcase was the reason this all happened. Barry always liked mine so much—the way it felt—that I bought him one just like it last summer for his birthday. I should never have done it, but how could I know? I just wanted to make him happy.

"I didn't bring Barry to this kitchen to kill him, though. We were walking out together after DIRNSA's Friday night meeting, on our way to Gatehouse 2. A car was meeting him there to take him home. He was telling me about listening to the tape that Katie made. This was just a good detour, a quiet place to talk. In case anyone else came along."

He was silent a long time, still gripping my arm. "I didn't want to kill Barry," he moaned. "He was my friend. I loved him. I didn't want to kill the girl, either. It all spiraled out of control. I had no choice."

I turned toward his voice, my movements slow in the thick black air. "Why did you do it then, Paul?" I asked quietly and carefully, as you would to a small child. "There must have been another way."

"I tried to explain to Barry what would happen if he turned me in to Security—that Katie would die. I thought he might help me. But he wouldn't listen. He just kept saying he would tell them the truth if I didn't. I couldn't let that happen. I begged him to help me. It didn't work."

"But, Paul, wouldn't it have been better to tell Security what was going on from the beginning? Think about what you've done to Katie and to the Agency. Maybe to the whole country."

"I couldn't risk it." He shook my arm. "You don't have a child, damn it. You don't know how I feel. She is so special. She's all I have left in my life to love."

"The dog?" I asked quietly. "Why didn't you kill the dog?"

"I couldn't. I just couldn't. She looked at me with

those big eyes and I couldn't kill her, too. I told you, I didn't want to kill *anyone*." A pause, then, "I forgot they shredded burn bags at that time of night. Perhaps," his voice fell away to a whisper, "I wasn't thinking very clearly by then."

I couldn't think of a thing to say. I sat in silence, listening to Paul's anguished breathing.

He groaned. "Katie's probably dead by now anyway. They're not going to send her back. I was stupid to think they would."

"Paul, thirty minutes ago Katie was alive and on her way to Pakistan," I said, hoping it was still true. "Let's take the tape to Security together. If you give it to them, you'll have some proof that you were forced to do what you did. And at least Katie will forgive you. That's what you really care about now, isn't it? You can't possibly imagine you can get away with all this."

In the blackness, I could feel Paul's emotions flash from hope to despair to anger.

"On the way to Pakistan? Right," he spat. "You're lying. What do you know about it anyway? How do you know where she is?" He shook my arm again, harder. "Who in God's name are you? And how do you know so much?" His hand on my arm was jittery, his words shaky and disturbed. "Damn you, you've been everywhere. You have been my curse from the beginning."

"Paul, you've got to listen to me." I was pleading, there's no denying it, for my life, but also for Katie, for NSA. "You have a chance to explain it all. You have a chance to be honorable about it. And you have a chance to get Katie back. Come with me." I tried to stand. Paul banged my head against the wall and a crack like thunder jolted my brain. I twisted away from him, hard, but he had too tight a grip.

"Just give me the tape now, Alex. We don't have time for this." He shifted his body and slid his hand down my arm to my hand.

"All right," I said. I flicked on the flashlight with my left hand and shined it directly in his face, only inches from mine. He brought his hand up to his eyes and I tossed the tape back into the under-floor area as far as I could. I knew if it slid back more than about four feet, it could be impossible for him to retrieve. Paul was a big man. He could never squirm his way through that space, no matter how desperate he might be.

He knocked away the flashlight, and if I hadn't moved so quickly the knife he struck me with would surely have hit a more lethal target. Instead, he buried the steel blade deep in my left shoulder. A surge of cold fire ran through my side and down my arm. I could feel the blood in my body rush to the wound and pulse down my side as he pulled the knife out to strike again.

More calmly than I thought possible, I moved my right hand over the floor, searching for the carving fork I had used to drag the tape from under the tiles. When I found it, I picked it up and lunged toward Paul. The tiny penlight still shone dimly from across the room, and I could see a shadowy outline of his face. He was reaching for me, a grisly look of resolve in his eyes when I struck out with the fork. I hit his jugular on the first try, an unnecessary blessing, really, since I would have kept stabbing him until I caused a fatal wound. He gasped as he felt his own warm lifeblood bubble and then burst from his vein, and he grabbed at his neck, trying to hold back the flood. I could hear him choke, once, twice, more, until his breath sounded frothy and weak.

"I'm so sorry," he whispered. "I had to save Katie."

44

Jamal Rashiq parked his car near an opening in the fence surrounding the NSA complex. Two lights mounted high on poles stood nearby, but both were either burned out or turned off. He rolled his eyes at such a lapse in security. It fit with the tone of the rest of the place, however. The sign that announced "Gatehouse 2" was held up by four aging and rusting iron struts; the assembly looked fifty years old and probably was. The faded green facade of the building had clearly reached the winter of its life, and everywhere the arrays of aging windows had broken panes taped into place. It was quite a different presentation from the gatehouse the visitors had entered for the promotion ceremony the past week: there, despite the dilapidated Visitors' Center, the OPS 2A building facade had been covered by a cream-colored stuccolike material and the broken windows had been replaced with large, modern panes of dark reflective glass.

Rashiq looked at his watch: three-forty-five in the morning. He pulled his coat around him and clutched his briefcase full of tiny anthrax packets as he opened the door and got out of the car and began his walk toward the gatehouse. He knew some of the lampposts had cameras attached, and he was careful to keep his head bowed and covered as he walked through the open gate in the fence.

Soon they will close these gates for good, he mused. *They will be very sorry they hadn't done it earlier.*

He reconsidered. *No, it won't be soon. It will take months, maybe years before they can decontaminate this place when I am through with it.* It was cold, and he pulled his coat tighter at his throat.

Only one FPS officer was stationed at the gatehouse. Rashiq watched him yawn as several shift workers reporting for duty at one of the specialized crisis action centers slid their badges into one of the four CONFIRM machines, punched in their PINs, and walked past the guard and out of the gatehouse's rear door. He was relieved to see that no new entrance examination procedures had been put in place.

Rashiq followed closely behind the group, stepped up to the machine farthest away from the guard, slipped in his sister's badge, and tapped in the PIN he had seen her use a week earlier. He was calm as he waited for the green signal light telling him to go forward. If a problem arose at this point, Rashiq would pull out the small Glock pistol from his pocket and shoot the guard and anyone else who stood in his way. But there was no need for such extreme actions. The green light flashed, and the doctor walked nonchalantly past the still yawning guard into the breezeway that separated the gatehouse from OPS 1.

Inside the building, the area was very different from the one he had entered the previous week. There, flags flew and pictures hung on the newly painted walls, and the floor tiles sparkled. Here, the whole area was in the throes of reconstruction. The linoleum floor had been torn up except for spots around the edges, and the doctor walked across old concrete streaked with black stains and marked here and there with orange numbers and arrows that presumably applied to the ongoing work. Plasterboard walls cried out for paint, and an aluminum framework bereft of ceiling tiles exposed dangling electrical cords and pipes of all sizes overhead.

Rashiq walked slowly, and soon the few others who had arrived for work had disappeared into the distance. Up ahead where the hallway narrowed was a men's room. *Perfect,* he thought. *I'll duck in there and activate the timers on the four anthrax containers.*

The timers were set for nine that morning, maximizing the number of employees who would be in the buildings and who would inhale the deadly spores as they floated invisibly through the air to all corners of the complex.

45

I crawled away from Paul's body and sat shivering against the wall. The little flashlight had burned out and the room was in almost total darkness. My shoulder throbbed with such fiery pain it caught each breath I took and twisted it with a cruel intensity.

Finally, I forced myself to stand up and start my trek to find the nearest guards and report this very unlikely sequence of events. *If only I could have a damn cell phone in here*, I thought. My body was shaking, probably from shock, as I fumbled my way to the snack bar doorway.

As I stepped into the hallway, which seemed brilliantly lit after the cavelike darkness of the old kitchen, a slightly built figure carrying a briefcase walked, limping very slightly, out of the men's room directly opposite me. I looked at him, surprised to see anyone around at this time of night and in this secluded part of the building. At first I was delighted; someone was here who could help me.

Then I looked again, closely, shocked beyond belief.

"My God," I gasped. "You're Mariam Rashiq's

brother." I groped for his first name. "Jamal." I was beyond confused.

He glared at me, black eyes flashing with a fearsome intensity as he got closer to me. "Shut up," he said, a menacing edge in his voice.

"What are you doing here?" I whispered. "How did you get in the building? You have to have a badge to do that." I was now close enough to clearly see the blue-edged NSA badge hanging on a chain around his neck. "That's Mariam's badge," I said, pointing at her smiling picture centered on the laminated, thick plastic. "My God, *you* killed her, didn't you?"

As I spoke, Jamal Rashiq pulled a handgun from his pocket and aimed it at me. I lowered my head and lunged toward him, striking him hard in the chest, knocking him off his feet as the pistol went off with a small *pop* and the bullet smacked into the wall behind me.

A silencer, I thought. *That gun has a silencer. This man came here prepared to kill.*

Jamal stumbled and cursed. "Don't make me drop this briefcase," he snarled. "You will be so sorry if that happens."

"Then I guess you would be sorry, too," I said. I kicked him as hard as I could in the groin and jumped away before he could shoot again. He groaned as he tried to get back to his feet. I turned to the left, to safety; Gatehouse 2 and the police were just fifty yards away.

It was too late. I could see through the glass doors that the gatehouse was dark. It had closed at four a.m. and wouldn't open again until five-thirty. I would be trapped if I went that way.

I spun around and took off like a bullet down the north hallway. If I could make it to the end of the corridor and turn right, I would end up in front of the door to DEFSMAC. Not only were there people working around the clock but a camera by the door alerted the mission director to visitors.

I glanced behind me. Jamal, still groaning, was placing his precious briefcase inside the ragged opening to the snack bar, but as I watched he stood up and started running after me. He was still holding the gun in his right hand.

I got about two-thirds of the way to the end of the hall before I knew I couldn't outrun Jamal. Despite the old injury to his leg and the new one to his genitals, he was amazingly fast, fueled by madness and fury.

I turned to the left and hurtled through the double doors and down the stairs to the basement. It wasn't my first choice, but I couldn't make it to DEFSMAC without getting shot. And anyway, the basement offered me an advantage: it was a convoluted jumble of meandering hallways, parked carts, and piles of construction material that I knew pretty well by now. I needed that edge, small as it was; I wasn't a slowpoke, but Jamal was quick on his feet.

If the hallway on the first floor was poorly lit, the one below it was nearly dark. Clearly the first place the Agency was saving money on electricity after hours was down here, below ground. *Excellent choice,* I thought gratefully. *Just what I need right now. Thank you, Logistics.* The corridor ahead was dim and ghostly, but I plunged down it like a frightened deer. I knew these hallways could dead-end or turn unexpectedly, and I tried to peer ahead to anticipate the worst, but the near darkness made it all a twisting labyrinth of shadows.

My thoughts raced faster than my feet. There was

only one place to go and only one hope to find. I zig-
zagged down the corridor, afraid Jamal might stop
and shoot.

As I had hoped, the dim light affected Jamal more
than it did me. I turned a corner fast, skidding as I ran.
Jamal was close behind me until he tripped over the
pink shrink-wrapped boxes stacked in the middle of
the walkway that I managed to avoid because I knew
they were there. He fell hard, and I heard the gun clat-
ter across the floor. I flew down the hall to the Project
Meridian office, punched four numbers into the key
box and pushed open the door whispering, "Please,
Jacks, please be here." Jamal was close behind me
again.

Jacks was sitting at his desk with his headphones on
and had no warning of the terrible danger until I fell
against him, yelling for help. He turned around to see
Jamal Rashiq as he burst into the office and raised his
pistol. I couldn't imagine how a man as large as Jacks
could move so quickly, but he was across the room
like a cat. Jamal shot at Jacks and missed, barely, as
the big sergeant slammed into him and pushed him
back against the other desk. Books, a coffee cup, and a
headset crashed to the floor as the two men fought.

Jamal's extensive physical training in France was
not enough to save him. Jacks had a hundred pounds
of muscle and mass on the doctor and he used it well,
grabbing Jamal's wrist with one hand and pounding
his other fist into the doctor's face. Jamal screamed in
pain, a deafening noise that filled the small room and
made Jacks stop his attack for just a second. I watched
as Jamal shrank into a despair-filled semblance of
himself, wrested his left hand free of Jack's quick
grip, and pushed on the Glock's trigger even though
the gun was pointed at his own head. The gun popped

again and blood spilled from a small hole between Jamal's eyes.

Jacks backed away and watched Jamal Rashiq crumble to the floor. The gun fell from the doctor's hand and Jacks picked it up. I turned away from the scene, trying not to throw up.

"Jesus Christ," Jacks said, mouth open, his large body rocking slightly as he stared at the body on the floor. Finally he turned and grabbed me by the shoulders, gasping for breath, and shook me until my teeth chattered. "What did I tell you?" he demanded. "No more of your wandering around this place in the middle of the night!"

"No," I agreed, wincing. "Never again."

He looked me over. "Sorry, guess I shouldn't have grabbed your shoulder like that," he said as the blood soaked through my shirt. "What in God's name have you done to yourself? And who is this son of bitch?" He peered at me. I was beginning to shake again.

"Never mind," Jacks said. "You can tell me all that later. Can you manage to walk up to the gatehouse at OPS 2A and tell the guards what's happened here? It's just down the hall and up the stairs. I'll stay here with him," he pointed to the very dead man on the floor, "and call Security."

I nodded.

The 2A gatehouse was open. One FPS policemen was on the phone; the other watched with wide eyes as I stumbled in, covered with blood and filth. His response was a peculiar mixture of chivalry and authority: he helped me sit in a folding chair in the corner, then pulled his gun and pointed it at me.

"Call General Murray," I said. "Tell him I know where the missing tape is. Tell him Paul Eckerd is dead."

I held up my hands in a helpless gesture. "Tell him there's a lot more, but he'll have to see it for himself to believe it." I looked at them and added, "Be careful of the briefcase in the snack bar. It might have explosives in it."

I sat silently then, waiting for the next scenes to unfold.

46

Gabe watched out the window of the C-130 Hercu-les as it began its slow climb from Quetta airport. The plane was owned by the United Nations and used for food flights into impoverished areas like Baluchistan. Its cargo had been unloaded the day before, and now it was returning to Karachi with its special passengers.

Below them, and to the east, a lake appeared, its startling turquoise water a sharp contrast to the sandy brown of the hills surrounding it. Gabe could see a picnic table on the shore, sheltered by pine trees, the only green spot in view. It surprised him; he couldn't imagine anyone having picnics in this remote and harsh area.

He shifted in his seat and closed his eyes. He had done all he could. He knew that. He had, in fact, done much more than CIA would have wanted, but somehow what he did still didn't seem like enough. He wondered what it all would mean for his future with the agency.

He made a tent of his fingers and rested his chin against his thumbs. Perhaps he should resign from CIA and try to do more to help Massoud's Northern

Alliance fight the cockroaches, the animals who ran
Afghanistan. He hated the Taliban and their sanctimonious self-righteousness, their hypocritical piety,
their revolting treatment of girls and women and anyone not like them. He could go back on his own, join
the Alliance and fight against the Taliban with
Babrack. Wouldn't that be better than just making a
parachute drop to set up intercept gear that had been
compromised almost as soon as it was installed?

Of course, now that Souria was dead, he needn't
tell any of them about her. He wouldn't have to face
the grim, censorious looks from the ████████████ at
Karachi when he turned up with an injured Afghan
woman he had taken enormous risks to smuggle out of
the country. A woman who needed even more American help. He would already have his hands full ex-
plaining what he was doing with the American girl.

He looked at the seat beside him. Katie was sleeping, a thin blue airline blanket wrapped around her
shoulders. She was holding a small pillow pressed to
her chest like a stuffed bear. Gabe mourned the death
of Souria; it was a crushing pain that throbbed in his
soul. But Katie broke his heart. How would she ever
recover from this terrifying experience? What had
they done to her while she was a captive? It was un-
thinkable.

Far below, the green-blue lake disappeared. The
landscape turned a relentless brown. Tiny vehicles
crawled along a dirt road, puffs of dust drifting behind
them.

Katie jerked in her sleep and woke up. She looked
at Gabe and started to cry. "I don't want to go home,"
she whispered.

He put his arm around her thin shoulders. "Everything's all right now, Katie. You're safe. I won't let anyone hurt you."

"This was all my fault," she said. "I was so naive and selfish. And my father. What will happen to him?"

"I'm not sure," Gabe said, although he could guess. Paul Eckerd would go to jail for the rest of his life, possibly even face the death penalty. "We'll deal with all that when we get back to the States. I'll be there with you, I promise."

"Really?" she asked, her eyes pleading. "I would like that."

"You're safe now," he repeated. "And nobody is going to blame you for any of this." He stroked her hair and told her over and over that it would be okay. Finally, she calmed down enough to drift off to sleep again. She still clutched the pillow to her chest.

The pilot had given Gabe an envelope as he boarded the aircraft. He pulled it from his shirt pocket and opened it. Unsigned, it read: *"Report to headquarters on Monday, seven a.m. The director of operations will see you then."*

It would not be a pleasant, supportive meeting like the last one, Gabe knew that. There would be plenty of questions and lots of censure. *I'll just tell them the truth,* he decided. *All of it.* After all, etched into CIA's main lobby wall were the biblical words:

"And ye shall know the truth and the truth shall make you free."

We'll see what they really mean by that.

47

The Anne Arundel Medical Center is not an en-
tirely cheerless place. My private room in the acute
care center had a carpeted floor in shades of green that
matched the blankets and a loveseat, darker green and
burgundy flowered, under the curtained window. Wall
fixtures provided muted lighting. But the beige walls,
plastic-framed pictures of boats on the Chesapeake
Bay, and pale ash laminate cabinets reminded me daily
of grim government attempts at interior decorating.
But I wasn't about to complain; I was lucky to be alive.

Very early Friday morning Gabe had managed to
track me down at the hospital and call me from the
consulate in Karachi. We spoke only briefly, just long
enough to tell each other the conclusions of our perilous ordeals and whisper a few words of tender concern. He would be back soon, he promised.

Clearly he was also lucky to be alive.

It took Security and the FBI a long time to sort out
what had happened to me in that old kitchen, despite
my repeated, weary recital of facts. Convincing them
the tape was under the floor was the easiest part, and
they finally pulled up the tiles and found it. Convinc-

ing them that Mariam Rashiq's brother had been planning to destroy the National Security Agency was impossible. I gave up and stopped talking. I had told them all I knew; let them figure it out for themselves.

The deep cut in my shoulder had become infected, and for the past four days I had been tethered to an IV full of antibiotics. I was not allowed many visitors, only relatives, a rule I liked. I needed time alone, without questions and without expectations.

For a while, I lived in a fog, helped along by painkillers and whirling thoughts. It wasn't so much that I had killed a man—in fact, under the circumstances, I would have killed both of them without hesitation if I had to—it was the unexpected realization that working for NSA wasn't the easy adventure, the game I had always thought it was. From the perspective of a safe office, I had always thought piecing together bits of SIGINT with other data was not only challenging but, in all honesty, exquisitely interesting and fun.

But now I knew the truth: it could also be dangerous. It was serious business. We were foolish if we thought the end of the Soviet Union meant the end of seditious and threatening enemies. They were out there in more forms than we could guess.

And some of them were us. Despite the background investigations and the polygraphs and the guards, the bad guys were not just outside the walls of NSA. At least one had been inside, and if there was one . . .

My mother, Molly, came to the hospital every day, sometimes just sitting on the loveseat and reading for hours. She rarely spoke.

She watched me move through the various stages of my emotions; finally, on Sunday, she said, "Alex, it's time for you to stop brooding and start planning what comes next."

"I'm not brooding," I replied listlessly.

"Yes, you are. You're thinking that NSA is suddenly not the place you thought it was. The safe, perfect place that shuts out the rest of the world to solve issues affecting the greater good of international peace and justice. You thought you were special. That you belonged to a select group of exceptional, omniscient people blessed not just with jobs, but with missions. And now you don't know what to think, do you? But you know what? You still are special and NSA never was perfect."

"Well, of course not, but after what just happened we will never be the same again."

"Alex, do you think bad things have never happened at NSA before? How about Bob Donnelly? I know everyone jokes about it now, but it wasn't so funny when he almost got killed. And, let me remind you, *inside* the building."

Bob Donnelly was a powerful NSA executive in the early days of the NSA complex at Fort Meade. He was said to have been domineering, sexist, and rude. One day in the late 1960s a man with a knife chased Donnelly out of his office on the first floor, cursing at him for sleeping with his wife or destroying his career—no one seemed to remember exactly what—and screaming he was going to kill him. Donnelly ran up the down escalator, the man close behind, followed by a Marine guard who had been stationed at the bottom of the escalator. The Marine finally tackled the attacker, joined by several other guards who hauled him away.

Rumor had it that Donnelly was so disliked that NSA employees lined the hallway cheering for the man with the knife to catch up with him before the guards did.

It's the most infamous story in NSA history, repeated and embellished and delighted in by thousands. Many NSAers found it even more deliciously scandalous than all the bawdy rumors and legends of sexual encounters in various parts of the buildings.

Molly continued, "There were others . . ."

I interrupted, "Molly, those things happened years ago. Nobody's even sure those stories are true."

"Oh, they're true all right, at least in some form. And if you don't like 'years ago,' how about the senior executive who was attacked in the parking lot three months ago because he's in charge of DIRNSA's new Transformation Office and is starting to make big changes? Or the other senior who was threatened in her office last month for the same reasons?"

Molly took my hands. "Think about all the good things we've accomplished at NSA despite the occasional disasters. You can't let this shut you down. You have too much to do."

I was silent. My mother kissed me on the forehead and went back to her book.

DIRNSA came to see me every day, just for a few minutes. It wasn't until Monday at about noon that he sat beside the bed and talked about my actions over the past ten days.

"You know," he said, without much conviction, "that you broke a lot of rules." I sat up straighter. "Wait," he said, holding up a hand, "I didn't say that was all bad. Some of them needed to be broken. Under the circumstances, I mean. But not everyone agrees with me. Security and my advisers have suggested you be put on administrative leave until the Agency decides on an 'appropriate punitive action,' if any. They are concerned about the STU III calls, of course, and the breach of the intelligence directives and the report about the radars and the enormous fuss it's caused.

Also, you lied to the OCMC chief. And on top of all that, two men are dead and you killed one of them. Not that," he hurried to add, "anyone thinks it was anything other than self-defense. But, as I'm sure you can imagine, they want an investigation."

I leaned my head against the pillow. "I suppose they would," I said. "Damn bureaucrats. Well, maybe it'll give some of the Agency's twenty-some lawyers something useful to do for a change. Fine with me. Put me on admin leave. I won't have to use up my sick leave."

General Murray smiled. "I thought you might take it like that. And I wouldn't worry if I were you. Personally, I think you should get a medal. The cassette tape you found makes everything clear. This will all work out. I do carry some weight around here. Although I must tell you," he said, an amused look spreading across his face, "you have stretched the term 'empowerment' much further than I intended it to be stretched."

"Yes, Sir," I said, with a crooked grin. "But I always tried to ask myself first what you would do if you were in my shoes."

"I'm sure you did."

I got serious. "Sir, what about the other man, Mariam's brother? He told me he had explosives in his briefcase. Was that true?"

General Murray's eyes turned grim. "The DCI has ruled that nobody but a very few of us will ever know about that part of the story. It's just too sensitive. He told me I would have to decide whether to tell you. I'm not sure if I should, not because I don't think you can keep a secret, but because of the incredible damage the man was planning to do. I'm not sure you really want to know."

"But . . ." I started. He shook his head. He stood up

and walked to the window and stared out of it for several long minutes. I knew he wasn't fascinated with the view: a series of dark, dingy, gravelly rooftops with a series of protruding pipes and vents. Off in the distance, at the intersection of three highways, a wrought iron fence with pointy pickets corralled a tiny cemetery.

I waited. Finally, DIRNSA closed the door to my room, sat back down beside my bed, and said in a low voice, "If anyone ever deserved to know the truth, it's you. You saved a lot of lives, Alex, but nobody will ever know it. Do you want to hear about it?"

I nodded.

He told me about the small anthrax packages, each wrapped with its own small explosive charge on a timer. The timer had been set for nine o'clock Friday morning, when the buildings were full of people. The bomb squad had taken the envelopes away to a special facility to defuse them.

"We're pretty sure he was going to put them inside the air handlers," DIRNSA said. "He must have discovered where they were located on his visit to NSA last week. The anthrax was mixed with a silicon additive to make it buoyant enough to float around in the air for a long time. The air vents for all four main buildings are interconnected, and the spores would have killed hundreds. Maybe thousands. And," he sighed, "the buildings would have been so contaminated it could have taken a very long time to clean them up. Think what that would have meant to us all."

I couldn't; it was beyond imagining. "Why?" I asked.

He shook his head again. "We don't know yet. There's an awful lot we don't know. But we're working on it." His eyes narrowed. "We're praying that there isn't any more of this anthrax out there someplace. That it was all in the briefcase."

I nodded. God help us if there was more. The deadly spores were bound to show up sometime, somewhere.

On Monday afternoon three visitors arrived. A girl, pale but self-assured, came into the room followed by a woman, almost certainly her mother, I thought. A curly-headed man with dark eyes stopped at the doorway, flashing a smile.

"Gabe. Thank God you're back." A huge weight fell from my shoulders and my eyes danced as I smiled back at him. I had been waiting for this moment, but even I couldn't believe how elated I was to see him again. My heart thumped and I could feel my face flush with joy.

I smiled at him again and turned to the girl. "You're Katie, aren't you? I'm so glad you came to see me. You look awfully good for all you're been through."

"Thank you, Alex." She turned to introduce the woman. "This is my mother, Fran Eckerd. I'm going to go live with her in Denver now, but I had to stop and talk to you first." She took one of my hands shyly and said, "I wouldn't be alive without your help, you know. I don't know how to thank you." Behind me, tears trickled down her mother's face.

"I'm sure you don't even have to try," I said, pressing Katie's hand. "I'm so pleased you're home safely."

"I'm so sorry about what my father did. I think he must have lost his mind."

I nodded slowly. "I think you might be right."

We talked quietly for a while, but soon Katie's eyes were bleary with exhaustion. Her mother took her shoulder and led her away.

"I'll stay in touch with you, Alex. I promise," the girl said as she walked out of the hospital room. She stopped briefly and whispered something to Gabe. He hugged her and she disappeared down the hall after her mother.

Gabe left the doorjamb he had been leaning on and sat on the bed next to me. We looked at each other for a long time without speaking.

"I am so glad to see you," he said, stroking my arm. "So glad."

I shivered at the whispery touch and grinned. "I'd say I missed you, but that's not quite true," I said. "After all, we talked on the STU every day. Sometimes often. But you know—I missed *you*. The real Gabe. I hope you're going to be around for a while now?"

"Oh yes," he snorted, "I'll be around for quite some time. The Company has put me on admin leave while they figure out what to do with me. I broke a few rules over there."

I jerked my head up. "That's very strange. NSA has done the same thing with me. Special admin leave while they 'investigate.'" I snorted. "Do you think there's any chance they've worked this out together? That it's really some kind of backhanded reward that they can't really give us otherwise?"

"God, wouldn't that be funny," Gabe said. "That would be the best piece of coordination our two agencies have had in a long time. Except, of course, for what you and I gave them." He looked at me affectionately. "When do you get out of here anyway?"

"Twenty-four hours after I stop spiking a fever. Which, I must say, you're not helping with."

"Hey," he said, touching my cheek, "sign yourself out. They can give you those antibiotics in pills and I'll look after you. We'll go away to a nice warm beach someplace and wait to hear from our bosses."

I closed my eyes for a moment. "Yes," I said, "yes, let's do that. We are certainly entitled to some time together."

I reached out and took his hand. "Gabe, I'm so sorry about your friend Souria. It's terribly sad. It must be hard for you to handle."

He grimaced. "Yes, it is. She didn't deserve to die. She never deserved to live like she did. Afghanistan is a country filled with fear and death and despair, and the world doesn't know what's going on there. Or doesn't care."

I pursed my lips. "When we get back to work, we have to do something about it. We have to figure out another way to find out what the madmen in Afghanistan are doing. CIA needs to have agents on the ground. Someone who can tell us what's happening over there . . ."

"Are you going to send me back so soon?" Gabe raised his eyebrows and grinned.

"No, not you. You've probably been compromised anyway. CIA needs to recruit natives or Afghan emigrants. People we can trust. We have to make our agencies understand this is important. We have so much to do." I sat up straight, my blue-and-white checked hospital gown sliding down one shoulder. I could feel my face was flushed and full of determination.

"Calm down, babe. Remember the fever. I want you out of here tomorrow."

I took a deep breath. "You're right," I said. "But we do have to try to fix this mess. There's so much to do it's hard to know where to start."

Gabe kissed me gently on the lips and smiled. "I have an idea," he said.

EPILOGUE

Pentagon, Central Plaza
September 11, 2001
Eight a.m.

It was a beautiful, sunny September morning. Kai and I sat at a picnic table in the five-acre central plaza, a heavily treed, grassy area surrounded by the five-sided, huge headquarters of the Department of Defense. We were drinking coffee we had just purchased from the snack bar nearby and checking the day's schedule.

We were about to participate in a conference on terrorism, hosted by a tiny, secret organization buried deep in the Department of Justice. It was an unusual meeting, attended by a group of Intelligence Community analysts called together by invitation only. A participant at the Pentagon graciously offered a SCIF—an area designed for discussing Sensitive Compartmented Information—in a room in the B Ring that was large enough to hold the gathering. Rumor had it that the chief of Alec Station, a subsection of CIA's Counterterrorist Center that had been cataloguing information on Usama bin Laden and issuing warnings for years—and sparking very little interest from other members of the IC in the process—was going to attend. Even the FBI was sending a representative;

someone, we had heard, had some new information to present. It was all very promising.

Kai was going to give her briefing at ten o'clock. We hoped this time someone would listen to our warnings of an impending attack.

The two of us had spent much of our time in the last eight months, with the blessing of DIRNSA, trying to convince others in the Intelligence Community as well as policy makers and military leaders that a terrorist strike against our country was not just real, but imminent. We still didn't have any idea if it was biological, nuclear, or some sort of massive scale of suicide bombings—or, indeed, where it was going to be. We just knew it was coming.

With no more intercepted comms in our back pockets, we had to use what I thought of as "Kai's radars" to prove our point. Months ago, the two of us put together a presentation that started with bits and pieces of intercepted al Qaeda communications from the days when Project Meridian was up and running and the terrorists were talking about *al-Buraq*. The terrorists' words were brutally clear: something big was in the works. We ended that part of the briefing with a recording of UBL's last intercepted words, bitter and angry: *"You will pay for this."* Jacks provided the translations; one of the anchors from the NSA news studio did the voice-overs. It was chilling.

We explained that the comms were gone, probably forever, but that we had clear proof that the terrorists' plans continued. Kai described the buildup of the enhanced SA-2 missile system near Kandahar, and the changes made to the radars to make them more capable in an ECM environment. She included a map that showed the locations of the missile launchers and imagery of the wicked-looking missiles uploaded and pointed toward the sky. She had charts and graphs of the SAM radars as they tracked aircraft flying over the nearby airfield. This testing continued, at least once, sometimes twice, each week.

"There is only one reason for this kind of activity that I can think of," Kai said. "The Taliban is expecting to have to defend their stronghold in Kandahar as well as that in Kabul, where they already have a missile system. They expect an attack by a modern air force, almost certainly ours. Why do they think this will happen?"

At this point in the briefing, Kai stopped and looked hard at her audience. "We believe they are planning such a terrible act of aggression on either U.S. soil or on our assets elsewhere in the world that they know we will retaliate by attacking their country."

We ended by showing a picture of bin Laden and repeating the recording of his words, *"You will pay for this."* And then we asked the audience to help us figure out exactly what the threat was.

We started by presenting this evidence to our own Office of Counterterrorism, where we found that, although there was skepticism among those unable to make the leap from radar tracks to world events, there was plenty of interest.

We worked our way through the Intelligence Community analysis organizations, with much the same reaction. No one was more eager or innovative than the State Department's tiny Bureau of Intelligence and Research; no place more lukewarm than the staid and self-directed FBI.

But in general, counterterrorism analysts in various agencies started taking notice of our persistent arguments and began forming special teams to push for more collection and more recognition of our warnings.

Finally, in June, the DCI convened a meeting at the CTC for us to present our claims and their associated evidence. Our audience was a small number of very important people, including a rep from the National Security Council's Counterterrorism Security Group, seated around a conference room table. We presented our interpretation of events that had convinced us the U.S. was about to be attacked. "It's coming," I insisted, wrapping up our presentation. "It's going to happen."

"How can you know that, Alex?" Louis Hahn, the DCI, asked me quietly. "How can you be so sure?"

"The radars," I said. "They are the key. The radars are still testing at Kandahar. At least once a week, just like before. They are proof *al-Buraq* is still alive."

The S&TI Center had sent its chief scientist to the meeting. He rolled his eyes and chimed in. "My analysts assure me that the radar activity in Afghanistan means no such thing. They think it's likely the Pakistanis want a new place to test their system outside their own country. Perhaps just a change in environment or topography."

To his credit, the CIA ELINT expert tried to support us, but by mandate the S&TI Center had the final say. After that June meeting, most of the special teams were disbanded and counterterrorism groups throughout the IC sank back into their stovepiped, reclusive activity.

Kai and I were devastated. We stopped briefing and went back to our "real" jobs. One morning in late July, though, Kai called me, excited nearly beyond words. "Alex, you have to come down to the lab right away. They'll have to believe us now. It's all changed."

And it had. The radars were no longer tracking the old, slow Russian Antonov aircraft. The SA-2 missile system commander had brought in high-speed fighter jets, no doubt to stress the system's capabilities and prove its skill against a much more powerful and cutting-edge adversary. To us, the change was chilling. To us, it meant an attack against this country was imminent and their preparations for a counterattack were even more serious.

And, in a way, bizarrely amusing. I looked at Kai and raised my eyebrows. "Who's flying these jets, anyway? The Taliban Air Force?"

Kai giggled. "Very funny, Alex. No, it must be the Pakis again, helping them out. Or maybe the Saudis. They're about the only countries that actually support those monsters."

"Yes, or . . . maybe they've hired some Russian ex-fighter jocks. That would be ironic."

"What should we do?" Kai asked. "I've talked to the S&T Center already. They want to look at the tapes and study the changes. Make sure we're right. They ordered me not to report this until they have time to see what's 'really' happening."

I thought of Gabe, parachuting into an ancient and dangerous land, risking his life to get information on the terrorists' plans. I thought of Souria, defying the Taliban for years and finally dying when she tried to escape their savage rule. I thought about the trouble another report would cause. It didn't compare.

"Kai, no one can order you not to report your analysis. NSA is this country's SIGINT agency, and ELINT is SIGINT. Write it up," I said, jaw set. "I'll edit it, and when the dayshift is gone, we'll take it to NSOC to release. Management can't hold it up that way."

Kai grinned. "You bet," she said.

A few analysts out there responded with interest, but soon the S&TI Center sent another blistering message to DIRNSA, the DCI, and just about everyone in the IC disputing not just our conclusions but our analysis as well.

I had a feeling, though, that our report may have been the catalyst for this meeting today at the Pentagon. For the first time in two months I had a glimmer of hope that someone cared what we had to say.

At eight-thirty, we stood up, threw away our coffee cups, and headed for the SCIF conference room. "Go ahead," Kai stopped and said, "I'm going to walk over to the drugstore and get some aspirin." She rubbed her temples. "Headache," she said. "It's probably stress."

I looked up at the perfect, blue sky. "On a day like this?" I said.

She shrugged and smiled. "I'll be right back."

"Okay," I said. "I'll save you a seat."

I found the conference room, made sure our briefing materials had been couriered over from the Agency and were ready for our ten o'clock presentation, and reviewed them as I sat and waited for the meeting to begin.

At about five minutes until nine, I heard people in the hallway yelling something about an airplane crash. Those of us already seated in the conference room ran out to see what it was all about. "This way," a woman called out, pointing to a large room with a television set. At three minutes past nine, we watched a second jetliner that morning fly into the World Trade Center. It was clear this was a terrorist attack—almost certainly the terrorist attack we had been predicting.

I ran out and across the grassy courtyard, shouting for Kai. So many people filled the place that I was swept backward and fell against a heavy wooden bench. Someone reached down and pulled me up, gripped my arms, and ran with me through the grass to an exit. "We're next!" he shouted. "We're damn sure next."

I finally worked my way through the throngs of people to my car, parked far away from the building on the south side, praying for Kai the whole way. I got my cell phone from the glove box and called Gabe's number at CIA. "Alex," he said, his voice trembling, "where are you? Are you at the Pentagon at that meeting? You've got to get out of there. We're being attacked. The Pentagon has to be a prime target."

"I'm out," I said, "but I have to go back and find Kai. She went to the drugstore. Gabe, I have to find her!"

"No," he said firmly, "you have to get away from there. We know there are at least two more hijacked planes that are heading for the east coast, either D.C. or New York. You may only have minutes to escape. Leave—now." He paused. "And don't go to NSA—it's being evacuated. Drive to my town house. I'll be there as soon as I can."

"Two more planes? My God, are you sure?" I said. My next words were drowned out as a jetliner flying just above the ground roared over a hilltop to my left and exploded in a huge fireball against the Pentagon's west wall. An enormous boom shook the ground. After a few seconds the black smoke cleared just long enough for me to see the gaping hole where the aircraft had hit the building.

In minutes, sirens screamed and waves of people filled the parking lot, running toward their cars. My cell phone was dead. I got out of the car, stood beside it with my fists raised, and swore an oath of revenge at the fiery plumes of orange and black filling the sky in front of me.

Late in the afternoon, a uniformed man pushing a large trolley filled with cases of Coke rumbled through the Pentagon's smoke-filled courtyard, bottles rattling as he headed to refill the red and white machine standing in the shade of the small snack building as he did every afternoon. Somehow he had walked unchallenged past all the police and road blocks. A fireman yelled at him, "What are you doing here, man? You could die in here."

"It's the only thing I can do to help," the man answered. He reached in his pocket, pulled out a handkerchief, and wiped the black soot from his eyes.

When he reached the snack bar he put the cases of Coke on the ground. He opened the door of the soda machine with his key. Smoke billowed around him as he printed a sign and propped it against the bottles. "Free," it read.

GLOSSARY OF TERMS AND ABBREVIATIONS

al-Buraq: Fictional al Qaeda cover name for their 9/11 plot.

Anchory: Database of NSA reports.

Antonov AN-26: Twin-engined light turboprop aircraft built in the USSR.

Ariana Airlines: National airline carrier of Afghanistan.

Burka: An enveloping outer garment worn by some Islamic women outside the home. During the Taliban's reign, women were required to wear a burka with a full face covering whenever they appeared in public.

Church Committee: U.S. Senate committee (precursor to the Senate Select Committee on Intelligence) chaired by Sen. Frank Church in 1975 that investigated CIA, FBI, and NSA for questionable information gathering. Resulted in the Foreign Intelligence Surveillance Act (FISA) of 1978 and several other restrictions limiting intelligence gathering and dissemination.

Cipher: A cryptographic system in which each letter of plain text is replaced by other numbers or letters according to a predetermined algorithm.

Code: The replacement of a word or phrase in a message with a different word or phrase not necessarily on a letter-for-letter basis. For example, "Attack at dawn" in a message might be replaced by "Come to breakfast," a prearranged substitution that the recipient understands.

Collateral Information: Within NSA, any information other than that derived from SIGINT (such as press articles, imagery, HUMINT, etc.). Often considered to be suspect by Agency analysts unless confirmed by NSA intercepts.

COMINT: Communications intelligence. Spoken or written words transmitted electronically and collected by a nonintended recipient.

CONFIRM: NSA's electronic access control system that identifies and time-stamps the entrance or exit of anyone in the NSA complex.

CRITIC: An emergency report sent by any U.S. military or government entity at Flash precedence to alert the president and other senior officials and agencies of a significant event or potential crisis situation.

Cryptanalysis: The steps or processes involved in converting encrypted messages into plain text without previous knowledge of the encryption techniques.

Cryptography: The practice of encryption of plain text to conceal its meaning from all except the intended recipients.

CTC: Counterterrorism Center, located at CIA, with analysts integrated from throughout the Intelligence Community; precursor of the National Counterterrorism Center.

Dari: One of the two principal languages in Afghanistan; official name of the Persian language in Afghanistan.

DCI: Director of Central Intelligence, who was also the director of CIA. During the timeframe of this book, the DCI was responsible for coordinating intelligence activities among the sixteen agencies in the Intelligence Community. In 2005, the DCI position was superseded by the Director of National Intelligence (DNI).

DDO: NSA's deputy director for operations.

DEFSMAC: Defense Special Missile and Astronautics Center. Joint NSA-DIA organization that directs collection of intelligence against foreign missile and space launches.

DIRNSA: Director, National Security Agency.

DO: Directorate for Operations. NSA's organization where SIGINT is collected, processed, analyzed, and reported.

ECM: Electronic countermeasures. A form of warfare in which electronic means are used to deny targeting information to enemy tracking devices such as radar or sonar. Jamming is a common form of ECM.

ELINT: Electronic intelligence. Focuses on noncommunications data, such as radar tracking, to assess capabilities and locations of foreign weapons systems. One of SIGINT's three pillars, along with COMINT and FISINT.

Encryption: Process of transforming information to make it unreadable to anyone without a "key." During the early twentieth century, electromechanical machines performed encryption and decryption using a combination of transposition, polyalphabetic substitution, and "additive" substitution. Today, most encryption is done digitally, at the "bit" level.

Finished Intelligence: Intelligence report based on all available sources that has been staffed and coordinated and represents the official opinion of the IC.

FISA: Foreign Intelligence Surveillance Act (1978). Prescribes procedures for requesting judicial authorization for electronic surveillance and physical search of persons engaged in espionage or terrorism against the United States on behalf of a foreign power.

FISINT: Foreign instrumentation intelligence, usually telemetry. One of SIGINT's three pillars, along with COMINT and ELINT.

FPS: Federal Protective Service. NSA's police organization.

GCHQ: Government Communications Headquarters. Great Britian's equivalent of NSA, located in Cheltenham, England.

GlobalSat: The fictional satellite phone system used by al Qaeda in this book.

GLOBE: Gay, Lesbian, or Bisexual Employees. NSA-blessed organization that addresses the concerns of gay and lesbian people who work at the Agency.

GPS: Global Positioning System. Aids in precise navigation by integrating line-of-sight positional data from multiple orbiting satellites.

HALO: High altitude, low opening parachute jump at approximately thirty thousand feet; freefall to fifteen thousand feet before chute is opened.

HEU: Highly Enriched Uranium. Essential ingredient in producing nuclear weapons.

HQ-2: The Chinese Hong Qi-2 (HQ-2) is a medium-range, medium-to-high-altitude surface-to-air missile (SAM) based on the Soviet SA-2 SAM. The HQ-2 has been upgraded with modifications to improve the missile's accuracy and resistance to enemy electronic jamming, as well as to increase the missile's operational zone.

HUMINT: Human intelligence. Collected primarily by defense attachés attached to U.S. embassies and CIA agents in the field.

IC: Intelligence Community. Consists of sixteen agencies within the U.S. government that collect, analyze, or report intelligence.

INMARSAT: International company that operates a fleet of geosynchronous telecommunications satellites to provide telephony and data services to users worldwide, through special digital radios called terminals. The terminal users send and receive information by relaying signals through the satellites. Various encryption methods can be used to ensure privacy.

INTELINK: Classified Internet for intelligence producers and users.

Jamming: Interfering with the operation of an electronic transmitter, often a radar, by saturating the receiver with false electronic emissions or with chaff or decoys.

JUMPSEAT: According to press, a code name for a class of SIGINT reconnaissance satellites operated by the National Reconnaissance Office (NRO).

KSM: Khalid Sheik Mohammed. Self-confessed mastermind of the 9/11 attacks, colleague of Usama bin Laden. Currently in U.S. custody.

MD: Mission director. Designated person in charge of a shift of workers at several of NSA's twenty-four-hour operation centers.

Microwave Communications: The transmission of signals by sending microwaves, either directly or by a satellite through a series of antenna sites. The microwave range includes ultrahigh frequency (UHF) (0.3–3 GHz), superhigh frequency (SHF) (3–30 GHz), and extremely high frequency (EHF) (30–300 GHz).

MOD: Ministry of Defence. British equivalent of U.S. Defense Department.

Mullah: A name commonly given to local Islamic clerics or mosque leaders in many parts of the Muslim world.

Myers-Briggs Personality Test: Test for measuring a person's decision-making preferences, using four basic scales with opposite poles. The four scales are extraversion/introversion, sensate/intuitive, thinking/feeling, and judging/perceiving. The various combinations of these preferences result in sixteen personality types.

Need to Know: Limitation on sharing of data within the Intelligence Community that forbids the sharing of any information without assurance that the recipient must know it to do their job. "Need to Know" is a mantra at NSA.

NIE: National Intelligence Estimate. Defined by the U.S. Department of Defense as a strategic estimate of the capabilities, vulnerabilities, and probable courses of action of foreign nations produced at the national level as a composite of the views of the Intelligence Community.

Nightstalkers: 160th Special Operations Aviation Regiment (Airborne). Missions include attack, assault, and reconnaissance and are usually conducted at night, at high speeds and low altitudes, on short notice, and in secret. Headquartered at Fort Cambell, Kentucky.

NIMA: National Imagery and Mapping Agency. During the timeframe of this book, NIMA was tasked to provide imagery and intelligence in support of the national security objectives of the United States. Now called NGA—the National Geospatial-Intelligence Agency.

NRO: National Reconnaissance Office. According to its Web site, "The NRO designs, builds and operates U.S. reconnaissance satellites."

NSOC: National Security Operations Center. NSA's primary twenty-four-hour watch center and the soul of the Agency after normal working hours and during crises.

OCMC: Operations Collection Management Center. A fictional NSA organization.

Operation Minaret: The fictional operation to send an agent into pre-9/11 Afghanistan to tap into the microwave communications owned by the Taliban (and also used by al Qaeda).

Operational ELINT: The category of electronic intelligence concerned with the introduction, disposition, movement, utilization, tactics, and activity levels of known foreign noncommunication emitters (such as radars) and, where applicable, associated weapons systems.

OPM: Office of Personnel Management.

OPSEC: Operations Security. OPSEC engineers design and implement security solutions to protect U.S. communications from those who might try to intercept them.

Oscilloscope: A device that allows an analyst to measure a signal for time, voltage values, frequency, distortion, signal-to-noise ratio, and other components.

ParagonReporting, Inc.: A fictional company that gathers "publicly available" information about Americans to sell to marketers and local and federal law enforcement agencies.

Pashtu: Language of the Pashtuns, the largest ethnic group in Afghanistan. Primary language used by the Taliban.

Pentagon: Headquarters of the Department of Defense in Washington, D.C.

PIN: Personal identification number.

Pixels: Short for picture elements. The smallest complete sample of an image.

Project Meridian: Fictional cover name for the program to intercept al Qaeda's pre-9/11 satellite phone system.

Raw SIGINT: COMINT that has not yet been analyzed and officially published by NSA. Unlike

ELINT or telemetry, raw COMINT cannot be shared with others in the IC. SIGINT may have three pillars, but they are not accorded the same status or treatment.

Read in: Present background and safeguarding rules for special accesses to those who have the Need to Know. For example, Alex would have been "read in" to the VRK program protecting Project Meridian.

SA-2: Medium-range, medium-to-high-altitude surface-to-air missile system built by the Soviets in the late 1950s. Most famous for shooting down Francis Gary Powers and his U-2 "spy plane" in an overflight of the U.S.S.R. in May 1960.

SAM: Surface-to-air missile.

Satellite Communications: Sending voice or other signals from the ground up to a geosynchronous satellite that relays them to other satellites until they can be sent down to the intended recipient.

SCI: Sensitive Compartmented Information. Classified information concerning (or derived from) intelligence sources, methods, or analytic processes that, because of its sensitivity, is required to be handled within formal access control systems.

SCIF: Sensitive Compartmentalized Information Facility. Uniquely designed and electronically fortified rooms where those with SCI clearances discuss especially sensitive reports and plans.

SCO: Senior collection officer on duty in NSOC.

Senior Executive: Managers who rank just above the GS scale and just below presidential appointees. According to the Office of Personnel Management, senior executives are men and women with "well-honed executive skills" who are charged with leading the continuing transformation of government.

Sidelobes: A secondary energy reflection of the main radar (or microwave) beam; spillover.

SIGINT: Signals intelligence. Intercepting signals for intelligence purposes. SIGINT comprises three subgroups: COMINT (the largest), ELINT, and FISINT. Collecting SIGINT against *foreign* targets is NSA's primary mission.

SOO: Senior operations officer. Chief of NSOC during daytime working hours and of all NSA during evenings, nights, weekends, and holidays.

SRO: Senior reporting officer on duty in NSOC.

S&TI Center: Scientific and Technical Intelligence production centers that produce assessments of the scientific and technical characteristics, capabilities, and limitations of all foreign military systems and weapons systems based on all source intelligence information.

Steganography: Art and science of hiding written messages or pictures within other, seemingly harmless messages. One simple example is using invisible ink.

STU III: A family of secure telephones introduced in 1987 by NSA for use by the United States government, its contractors, and its allies. The system's terminals are designed to operate as both ordinary telephones and secure instruments over the dial-up public switching telephone network.

Subscriber Identification Module (SIM): SIM cards store network-specific information used to authenticate and identify subscribers on the network, a satellite communication system in the case of this book. It is a removable "smart card" that allows users to change phones by taking out the SIM card and inserting it in the new phone.

Technical ELINT: ELINT that provides detailed knowledge of the technical characteristics of a given emitter that permits evaluations of its primary function, capabilities, modes of operation, as well as its specific role within a complex weapon system or defense network.

TRUMPET: According to press, TRUMPET is part of a fleet of intelligence-gathering satellites that monitor everything from missile launches and troop movements to mobile phone calls.

TSZ/TKC: Top Secret Zarf/Talent Keyhole Channels. A classification and handling procedure used by NSA for certain sensitive information.

UBL: Usama bin Laden.

USSID 18: United States Signals Intelligence Directive 18 ensures that NSA SIGINT collection and reporting are conducted in accordance with procedures that meet the reasonableness requirements of the

Fourth Amendment and do not violate the privacy of U.S. citizens anywhere in the world.

USSTRATCOM: United States Strategic Command. Controls the nuclear weapons assets of the U.S. military. Headquartered at Offutt AFB, Nebraska.

Voice Recognition Software: As it applies to NSA, this is a filter placed on voice communication intercepts to attempt to identify the speaker(s).

VRK: Very Restricted Knowledge. NSA programs for extraordinarily sensitive SIGINT collection operations. Each VRK is limited to access by those who *must* have it.

WAC: Weapons Analysis Center. A fictional S&TI Center.

Wrangler: Database of ELINT intercepts.

ABOUT THE AUTHOR

M. E. Harrigan is a former National Security Agency technical director of the Defense Special Missile and Astronautics Center (DEFSMAC), a joint NSA/ Defense Intelligence Agency organization. DEFSMAC is one of the most vital providers of intelligence information at the NSA complex.

During her twenty-seven-year career with NSA, Ms. Harrigan worked as an intelligence analyst, specializing in foreign weapon systems and missile testing. Intelligence Analysis is a profession that demands well-developed problem-solving techniques, research ability, writing skills, ingenuity, plenty of common sense, and, often, proficiency in physics, math, and mind-reading.

Ms. Harrigan is a recipient of NSA's highest "Master" level award for her work in the Intelligence Analysis field.

Perhaps her most immediately rewarding work at NSA occurred in July 1996, when she led a tiny team of analysts that determined the initial sequence of the explosion and crash of TWA-800 into the Atlantic Ocean off the south shore of Long Island. This time line of events was sent to the FBI within forty-eight hours of the crash and was used for victim and aircraft recovery. According to the assistant director in charge, New York office, Ms. Harrigan and her team provided the most critical early information the FBI received from anyone in the Intelligence community.

But reconstructing the accident was also her most heartbreaking task at NSA: sixteen members of a high school French club in Ms. Harrigan's hometown of Montoursville, Pennsylvania, and their five chaperones died in the crash of TWA-800.

Betsy Harrigan lives in Arizona with her husband and two German shorthaired pointers.